Pen Pal

ISBN 978-1-49-426463-5

Pen Pal

Francesca Forrest

I would like to offer heartfelt thanks to the friends who read and commented on the earliest version of this story—an exchange of letters that ran on Livejournal in 2009—and to those who beta read later versions and offered encouragement and wise words, especially Lisa Bradley, Caroline Ellis, Miquela Faure, Merrie Haskell, Julie Just, and Sherwood Smith. I'm also extremely grateful to Khiem Tran, who provided the cover image, and to Aubrey Rose, who created the cover. My humblest and biggest thank you goes out to my husband, who supported me through this entire process—even traveling to hot places he had never envisioned going to—and to my children, who put up with my obsession and my neglectfulness. Warmest hugs also to my father (always an inspiration) and my brother and sister, and a prayer and an offering to my mother, grandmother, and LA, who are no longer with us, but whom I think on every day.

Table of Contents

Chapter 1. Letter in a Bottle

Dear person who finds my message,

I live in a place called Mermaid's Hands. All our houses here rest on the mud when the tide is out, but when it comes in, they rise right up and float.

They're all roped together, so we don't lose anyone. I like Mermaid's Hands, but sometimes I wish I could unrope our house and see where it might float to. But I would get in trouble if I did that, so instead I'm sticking this message in a bottle. If you find it, please write back to me at this address. Tell me what the world is like where you are.

Yours truly,

Em

June 27 (Em's diary)

Today Ma used up the last of the cough medicine on Tammy, and I rinsed out the bottle. It was a good, small size, and I decided today was the day to send out my message. Small Bill helped me row out far enough to see the free and open ocean.

"It's probably just gonna bob around here. Least it won't sink," he said, examining the corks that I put all around the outside of it, held on by electrical tape. "Not until the stickum wears off the tape, anyway. Maybe the dolphins will play with it. Maybe they'll pass it on to the seapeople. You want it to go to the seapeople, or people up here?" He waved his hand at the sea, but he was meaning the folks on the shrimp boats and the big cargo ships, and the ones out on the oil rigs, too.

"Well, either way, but I want someone to write back," I said. "Wish I could be the message ... Go visit the seapeople, or go see some new place above-water."

"You want to leave here?"

"Not for good! Just to look around. Just to see stuff with my own eyes. Haven't you ever wanted to visit the seapeople?"

Small Bill shrugged. "Maybe the seapeople. Don't think I need to meet any more dry-land people, though. You want me to throw that for you?"

"No, I want to do it myself." I stood up real carefully, so I wouldn't capsize the dinghy, and threw the bottle as far as I could. "Don't say, 'Not bad, not bad,' like you're the king of good throws," I warned.

"Not sure you threw it far enough for 'not bad,'" Small Bill said, grinning, and then I nearly did capsize the dinghy trying to spill him out of it, but he was lodged in as good as a hermit crab in its shell. So we rowed back and played tag with everyone else for a while, and Small Bill's mom gave me a bundle of dried leaves tied with cordgrass twine. Ma only likes dry-land medicine that comes in bottles, but Dad'll make those leaves into a tea for Tammy.

And now I wait to see if anyone gets my message in a bottle.

June 28 (Loop Current Charter Fishing Tours log entry)

Nice family today; a father, two sons, and one daughter. Calm seas, plenty of fish. The family took home a couple good-sized red snapper. My own line snagged at one point on some rubbish—it was a little bottle wearing a life jacket of corks, and would you believe, it had a kid's message in it. Decided to send it to Matt. He's shipping out next week; maybe he can drop it in the Straits of Malacca or something. If someone over there finds it and writes back, the kid'll really get a thrill.

June 28 (Em's diary)

I won't go to the post office today. There couldn't be a letter for me there yet. I hope not, anyway. I don't want nobody to have found my message in a bottle yet, because if they have, they're probably from around here. Unless the bottle really does go under the waves, to the seapeople.

Things I wonder about: What would happen if the Seafather himself found it? Would he harness up a seadragon and come riding right into Mermaid's Hands, to find out how we're all doing, here? Would he give me gills and invite me to come with him and have adventures?

But if he came in this close to shore, he might make a tsunami, and that would be bad. Small Bill says he wants a tsunami to take out Sandy Neck, but if a tsunami came, it would hit our houses first. Small Bill thinks we could float through it. It's not like a hurricane, he says. There's no wind. There's no rain.

Small Bill hates Sandy Neck because a lot of folks there are mean. They don't like people from Mermaid's Hands.

"It's because they're jealous," Dad says. "Scratching away at a hard, dry life on their hard, dry ground while we live life floating. What we need comes to us."

But some of the Sandy Neck folk go shrimping and fishing, too, so I don't think Dad is one hundred percent right.

"It's because they're afraid," Mr. Ovey says. "They're afraid of people with seablood. People who came out of the water, or are called into it."

That's what people in Mermaid's Hands have: seablood.

“Especially people with marlin blood, right Dad?” Small Bill says.

Things I need to remember: Not to be jealous of Small Bill’s genealogy. Mr. Ovey’s six-greats-ago grandfather was a marlin, and Mrs. Ovey’s seven-greats-ago grandmother was a sea turtle. But all of us got seablood, even if it’s not from creatures with gills or shells. We’re either born with it or it’s sung into us. The Seafather gave it to the Choctaw and Biloxi and Pensacola people who hid out in the salt marshes, so no white folks could find them, and to runaways and other slippery folk who were happier on the sea than the land—like Vaillant, who swam from Haiti to Cuba and Cuba to here, to get away from slavery. Gran said that when he found out there was slavery here, too, he decided to give up on dry land altogether and pledged allegiance to the sea. The Seafather admired Vaillant so much he gave him fins. Whenever Small Bill starts talking about his marlin ancestor, I start bragging on Vaillant’s fins. The marlin was just born with fins, but Vaillant earned them.

Vaillant’s one of my ancestors because of Granddad. Granddad died when I was little, but Gran tells the story of how Granddad came to Mermaid’s Hands: he swam in, just like Vaillant. He never would say where from. They sang him into Vaillant’s line when him and Gran got married.

Getting sung into a genealogy proves that not everyone on dry land is bad. Some of the best seachildren started out as dry-landers.

Ma came from dry land. Dad worked away from Mermaid’s Hands in a cannery the summer he turned eighteen, and he met Ma there. She told us how he brought her bouquets of whitetop sedge and milkwort and other wildflowers each morning, and at the end of the summer he brought her back to Mermaid's Hands to meet Gran and Granddad. When Dad married Ma, she got sung into a brand new line: red-winged blackbird. Tammy loves that, because she loves birds. And red-winged blackbirds are pretty, but they're land birds! Even if you can see them in the long grass in the water, sometimes.

It's true nobody would say Ma's one of the best seachildren. Ma don't even call herself one. Sometimes I think if only she'd of been sung into a petrel line, maybe it would of put a bigger love for Mermaid's Hands into her. I worry sometimes, that Ma don't like it here all that much. Dad and her argue a lot. But Dad says so long as he can get Ma to smile, everything'll be all right. Mostly I believe that.

July 1 (Em's diary)

There was nothing for me at the post office. There was only a letter for Ma from Aunt Brenda. Next time we go, I think it would be okay for me to get a letter. By then the bottle will of been floating long enough to reach someplace far away.

Person who gets my message, will you be a grown-up or a kid? Will you live right by the sea, or will you be visiting it? Will you be excited to find my letter?

I should of put a treasure map in my bottle, along with my note. A treasure map would of made it more exciting. But I'd need to have a treasure to do that, otherwise the map would be a lie, and I don't have a treasure.

Maybe tomorrow Small Bill will want to go looking for Sabelle Morning's treasure again. Just because we haven't found it yet don't mean it's not out there somewhere. We just need to look harder. Tammy can come too, and Skinnylegs and Clara, if she ain't busy watching her brothers.

Chapter 2. A Response

July 4 (Kaya to Em)

Dear Em,

It was a pleasure to get your message. Sumi, my pet crow, brought it to me.

You ask what it's like where I am. I'm a prisoner, actually. My prison has the poetic name "Lotus on the Ruby Lake." You mentioned in your letter that your house floats when the tide comes in. My house floats too, in a manner of speaking. It sits on a long wooden platform, which hangs from thick chains that are bolted into the sides of the crater of a volcano. If I lean over the rail at the edge of the platform, I can see the glowing lava of the Ruby Lake. It's not anyplace you'd want to swim, that's for sure.

My captors bring me supplies by helicopter once a week, and they let me send notes to my mother. I will include this message in my weekly note, and my mother will post it on to you.

Please do write again; it's very lonely here by myself.

Yours,

Kayamanira (Kaya) Matarayi

July 4 (Kaya to her mother)

Dear Mother,

You will see I am enclosing a little note in English; you will see an address in the lower corner—a wonderful-sounding place, with a name from a fairy tale, looking out on the great bowl of the Gulf of Mexico. If they hadn't confiscated my computer, you could go online and look for the place. Maybe you can go to the research station and ask Piyu (he's the friendly one) to find it for you, then write and tell me what it's like.

It's a reply to letter I've received from someone in America. Is it hard to believe? The way the letter came to me is even harder to believe. Yesterday, I was resting my elbows on the guard rail, just woolgathering. I was staring at the fires of the Ruby Lake and thinking that it's like a heart, an exposed heart. The mountain seems strangely vulnerable, when you think of the Ruby Lake that way.

I couldn't keep looking at it for long, though. It's too bright. It paints itself permanently on your eyes, the way the sun will if you stare at it. I closed my eyes and saw black spots where the lava had been especially bright, and when I opened them, one black spot remained, seeming to rise right out of the lava.

It was Sumi. Seeing her flying toward me that way put the old stories in my head, about crows being the tribute the Salu evergreens sent to the Lady of the Ruby Lake, and how they've been the Lady's messengers ever since.

But for all that Sumi seemed to be to flying up from the depths of the Ruby Lake, she must actually have been returning from a trip to the coast, because she brought me a present from the sea. It was a little bottle, and in the bottle, all soft and damp with seawater, was a piece of paper, a letter, still legible in spite of its soaking.

A letter in a bottle, can you imagine that? I remember Tema and I talked about messages in bottles the day I found Sumi, and now, years later—and I in these circumstances—Sumi brings me one! I'm laughing as I think about it, and when I laugh, Sumi cocks her head and looks at me sideways. Maybe she's smiling? She seems pleased with herself.

And the letter is from America. The bottle somehow traveled all the way from the Gulf of Mexico to here! Ocean currents should have sent it to England and Europe, if it ever made it out of the Gulf. And yet, here it is.

The writer seems young, maybe twelve or thirteen. The letter's in pencil and the handwriting is neat but not mature. She's looking out across the sea for a friend. I hope she does write again. If she does, you will be the one to receive the letter. Could you slip it in with your letter to me, so I can keep corresponding with her? You will be our go-between.

If you do see Piyu, ask him how the tobacco is doing. Are the plants healthy? Oh—and the orange seedlings. Have the orange seedlings taken?

Also, you have not sent me any news about Ramiratam and the others for two letters now. Is it that you have no news, or there's no progress, or has there been news, but it's bad? You must tell me everything you know, even bad things.

I am so sorry to be such a fountain of ceaseless demands. I wish there were some way I could ease your burdens and make your days happier.

Your loving daughter,
Kayamanira

July 4 (Kaya's memoir)

It's no good; I can't pretend any longer that I can continue my research here. I need something else to fill up the days and keep me from staring too hard and long at the Ruby Lake. So: a memoir. I will write down my thoughts on how I came to be here, what it all means. I don't expect that anyone will ever see what I write, but perhaps I can gain some certainty by writing things down, some strength.

Then, if Em should write again, if she asks questions, maybe I will be better prepared to answer her. A village of floating houses, roped together—I've never heard of such a way of life in America. Could it be that Em's people are as much outsiders in her country as mine are in mine? In which case, part of me can't help thinking that somehow the Lady of the Ruby Lake really does have a hand in Em's message coming to me. A superstitious, wishful part of me! When did that part get so strong? It must be the sulfur fumes.

July 10 (Em's diary)

I got a letter! I got a letter today—it was in with a doctor bill and ads, a letter for me! *And it came from a different country.* The stamp has a picture of flowers and mountains. Dad was talking with Ma about the bill and Tammy was looking at the picture of the hummingbirds in the ad for hummingbird feeders, and I was just turning the letter over and over in my hands, not quite believing it was real.

"What's that you have?" Dad asked. "Something else from *Kids Speak*?" He asked that because last fall my teacher made us all write essays on Best Family Traditions and sent them in to an essay contest. After that, everyone in class kept getting letters asking if we wanted to buy a book with all the essays in it. The book was called *Kids Speak.* I think I got three letters from them, but that book was way too expensive. Really the only good thing about writing that essay was getting the idea to have this diary: What it's like being Emlee Baptiste, living in Mermaid's Hands. One day I'll make a book of it that anyone can afford to buy.

"No, it's a letter from far away," I said, but Dad wasn't paying attention anymore, because Ma was talking to him about the bill again.

I knew next Ma and Dad would go back out to Mermaid's Hands to see Mr. Tiptoe to find out if there was any extra money from the sale of the last catch. If there was, then probably he'd give them some, and then they'd take it to the doctor's office.

I wanted to go read my letter by myself, but I also didn't want Tammy to have to tag along with Ma and Dad for all that. She can't help it if she's always coughing, and it's not her fault Ma wants her to see a dry-land doctor that costs a bunch of money instead of just using sea remedies. So I told her she could come along with me.

"We're going to Foul Point," I told Ma and Dad.

"Just be home before it gets dark," Ma said.

Foul Point is called Fowl Point on maps, but we call it Foul Point because it stinks sometimes. Pretty often, really. It stinks because of all the birds that flock there, but that's why me and Tammy like it, too, for the birds, and for the no-people. No dry-land people go there, because it's hard to reach if you don't want to get wet, and no fishermen go there because of the cordgrass and the rocks, and not so many fish, and not even other kids from Mermaid's Hands go there much, because Mrs. Ovey said in the olden days it's where we seachildren would take all the chamber pot stuff from our houses to dump. Ewww, go wading through long-ago this-and-that? No thanks! That's what they're thinking.

But long ago is long ago. Now it's just bird doo that makes Foul Point foul. Mainly terns. Terns like to nest there.

We didn't see many terns there today. Instead we saw lots of red-thread dancers, so delicate! Red-thread dancers is our name for them, because their legs are as thin as red threads, and their walking looks like dancing, but I got a bird book out of the library once, and their book name is black-necked stilt. They do look like they're walking on stilts. And today there were also brown willet birds there. Tammy went looking for abandoned nests in the grass, and I sat on a rock and examined my letter.

There was my name on the envelope, written in thin letters and wobbly. Maybe a grandmother or a grandfather wrote it. I used my finger like a knife to get into the envelope, and then I took out the paper inside. It was in different handwriting. Pretty writing, darker and stronger than what was on the envelope. I read the letter.

"Who is it from?" Tammy asked. I hadn't even heard her come up. I was thinking about volcanoes. I was imagining a platform hanging from chains over a lava lake, and a house on the platform, and someone in the house, writing me a letter.

"A prisoner. It's from a prisoner in …" I had to look at the envelope again. The country name came at the bottom of the return address: W—. That was the word on the stamp, too, in small letters under the picture.

"A prisoner in W—," I said, "Want to go to the library? I want to find out where W— is."

"Can I see the letter? I'll show you what I found." I let her look at the letter, and she gave me two long straight feathers, one small fluffy one with speckles, and a bottle cap.

"I like the bottle cap 'cause it's purple," said Tammy, leaning in to share my looking at it. She reached for it again. It was purple with a mark sort of like a butterfly on it, in white.

"It's a good one. You don't have many purple ones, do you?"

She shook her head.

"Those two come from the red-thread dancers, I think," she said, pointing to the long straight feathers. They were white with black tips.

"Matching, too," I said, holding them both up. "One for each hand. You can make wing magic."

Tammy nodded. "I can't read the writing," she said, handing the letter back to me. "Will you read it?"

I read it to her. Tammy frowned.

"That's a bad place to live. I wonder why they put her there."

"I wonder too. I feel sorry for her," I said. It made me think of Jiminy, since he's a prisoner too. Dad don't want us to feel sorry for him, but I do.

"She has a crow, though," Tammy remarked. "Crows are witchy birds. You think maybe she's a witch? Maybe they put her over the volcano because she's a witch."

"You think? I don't think having a crow makes you a witch. Sabelle Morning had a crow, and she wasn't a witch."

"But she was a pirate."

"But she was a good-guy pirate. A Mermaid's Hands pirate."

Tammy shrugged. "Ma says there ain't no good-guy pirates."

Yeah, that sounds like Ma all right, not believing there's such a thing as good pirates. And Tammy spends too much time with Ma on account of always being sick, and so she don't understand about good pirates versus bad ones.

"I'm just saying that having a crow don't make you a witch," I said. "And crows are smart, too. Were you around when Uncle Near told the story about Sabelle's crow?"

Tammy shook her head.

"It could talk, just like a parrot. Government revenue agents—those were who chased pirates and smugglers, back in olden times—captured the crow and tried to get it to tell them where Sabelle was, but instead the crow took them up and down the coast and made their ship run aground in shallow water."

Tammy grinned.

"Uncle Near says that the grandchildren of that crow could tell us where Sabelle's treasure is, if we knew which crows those were."

"Okay, so they're smart," said Tammy. "But they ain't as pretty as hummingbirds, or red-thread dancers."

Tammy loves pretty things. I think crows are kind of pretty, with their shiny feathers, but it's hard to compare them with hummingbirds and red-thread dancers.

"So you coming along to the library with me?" I asked. She nodded.

At the library I found out that the country the letter came from, W—, is an island right mixed in with the islands that are the country of Indonesia, which is not the same place as India. India is a big diamond shape that sticks down from Asia into the ocean, but Indonesia is a long splash of islands further to the east. At first I couldn't find W—, but the librarian showed me how one island on the map was colored blue when all the islands of Indonesia were colored orange.

Then she showed me how I could find photos of W— on the computer. There were photos of towns and villages all around the edges of the island, and there were photos of the capital city, a jumble of grand-looking buildings and patched-together ones and streets crowded with people and cars and even long-horned cattle, and then photos of mountains in the middle of the island, dark green with trees. Then she typed in a different search, and it showed people. Some were fishing, in small boats no bigger than ours, not big ones like the dry-land people use, and some were bending and planting stuff in fields, and some were selling things on the street in the city. One photo was of some girls all dressed up in fancy costumes, doing a dance.

"Ooh," said Tammy. "I'd like a dress like that. Do you think the lady who wrote to you wears things like that?"

"Probably not unless she's a dancer," I said. I wanted to see if I could find pictures of Kaya's volcano, but when I typed "Lotus on the Ruby Lake," the computer just gave me pictures of flowers and lakes and other things. So then I tried typing "W—" and "volcano," and this time a bunch of pictures came up, pictures of bright redness, with veins and streaks of gold across it, sitting in a dark black dish—that was the crater. None of the pictures had a hanging platform in them, though. I guess they only built Kaya's prison recently.

I switched the computer back to the library's home page. It made me feel kind of funny in the stomach to think about a house above all that lava.

"Library closes in ten minutes," the librarian said.

"Let's go," I said to Tammy.

July 11 (Em's diary)

Today while the tide was out and we were helping to make some cordgrass sun capes at the Oveys' house, I told Small Bill about the letter.

"Do you have it with you?"

I pulled it out of my back pocket. It was kind of damp, but the words hadn't blurred.

"Wow," he said, after he read it. "Wow. A volcano." He frowned a little. Maybe he was trying to imagine the scene. I had an idea of it. I had an idea that Kaya's house was like one of ours, only where we have the sea around us, she has air, and under that, lava.

"It made me think of Jiminy," I said. "But I guess Jiminy's lucky compared to her. Least he's not sitting over a volcano."

I never thought of being in Clear Springs Prison as being lucky before.

"Yeah, it's gotta be easier to break out of Clear Springs," said Small Bill. He plied some more cordgrass into his length of twine.

I'm glad I can talk to Small Bill about Jiminy. Dad won't ever talk about him at home. When we heard that Jiminy confessed, Dad said, "I guess he ain't a seachild after all." And that was the end of it. We didn't get to go to the sentencing or anything.

Dry-land folks think Mermaid's Hands folks are all lazy and criminals, but we're not like that at all! Not since Sabelle Morning's time, and she only stole to help those in need. Like I try to tell Tammy, she was a good-guy pirate. Jiminy, though, wasn't stealing for nobody but himself. He gave everybody in Sandy Neck a reason to say *See? We knew they were like that.*

But I still think Dad should of stuck up for Jiminy. Not turned on him like that.

Small Bill's dad ain't so cold as our dad is. "Everybody makes mistakes," Mr. Ovey told Dad once. "You gotta release your anger and keep your son." But Dad don't hear him. Mrs. Ovey told us we should say his name to the waves when the tide's going out, so the Seafather knows we want him back. Ma won't do that, because she don't believe in the Seafather, but me and Tammy do it, and Gran does it.

I wrote some letters to Jiminy, but he don't like writing much. He's only written back once. He said he wanted cigarettes, but inmates can only get care packages three times a year, and you're not allowed to send things like cigarettes.

"I'm gonna write Kaya back," I told Small Bill. "She needs a friend. I'm gonna make her my pen pal."

I hope Kaya writes back.

Tammy and I wove the last of the loose grass into the wide zigzags of twine that Small Bill had made. Sun cape, done! I held it up.

"How's it look?"

Small Bill nodded, good, it looks good, and Mrs. Ovey came over, and she said it was good too. That one'll be for Mr. Winterhull, who'd be burned as red as a dry-land farmer if he didn't cover up, out there fishing, but anyone who goes out fishing all day should wear one, even people like Dad, who are as black as nighttime. A sun cape keeps you good and cool.

"How are you doing, Tammy? Still struggling with the air above the waves?" Mrs. Ovey asked. She likes to say that Tammy has a little too much seablood in her, and that's why she coughs and wheezes: she's not used to air. Tammy loves this because it makes her feel like a true mermaid.

I get a little jealous, though, because who can swim from our house to the Oveys' when the tide's in and not even come up for air? Me. And who can guess right (most of the time) about when a storm's coming from where the redfish gather? Me! I can do it as good as Small Bill's granddad, and he's the oldest in Mermaid's Hands. So don't that make me pretty full of seablood?

Things I need to remember: It's no fun for Tammy to be stuck at home wheezing and coughing while we're out exploring. When I remember that, my jealousy dries right up.

I cringed inside when Tammy told Mrs. Ovey about Ma and the doctor and the dry-land cough medicine, but at least she also said that she liked the tea that Mrs. Ovey gave her.

"Of course you did, my mermaid miss," Mrs. Ovey said, after raising her eyebrows and pursing her lips like she's never heard such nonsense, when Tammy was telling her the other part.

Why does Ma have to be such a red-winged blackbird? But also, why does Mrs. Ovey need to be so surprised? Ma and Dad've been together for nineteen years. Mrs. Ovey knows what Ma's like.

We made one more sun cape from scratch and repaired a couple others, and then Mrs. Ovey said she didn't need no more help and we could run along, so we went back to our house, and I wrote a letter to Kaya and Small Bill made a map for a game we made up before, called Jellyfish Invasion, and Tammy drew a picture of what a red-thread dancer would look like if it turned into a person.

Chapter 3. Seagulls and Crows

July 11 (Em to Kaya)

Dear Kaya,

Wow! I never thought my bottle would go all the way to another country! I never got a letter before with a stamp from another country. It's pretty.

I'm sorry that you're a prisoner. Did you commit a crime? My big brother Jiminy did. He snuck into a floating casino and was stealing from the people there, but they caught him.

I would visit him if I could, but his prison is not even in the same state, and Dad would never let us go, because he thinks Jiminy threw away his family when he started stealing things. Ma says we should keep him in our prayers, and Gran says the Seafather will find a way to free him, because no seachild should be stuck so far away on dry land, even if he's a thief.

Ma shakes her head when anyone talks about the Seafather. She doesn't believe in him, but that's because she came from dry land herself. "I loved your Daddy so much, I gave up a proper house to come live out here on the mud," she tells us, but Dad smiles and says, "No, Josie, that ain't how it is. I rescued you. From a hard stiff land life, and brought you here to be rocked by the sea each day. Now that's love."

I went to the library and asked the librarian to show me where your country is on the map. It's very far away. It's got the ocean all around it, though. Maybe the Seafather can send seagulls to you.

One time when I got to talk to Jiminy on Mr. Tiptoe's phone, he said he saw seagulls twice in the prison yard, even being hundreds of miles away from the sea.

I will keep writing to you.

Your friend,

Em

P.S. Here is a wing feather from a laughing gull. If you keep it, then any seagulls who visit will know you're a friend.

July 20 (Kaya's mother to Kaya)

My dear girl,

Look what came for you—a letter from your new friend in America. I am doing as you suggested and sending it along with my note to you. Do you see your friend has drawn a stamp, next to the actual stamp, on the envelope? Pretty, isn't it, the curling vine and the red flowers.

Still nothing to report about Ramiratam and the others, I'm afraid. The media doesn't mention them at all—nothing about charges or a trial—not even any rumors make it to our ears.

With Ramiratam and the others detained and you in that suspended prison, everything has become very quiet here once again—no separatist talk, no old songs for the Lady of the Ruby Lake, nothing. It's as if the celebration and all the ferment at the beginning of the year never happened. As for the government's story regarding your "elevation," most people recognize it as mockery, just another insult that must be borne. There are some, though, who really seem to think the government is sincere, and take this as proof, somehow, of your connection to the Lady! I don't know whether to laugh or groan. I wish I could inhabit their pleasant reality.

Try to keep your spirits up. Don't fret about me and whether I'm well. You know I'm proud of you, and if your father could have lived to see the path you've taken, he would have been too. Yes, even though he never spoke about politics.

The man from the security services who brings me your letters has permitted me to send you the enclosed book of poems. Remember when you went off to St. Margaret's? You wouldn't let me pack this book; you insisted on carrying it with you. You were so determined to show your new lowland classmates that we in the mountains were not the primitives they imagined, but cosmopolitan and cultured. I doubt you mentioned the Lady of the Ruby Lake to them! How different things are now.

Stay well, Kayamanira
With love,
your mother

P.S. Did you know that Sumi sometimes visits me? I always give her a little treat.

July 26 (Kaya's memoir)

This evening I feel parched, though they've left me plenty of water. I think it's green things I'm thirsty for, and birdsong. Poor Sumi. You're a fine bird, but you can't help me there.

But they left a different sort of refreshment, better than water in its way: a letter from Em, this time by post instead of ocean waves and Sumi.

She asks if I committed a crime. Such a direct question! How can I answer her? The law says I did, but if the law itself is criminal, then is it a crime to break it?

She mentions the Seafather. He must be a sea spirit or deity, I guess, but not one I ever heard of when I was studying in America. Perhaps it's only people in her floating village who know him. Maybe, then, if I ask Em to imagine what it would be like if one day it became a crime to honor the Seafather, she would understand what it's like here, never being able to celebrate the Lady of the Ruby Lake.

But Em probably doesn't spend much time thinking about grand ideas like freedom of religion any more than I did, when I was her age. I didn't care, in primary school, that the teachers told us not to sing our songs on the school grounds. Why should I, when we could sing them on the walk home? Just as I never wondered why it was that our people only appeared in the history books at the point when the lowland kingdom extended its reach up into the mountains, as if we didn't exist before then. That was just the way it was: school was where we learned about distant, confusing lowland history. For our own history—the exciting stories about the Five Sister Kingdoms of olden days—we relied on grandparents and parents. That was the ordinary pattern of life.

We weren't thinking about olden-days stories in our final year of primary school, though. What excited me and Nawalam and Dinasha that year was the thought that if we studied very hard, we might win a scholarship to one of the prestigious secondary schools in Palem, the capital city, down on the coast. We were the first cohort of students from the mountains to be required to learn the national language from our first year of school, so we were the first to whom the scholarship was offered—and we were thrilled. That's how far from activists we all were!

Some of our classmates, the ones who suffered more in trying to master the national language (it was three switches on the shoulders anytime we lapsed into our native tongue), no doubt felt more bitter about how things were, but not us: we were the ambitious ones. We were going to remake ourselves as lowlanders. The separatist movement that had been crushed when we were small children was a severe embarrassment to us. How could our aunties and uncles have participated in something so shameful and foolish, so damaging to our nation?

Every now and then we'd overhear the grown-ups talking about those days, among themselves, but then they'd notice us listening and the talk would die. "We have to think of their future," they'd say, nodding in our direction, and, "It's just the way things are." Always with a note of regret in their voices that we didn't want to hear.

I wonder how Ramiratam felt, back then. None of us knew—not in primary school—about his parents. Our parents would never talk about it—certainly not my father, who hated political talk, or my mother, whose brother had been detained, but then released. But Ramiratam must have known. Was it hard for him to keep silent? Or was it like second nature, self-preservation? Rami, if I could be granted one wish, it wouldn't be to change anything that's happened in the past year. I would wish to have been a better, more perceptive friend to you back when we were all younger.

Ramiratam wasn't even going to try for the boys' scholarship, and none of us understood why he held back, since we all knew that he was a better student than boastful Nawalam, who claimed to be the best in our school.

"Conceding the field?" Nawalam teased. "You're making things too easy for me." So then Ramiratam did try—and lost out to Nawalam. I couldn't believe it. Nawalam scored higher than Rami? My confusion grew deeper when I caught a glimpse of Ramiratam's exam on the headmaster's desk when I was dropping off the attendance. In the final box, neatly printed in red: ninety-five. Five points higher than the score Nawalam was bragging about to one and all. Ramiratam was the top scorer. Why didn't he say anything? His silence kept me silent too, for three days, until I could no longer tolerate the mysterious injustice. But when I finally worked up the courage to ask him about it, all he would say was that the exam score was only part of what determined who received the scholarship, and that he had never expected to win.

I wanted to ask Dinasha for her opinion on how this could have happened, but there was something about Rami's face, and voice, when he spoke to me, that kept me from sharing my secret knowledge even with her. I was left thinking about it on my own.

To thirteen-year-old me, it simply didn't make sense. It couldn't be bad character: Ramiratam was always helping the younger students with their work, never smoked, had never snuck off to steal a taste of Uncle Satmelelin's distilled Dragonfire. He did once jump from the shell of the abandoned dump truck into the flooded quarry on a dare, but I don't think the teachers ever found out about that, and anyway, that belonged in the category of bravery, not bad character.

Family circumstance? Nawalam's family owned so much land that they hired other people to help them till it. Ramiratam lived with his grandparents, not in our narrow valley but somewhere on the actual mountainside, far enough away that he had to leave before sunrise to reach school each day. You could see the sharp bones of Rami's shoulders through his uniform shirt where they had worn the cloth thin; Nawalam had a new shirt each year. But wasn't a scholarship meant to erase distinctions of wealth?

It made me wonder if maybe I hadn't deserved to win the girls' scholarship. Maybe it should have gone to Dinasha. I couldn't bring myself to ask her outright what she'd scored on the exam, but when I expressed my doubts about the scholarship, she just rolled her eyes.

"How could you have won the scholarship if you scored lower than I did? No, I'm sure you won it fair and square. I might have come close to you on the language questions, but I didn't finish the maths section, and I'm never good at identifying literary passages. You'll just have to live with the glory—and uphold mountain honor!"

Again I felt the urge to tell her about Nawalam and Ramiratam's scores, but again I held my tongue. Instead I vowed I'd be a second

Morakalan.

Morakalan, the one person from the mountains that the lowlanders know and admire, because he embraced lowland ways, learned the lowland language, wrote poems in the classical lowland style, and fought with all the lowland patriots for W—'s independence. That's who I wanted to model myself on. I wanted my new classmates to see me as accomplished, knowledgeable, modern, and as much a child of W— as they all were.

* * *

At St. Margaret's, I was lucky to have Tema as a bunkmate. She was bossy, yes, but she was a shield, too, against the other girls' careless (and sometimes deliberate) cruelties, and she became a true friend.

On the first day, girls were milling around, finding their bunkmates. Many of them gave me mistrustful looks or turned away entirely when I tried to meet their eyes, and my resolve to be bold and friendly was trickling away. Then Tema came over. I'm embarrassed to say I was intimidated—all the lowlanders are very tall, but she was exceptionally so. Most of the other girls had their hair in plaits or pony tails, but Tema had hers cut at an angle at chin length. It swayed like curtain fringe when she moved her head.

"You must be the girl from the mountains, Kayamarina … no; that's wrong, isn't it: Kayarima … no: Kayana—"

"Kayamanira," I said. "But you can call me Kaya."

"Kaya—that's much easier. I'm your bunkmate, Tema. Don't you worry about them," she added, waving her hand at the rest of the girls. "I won't let them pick on you. I know which ones are friendly and which ones are impossible stuck-up snobs. Come on; let's go. Here, help me with my bags—that's part of how it works in the dorms: first-years get a second-year bunkmate to look after them, but in return they have to do favors if the second-year asks. I'll be very reasonable, though; not like my bunkmate when I was a first-year. Ughh, she thought she was queen of the dormitory. And don't worry; we'll come back and get your stuff. Is that all you brought? Huh. That's not much. Is it true that all the mountain natives are poor? I heard the only prosperous people in the mountains are those who moved there from the lowlands. I suppose you must be here on scholarship. I pay full fees—my father runs Pearl Fin Consolidated Fisheries. He's got to be a millionaire at least."

That was the way she always talked: a continuous, quick-moving stream of words. I had been nervous about my accent, but at that moment I thought that perhaps I'd get by without having to say a word at all. After she had made her remark about her father, one of the other girls said,

"Phew, does anyone smell fish? Oh, I should have known: it's the fish oil millionairess. Did you know if you eat too much fish, it makes you monstrously tall?"

Several of the girls laughed, and I felt my heartbeat speeding up. But Tema didn't bat an eye, just said, "My goodness, Shim, all those sweets you hide under your pillow, and yet you're as sour as raw tamarind. Still hankering after an invite from the princesses? And yet you still haven't got one. Can't imagine why not!"

Some of the very same girls who had laughed at Shim's taunt laughed at Tema's retort. Shim lifted up her chin and wrinkled her nose and said to the girls near her,

"I really don't think I can bear the fish stink any longer. Let's go talk to the new English instructor. Peri says she taught in Japan before coming here and can sing both Spice Girls *and* Amuro Namie songs." She and two or three others girls wandered off.

"That's terrible, what she said," I ventured.

"Oh, Shim doesn't bother me. I have plenty of friends." She said it lightly, casually, but the way her eyes traveled after those girls and the way she pressed her lips together after saying it made me wonder.

"See them?" she said, pointing to two girls standing under the giant angsana tree in the center of the courtyard, heads practically touching as they looked at something one of them was holding. I nodded.

"Everybody calls them the princesses because they're both from the old royal family. You wouldn't believe how some of the girls fawn over them. It's ridiculous. Like the royal family ever did anything for W—. My father's done more for W— than any prince in a gold jacket and scarlet eyeliner." She made a face.

"And it's not as if it does girls like Shim any good to play up to them. They'll only ever associate with other former aristocrats. Stupid."

As if aware that they were the topic of discussion, the two girls looked up. Tema narrowed her eyes. "I don't believe it. They can't possibly be coming over here."

But they were. They stopped in front of us and stared at me.

"See, Sarei? Mountain people really are small, and so dark! Like black lacquer," remarked the one on the left, whom I found out later was called Vira. "Just like something out of an anthropology film." To me she said, "Tell me, is it really true that you people wear bones and feathers in your hair?"

I was at a loss for words. *Do you mean children's good luck charms?* I wanted to ask, and *Lowlanders don't have those? You don't call on birds by bone and feather, for protection, and plait the charm into children's hair?* But then I recalled how angry it made the headmaster whenever he saw any of the year-eight students wearing one. How he scolded! My mother had wanted to plait mine in my hair when we were taking the high school entrance exams, just for luck, but I said I didn't need luck, just more time studying.

"Doesn't she speak our language?" Vira asked, turning to Tema.

"Of course I do!" I said, finding my tongue at last. "It's my language too, you know. No, we don't wear bones and feathers in our hair, any more than you do."

That's how I sold out my home and my people that first day—erased our childhood good-luck charms, denied the tears we shed to master the national language.

"Oh, too bad," said Vira, almost pouting. "I guess we won't get to see an exotic costume on uniform-free days. Well, keep her in line, Tima—"

"It's Tema," Tema corrected, but Vira ignored the interruption.

"—and don't let her embarrass herself. You're such an expert on so many things that might trip a backwoods innocent up. Things like Western toilets and all—didn't you treat the whole dorm to an explanation of Western toilets last year? Fascinating stuff." Sarei laughed, and the two of them drifted away.

"Stupid princesses," Tema muttered. "Let's hurry up and get settled; no point in hanging around here. Grab that bag—no, that one."

She strode off at quite a pace; I practically had to run to keep up with her, which was hard, lugging one of her bags and my own.

"False praise is worse than jeers," she said, shoving underthings into the sliding drawers under the bunk bed. "Maybe the princesses think it's crude to talk about toilets, but some girls really don't know. If you don't come from the capital, you might never have seen one … have you seen a Western toilet?"

One thing I loved right away about Tema was that she would talk about anything, directly, and with her full heart. Even embarrassing things. Em reminds me of Tema in her directness.

"The headmaster told us about them before we left. One of about a hundred miscellaneous things he thought we should know."

Then I took the plunge and turned the conversation. "You said 'False praise is worse than jeers.' Were you- Did you know that Morakalan uses that phrase in the fourth of his *Sixteen Odes*?"

He's from the mountains, I wanted to add, *and he's in the literature textbook.*

Tema looked at me blankly, and I instantly wished I hadn't brought up poetry. Perhaps Tema hated poetry. Then her face brightened.

"Oh! you mean Kalan. We usually just call him Kalan. Why do mountain names have to be so long? Yes, I love Kalan's poems—he's not as good as Pirar, but sometimes he has just the right way of expressing things. So … you like poetry? Do you have literary aspirations?" She sounded almost anxious when she asked.

"I do like poetry," I said. "Literary … aspirations?" For a moment the meaning of the word escaped me, but then I remembered. "I-I don't think so. I like to write poems, but I need to do something more practical later in life. Something to help people where I live. I think I want to become a doctor or a biologist or something like that."

Tema flashed a radiant smile when I said that.

"Oh well, that's perfect then. Yes, you study sciences; I don't mind at all if you excel in science. In fact, it could be handy. Me, I intend to become a literary critic and a novelist and maybe run a newspaper one day—and I wouldn't mind recognition for poetry too, and it would be awkward if you and I both wanted to be school poet. But if you want to do well in sciences, you probably won't have much time for poetry, so how about you leave writing poems and winning literary contests to me, and I'll leave science contests to you? All right?"

On the one hand, Tema was including me in her imagined future of fame and greatness, and there was something intoxicating about her confidence. On the other hand—not write any more poems? Could I keep on writing them on the sly, maybe late at night or very early in the morning, without her finding out? And what about *reading* poetry?

My face must have given me away.

"What's wrong?" she asked.

"Nothing! But … you wouldn't mind if I still *read* poetry, would you?"

She laughed.

"Of course not! I'll want you to read my efforts, for one thing. How about we pick out a poem a night, to share? Come on; don't look so solemn! What do you say?"

I managed a smile.

"All right; yes."

And our futures did turn out as she imagined, more or less. When we finished high school, she entered a journalism program at W— National University, and I went to America to study agronomy. Tema wrote me while I was in America to say that she had a job with a TV news station. Just before I came back to W—, she wrote that she was engaged to be married.

I guess she'll have heard about what I and the others have done, about the "trouble." The "agitation." What must she think? My protector and friend, and now we stand on opposite sides of a deep gulf.

And what about my childhood friends, who let me lead them into this mess? "It's not political; we won't let it be political," I said, but we're in prison all the same.

July 27 (Kaya's memoir)

Just now I awoke with my heart racing and an indescribable feeling of *something* hanging over me. I jumped up from my sleeping mat and ran out to the platform rail for air and … and I don't know why else. To be reassured? By the Ruby Lake?

That makes no sense.

But I am not becoming unhinged. I'm not. It was just a dream haunt—the work of a cave bat, we'd say at home.

I never would have mentioned cave bats or any other such thing during my school days. It dismayed me to realize just how completely my classmates thought that mountain people were primitives—either primitives, or stupid and idle. It drove me to study harder and longer, so that whenever I was called on, I could answer intelligently. While the other girls were singing along to radio hits, I was listening to the announcers, repeating their phrases in my head, trying to get the trick of intonation and emphasis just right so that I could duplicate it when I spoke. My looks might reveal me for a mountain native, but I was determined not to sound like one.

I schooled myself to brush off slighting remarks from my classmates and dorm mates, but it hurt when Tema said something dismissive. I tried never to mention anything about home, so as to not let an opportunity arise, but sometimes I would let something slip, like at the midterm study session Tema organized for first-years in our wing. We were going over the complicated tribute and hostage situation between the princes of W— and the Johor sultanate, and I said it was like the arrangement among the Five Sister Kingdoms.

"Tribes," she said. "You mean tribes."

"No, they were kingdoms," I said, realizing even as the words were leaving my mouth that I was wandering into unsafe territory. I saw the other girls exchanging glances; a couple hid smiles behind their hands. Tema flipped to the index of the history book and ran her finger down the columns.

"Look," she said, pointing. Under the entry for the mountain region, along with "pacification of" and "tribal conflicts," was "Five Sister Tribes."

"The word we use is 'tribes,'" she explained. Just correcting a word-choice error on my part.

"We call them kingdoms," I said, hunching my shoulders. I couldn't stop myself. Memories of a certain day in the fifth year of primary school were filling my mind.

"But the word is 'kingdom,'" I said to Ramiratam, through furious tears, as we were leaving school that day. "I know what 'tribe' means and I know what 'kingdom' means. The word should be 'kingdom.' The book has it wrong."

"If it's in the mountains, it's tribes, not kingdoms, as far as lowlanders are concerned," Dinasha said.

"But that's the wrong word! They've got it wrong. They're not understanding our language correctly."

"They understand the language; they just have their own ideas of what makes a kingdom, and nothing in the mountains fits," Rami said, picking up a pebble and tossing it at a battered road sign. It pinged and fell. From behind us someone called. It was Nawalam, jogging to catch up.

"So you actually went and got yourself switched over the stupid history book," he said, panting a little. "That's very noble of you.

How're the shoulders?"

I evaded the clap on the back that he attempted to give me and scowled.

"I just think the textbook should use the right words," I muttered.

"Sure, me too," he said. "It's an idiotic textbook and an idiotic language. Hey, what say we get everyone in class to say 'kingdoms' instead of 'tribes,' as a protest? Can you imagine it?" He grinned. "It would drive Mr. Baktin mad." Then he shrugged. "It's probably not worth the sore back, though. Who cares whether lowlanders want to say 'tribe' or 'kingdom'?"

"I care!"

"I care too," said Ramiratam, "but you've got to just say 'tribe.'" He turned to Nawalam.

"You shouldn't joke about a protest. They can do more than switch you." His face was painfully serious; we all stared at him.

"I'm not afraid of old Baktin," said Nawalam, but his voice was uncertain.

"Just say 'tribe,'" Rami repeated. "You know they're really the Five Sister Kingdoms. For each time you have to say 'tribe' in school, say 'kingdom' five times on your way home. That's what I do."

Tema gave me her best big-sisterly smile. "I guess to mountain people they seemed like kingdoms, but if you think about the population and wealth they controlled, or the social organization, they really weren't at the level of kingdoms," she said.

I nodded, but I felt as if I had an ax blade stuck in my chest.

* * *

It wasn't until the day I found Sumi that I saw life in W— as maybe more complicated than lowlanders versus mountain people. That day, first-years and second-years took a field trip to Tasan Port, at the eastern end of Palem Bay, to see the annual boat races. Some of the boats were more than a century old, and all were beautiful, carved and painted to resemble dolphins, whales, and fantastical fishes with spiked and jointed fins. After the races finished, we had a couple of hours free to find food and explore the port before boarding the bus back to school. We were supposed to move about in groups of four, but I got separated from my group when my eyes were caught by a fishing net that seemed to be possessed by a spirit. All along the dock, draped from rails, yellow and orange nets hung limply, drying, but this one was rippling and writhing. The other nets were sleeping. This one was having nightmares.

Something was in there, tossing about like a fish. I came closer and saw it was a bird, but not a white-winged gull or tern. No, this bird was black as ink.

"'Sumi,' that's 'ink' in Japanese," I informed the creature as I got closer. "That's what you're as black as."

Sumi stopped struggling, fixed her left eye on me, and cawed. I saw her right wing was caught in the net's mesh. She went back to fierce fluttering as I tried to slide her wing free.

"Stop it! You're only going to—"

hurt yourself, I thought. She fell at my feet, still fluttering madly, her right wing spread at an unlikely angle.

Half a crab dangled from the inside of the net, no doubt the lure that had attracted Sumi in the first place. I pulled off a jointed leg.

"Sit still. Here have some of this," I said. Her sharp beak

snapped at it. I let her have the whole thing. She held it in place with one of her feet as she devoured it. What to do about the damaged wing, though? Was it merely dislocated, or broken? I'd have to feel the wing to tell, and Sumi would never let me.

Unless perhaps I wrapped her up in something? She seemed small, maybe a juvenile, but even so, our uniform neckerchief wouldn't be big enough …

I crouched down and spread my skirt over her. Holding her wrapped in its folds, I felt along her good wing, then the limp one, and found a break.

"Kaya, what are you doing? It's getting late. Where's your group?"

I looked up. Tema was standing beside me, one hand shielding her eyes from the afternoon sun, the other holding a paper shopping bag with turquoise tissue paper peeking over the top.

"This crow has a broken wing. I'm trying to think of how to help it."

"A crow? Those are carrion eaters! You shouldn't touch something like that. You could get sick."

"But it's hurt! And crows are the Lady's birds." Like at the study session, the words just slipped out.

"What lady?" Then, comprehension dawning, "Oh, you mean … the volcano. Mountain people— I didn't think— I—"

I could see her searching for the right thing to say, but we were both spared by the arrival of a fisherman.

"What's the problem, girls? What do you have there?" He spoke differently from the people in the capital, with drawn-out s sounds and without the staccato quickness. It was the first thing I noticed about him: that he spoke with an accent—like me—but a different accent. And he was dark, too, almost as dark as I am, from working beneath the open sun all day. Still tall, though, like all the lowlanders. The wind was ruffling his hair, and there were fans of lines by his eyes, sun-squint lines.

"My friend found an injured crow, uncle. She won't just leave it here, even though they're dirty birds," Tema said.

She looked at me accusingly, but any anger or defensiveness I might have felt was lost in surprise over the way she spoke: Tema answered the man in the very same accents he had used.

"Ah, crow, is it? Gulls are the usual thieves." He squatted down beside me. "You're from the mountains, aren't you."

I nodded.

"Thought so. My brother worked up there, in the eastern mountain district, at a logging camp."

"I'm from the western mountain district," I said.

"We have to go, Kaya. Let uncle get rid of the crow," Tema said, switching back to standard speech. "You heard—they're thieves, like gulls."

"I know that!" I flared. "They steal from fields at home, too, but you have to let them take what they need, because—" I stopped. I didn't want to bring up the Lady again.

"They belong to the Lady of the Ruby Lake," finished the fisherman. Tema and I both stared at him.

"You know about her? From your brother?" I asked.

"We know about her here," he said. "We always knew about her. Crazy sister of the Lady of the Currents."

"Not crazy," I protested, "just wild, and, and … powerful." But a question flashed into my mind, cutting through the memories of the stories of the Lady that my mother and grandmother used to tell me. *When is wildness craziness?*

"Don't worry, little daughter. I'm not speaking evil of her. The Lady of the Currents is crazy too, sometimes, just, she brings us more good than the Lady of the Ruby Lake."

"You believe in the Lady of the Ruby Lake?" Tema asked, disbelief in her voice.

"You didn't know that? You speak like you're from hereabouts. Haven't you ever been to the blessing of a new boat? Seen'm spill a few drops of blood over a flame as well as in the water? A little gift to both sisters, keep'm from asking for a bigger gift, later on."

He turned to me. "Now look, little daughter. If you want the crow to get better, you have to bind its wing right close to its body, just the way it always holds it, so it can heal up—but then you need to take the bindings off in good time for it to remember how to fly. Got something to use as a bandage?"

"I … I could use the extra cloth in the hem of my skirt, if I had something to cut it with," I said.

"Kaya!" Tema was scandalized.

"It was way too long for me; there's lots of extra cloth here," I said. "And I can hem the raw edge back in place when we get back to school. Do you have a knife I could borrow?" I asked the fisherman.

We got Sumi bandaged up, the fisherman went on his way, and Tema even had a few safety pins that I used to hide the ragged edge of my skirt.

"They aren't going to let you take that dirty thing onto the bus," said Tema, but she leaned over my shoulder and watched with interest as I gave Sumi another leg from the crab.

"I was thinking …" I glanced at the bag she was carrying.

"What, this? You can't use this! I've got souvenirs for people in here."

"Please? I'll carry the souvenirs for you. Look, I'll make a carrier with my neckerchief."

"No, it's … I wanted the bag especially for…"

She hung her head, fiddled with the tissue paper. It was strange to see Tema flustered.

"For?" I pressed.

"Vira saw me going into the shop where they sell local hand-dyed stuff. You know, with the wave-and-net pattern? This area's famous for it." She was speaking even faster than usual and still wouldn't look me in the eye.

"She called out to me and asked if I'd get her a couple of handkerchiefs. So I did, and had the woman at the shop put them in a special bag. I was going to pull out my own things at the last moment and give Vira the bag."

"But you've always said— she's one of the princesses! How can you let yourself run errands for her? You despise it when people fawn all over the princesses!"

"It's not running errands! It's doing her a favor, and I do, and I'm not! Fawning. I'm not fawning. I don't care a fly's eyeball about her. It's just being polite. You have to respect— I … She never talks to me, you know—but there's no reason why she shouldn't. I'm as good as she is. You're even as good as she is. I just, I just wanted to make a good impression. There's no reason not to make a good impression. I'm every bit as cultured as some twenty-generation aristocrat, even if my grandfather was a fisherman. And I bet I'm three times as rich."

Maybe Tema's grandfather sprinkled blood over an open flame.

I'd like to say that thinking that made me realize how odd it was that coastal lowlanders were free to honor the Lady, when we up in the mountains, up by her home, no longer were, but it didn't. No, I was too busy trying to understand what it meant that confident, self-assured, and wealthy Tema had a past with an accent and a grandfather who used to go out to sea each morning.

And there was still Sumi to think of.

"Could we maybe get a spare bag from the shop? And put the handkerchiefs in that, to give to Vira?" I asked.

"No, never mind," said Tema abruptly, kneeling down and emptying the contents of the bag into her lap. "I'll just wrap them in the tissue paper and give them to her by hand. She doesn't need a special bag. It would probably only be a bother for her, anyway. Here." She pushed the bag toward me. "But I still don't see how you're going to keep it a secret at school. You certainly can't hide it in the dorm."

"I was thinking of hiding her by the delivery entrance for the cafeteria kitchen. There are always boxes and things stacked there, and the teachers never go there."

Tema made a face.

"It's not very dignified to poke around back there. It's something a street urchin would do, not a student. People will think badly of you if they see you. Especially … well, it doesn't look good."

Especially when you're from the mountains, that's what she had been going to say. But the thought didn't sting as much as it might have even an hour ago, before I learned about her grandfather and heard her speak the soft coastal way.

"I'll be careful."

I lifted Sumi into the bag. She didn't even squawk, poor thing.

Tema was watching intently.

"Do you think it would like another bit of crab?" she asked.

"Maybe. Would you like to give it to her?"

"Oh no! No. I don't want to get my hands dirty. And its beak looks sharp." She hesitated. "I like watching *you* feed it, though."

I gave Sumi one more piece of crab. Then I wiped my hands off on the tail end of Sumi's bandage and stood up.

"It's funny," said Tema, watching, "I always hoped to find a message in a bottle, when I was little and we'd go to the beach. Sometimes the fishermen would show my brother and me odd bits of trash that they'd found in their nets. There were sometimes bottles, but never one with a message in it. But a crow. That's got to be the most unlikely thing I've ever seen come out of a fishing net. I should make a poem out of it. Something about the crow being a message."

"I always thought of crows more as messengers than messages, but maybe Sumi's a message, somehow," I said, untying my neckerchief.

"Now you be quiet on the bus," I said to Sumi, laying the neckerchief loosely over her.

"Yes, you be quiet." Tema used her scolding big-sister voice on Sumi. "Otherwise you'll be a messenger of disaster, and the message will be that little Kaya is expelled from school." We headed back to the bus.

Chapter 4. A Cup of Fortune

July 27 (Kaya to Em)

Dear Em,

Thank you for this second letter. I treasure it!

I'm glad you found my country—yes, it's an island, but I was born up in the mountains and never even saw the ocean until I was a little older than I imagine you must be now.

I suppose I did commit a crime, but I didn't mean to. I just wanted to celebrate the fire festival, the way we did when I was very little. We used to have a fire festival every year, on a night at the start of the rainy season. It was for the Lady of the Ruby Lake.

You have the Seafather to watch over you, and we, up in our mountains, have the Lady of the Ruby Lake. She lives in volcanoes. I guess you can say she's the mother of all fire. Volcano fires are special—-they can destroy things, but their ashes can make things grow. Maybe you know this from school? Any little fire that people light, it's a child of the fires in the Ruby Lake.

For the fire festival, people used to light huge bonfires. They'd carry flames from those fires all through the fields and orchards and then into their houses. If people wanted to beg some new fields from the forest, they'd use those flames to do it, because forest land cleared with those flames would be protected by the Lady. The flames would drive away evil spirits, things like sweat snakes and cave bats, and the sparks would prick the sky and release rain, so the ground and all the plants would have plenty to drink. People would sprinkle the ashes from the bonfires all around, to help the plants grow.

But then we stopped being able to celebrate that festival. In my country, the people who live up in the mountains have different traditions and customs and even a different language from the people who live on the coast. Some of the mountain people started saying we should have our own country, and that made the lowlanders very angry. There are many more of them than there are of us, and they made laws prohibiting our festivals, because the separatists were using them to stir up rebellious feelings.

So by the time I started school, we didn't have the fire festival anymore. I didn't think about it much as I was growing up. I was busy studying hard. I went to a special high school in the capital city, on the coast. And then I went to your country for university, though in a place far away from where you live. I wish I could have visited your lagoon home.

Some months after I came back to my country, I had a dream about the Lady of the Ruby Lake. I dreamed she had become a very old grandmother. She asked me why nobody celebrated fire anymore, and I didn't have an answer for her. She shook her head and said it was too bad, just too bad, and started to walk away. I felt so sorry. I said, "I promise we'll have a festival again."

And when I woke up, I thought how good it would be to have a celebration, like we had when I was little. I got my friends to help me, and we worked hard to recreate our childhood memories. I didn't think the government would mind, because we had no rebellious intentions at all, but I was wrong. The day of the festival, they arrested all of us.

I told them that we were only doing it because of my dream, that we didn't care about a separate country or any of that, but they didn't believe me. And meanwhile people in the mountains were angry about us getting arrested, so angry that they did start up the old talk about a separate country—which made the government all the more sure of our guilt. They put my friends in an ordinary prison, but they made this one specially for me. They said, since I was acting as the voice of the Lady of the Ruby Lake, they'd make a house for me right over the Ruby Lake, as an honor to her. It's a kind of taunt; they have no real respect for the Lady.

Sometimes I wish the Lady really had chosen me to speak for her, but I highly doubt it's the case. If she had, shouldn't I have more dreams and visions? What does she want me to say?

Truthfully, I don't know if I even really believe in her. Do you believe in the Seafather? Are you truly expecting him to rescue Jiminy? I hope somehow it can be so.

My regards to both your parents, and to your friends. As I fall asleep tonight, with this house swaying over the Ruby Lake, I will think of you, rocked by your house as the tide comes in.

With gratitude,

Kaya

August 10 (Em's diary)

This afternoon, all the time we were guiding our dinghies through the maze of little water paths in the hushing, shushing grass (me and Small Bill in his, Tammy and Clara in ours, and Wade and Skinnylegs in Wade's), I was thinking about Kaya's letter, that I got in the morning. The part about her country and its government made me a pricking, jellyfish stinging kind of mad. Not letting people speak their own language or sing their own songs? How can the government make rules like that?

That's one thing about being a seachild. Dry-land kids can tease and grown-ups can frown when we're up there on the dusty shore, but when we're in Mermaid's Hands, they leave us alone. The sea hold us cupped in its palm, and who'd fight the sea? You can never win against the sea. Dry-land people are scared of it. That's why their boats are so big. And the government never bothers about us. Mermaid's Hands ain't even written on maps. I looked.

The part of Kaya's letter that made me the angriest, though, was the part about sticking Kaya right over the Ruby Lake and pretending it was out of respect. It's like when a bunch of the girls at Sandy Neck High School told Small Bill's biggest sister, Jenya, that they wanted to crown her Mermaid Princess, and that it was like prom queen, only better. They made a crown of gulfweed and decorated it with fishing lures and put it on her head and said how pretty and took photos, and Jenya was flattered, because gulfweed *is* pretty, and so are fishing lures, but then they all started laughing and saying, "She believed it! She believed it! Wearing seaweed in her hair!"

Jenya had the last laugh, though. Those girls were jealous because

Cody Boyd was paying her so much attention, and now Cody and her are engaged, and Cody's going to come live with us in Mermaid's Hands and become a seachild.

I wish Kaya could have the last laugh, too. Being trapped above a volcano's way worse than having people make fun of you for wearing a seaweed crown.

Those questions Kaya asked in that letter … Some of them make me a little dizzy, when I try and think about them.

Do I believe in the Seafather? That's what I was pondering when Skinnylegs said, "Here's a good spot." The water lane had opened up into a wide pool, with grass walls all around it. He jumped in with a splash, and a heron at the other end of the pool flew off. "Coming?"

"How's the bottom? Soft or supersoft?" Wade asked. Skinnylegs was up to his hips in water, so we couldn't see how deep into the mud those skinny legs of his were.

"A good amount of soft," he said. "Not too slurpy." The rest of us jumped in too. I went completely under, so that the breeze would feel cool on my wet skin when I came back up. The soft mud squeezed my ankles. We spread out all across the pool and began dipping our umbrella nets.

"You ever hear of anyone talking with the Seafather?" I asked Small Bill. I was thinking about how the Lady of the Ruby Lake talked to Kaya in Kaya's dream. When the Seafather gave fins to Vaillant, did they talk, one to the other?

Small Bill looked surprised. "Well, when the tide comes in, and you hear the surf and the shells on the sand—"

"I don't mean that kind of talking," I said. "I mean with words, like you and me are using."

Small Bill dipped his hand in the water and ran it through his hair. Little drips came down the side of his face.

"Why does he need to talk in words?" he asked. "Don't everything talk its own language? Gulls talk a lot, and dolphins, but not in people words."

"I know, but—"

"Is it your ma again, saying that the Seafather's nothing but stories?"

"No, it's not her, it's my pen pal, Kaya. She was asking if I really believed in the Seafather. Where she lives, they have the Lady of the Ruby Lake, who lives in volcanoes, to look after them the way we have the Seafather. The Lady of the Ruby Lake spoke to Kaya in a dream and asked for a festival, and that's why Kaya got in trouble, because in her country they're not supposed to have any festivals for the Lady of the Ruby Lake."

"That don't make sense. If the Lady of the Ruby Lake looks after them, then how come they can't they have festivals for her?"

"It's something about politics. Not everybody in Kaya's country believes in the Lady. The people that live in the mountains believe in her, but there's not many of them, and there's whole boatloads of people living in the lowlands that don't."

"Like there's not many of us who know the Seafather, compared to people on dry land, who don't."

"Yeah, like that. Only worse, 'cause dry-land people don't pay no never mind to the Seafather, but in Kaya's country—"

"'cept for your ma. She minds," Small Bill interrupted.

"Ma's not a dry-lander! Don't call her that! What I'm saying is, nobody cares, here. We can call to the Seafather each morning, and the school don't care, and the police don't care, and the president and the army don't care. But where Kaya is, the government thinks calling to the Lady equals calling for rebellion."

"Uh oh."

"Yeah. That's why Kaya got arrested."

Small Bill waved his hand by his head, maybe to drive away gnats, maybe to drive away politics.

"So what's all that got to do with whether the Seafather talks in words?" he asked.

"The Lady of the Ruby Lake spoke to Kaya in words, in her dream. But in her letter, Kaya said she wasn't sure if she believed in the Lady … I don't know. If someone like the Lady talks to you, person to person, wouldn't it *make* you believe?"

Small Bill shrugged. "Well, you said it was a dream. That's not the same as when you're awake."

That's true, and when he said it, I nodded. But just now, writing it all down, I'm thinking, *but Kaya organized a whole festival because of that dream.* If you do something because of a dream, then don't that show you believe it even more? I wonder if Kaya believes and just don't realize it.

"Kaya also asked if I thought the Seafather would rescue Jiminy." I kept my eyes on the water when I told Small Bill that, so as to keep my feelings on the topic horizon-level.

Small Bill got his considering face on, the one where he sticks out his lower lip a little. A dragonfly buzzed between us. I could hear the others splashing and talking on the far side of the pool.

"I wish I could go see him," I added, watching the puffs of silt that rose up each time I put my foot down. Little underwater explosions.

There was a splash right by us, and up came Skinnylegs out of the water.

"You gonna check your net at all or just let it sit under there? We've already got half a bucket full."

We lifted up our net and put the good stuff into our bucket, then moved on a bit and put the net down again. It was getting headache hot, so I took another dip and let the water finger through my hair a bit. It feels good while you're under, but then your hair's just heavy when you come back up.

"There's Mr. Tiptoe's truck," Small Bill said, when I resurfaced. It took a minute for me to realize he was still trying to think of a way for me to visit Jiminy. "Maybe you could go with him next time he takes a catch to the restaurants inland. Then maybe he might …" He frowned. The thought was probably occurring to him that occurred to me, when I first thought of begging a ride from Mr. Tiptoe: that Jiminy's prison is hundreds of miles away, and across state lines. "Too far?" he asked. I nodded.

"Probably. I think it would take all day."

Actually, I ought to check that. I ain't sure exactly-precisely how long it would take.

"Anyway," I said, "Mr. Tiptoe has Cody to help him—I'd just be in the way." Ma's always telling us not to be in the way, and Cody has a driver's license and strong arms, so he's a better helper. He's always offering, too, to help Mr. Tiptoe or anyone else in Mermaid's Hands with anything that needs doing, and he'll do things no one else much likes doing, like dealing with folks on dry land.

Cody's the opposite of Ma: he slid right into Mermaid's Hands like we were holding a spot open for him. Mrs. Ovey says he must've been stolen away from the sea as a baby. "Good thing we've got you back now," she tells him. "Good thing Jenya recognized a sea spirit when she saw one."

It's hard not to like Cody. He has time for everybody and never loses his temper. There's lots of things he don't know about, growing up on dry land, but he's not bothered when there's stuff that even a little kid can do better than him. He just says, "Wow, you're so good at that," and he means it.

But what if the spot Cody slid into is the one that opened up when Jiminy left? Sometimes I get the feeling everyone else thinks if it's a trade, Cody for Jiminy, then Mermaid's Hands won out. It makes it hard for me to like Cody one hundred percent.

"Ready to go?" called Skinnylegs.

Tammy and Clara had already given up on fishing and were chasing each other in and out of the cordgrass, shrieking and laughing.

"Just about," I called back, and me and Small Bill pulled up our net one last time.

There was a battered tin cup in it.

"Sabelle Morning's cup," Small Bill said, eyes wide.

"*Sabelle, Sabelle Morning*

Catch her if you can

Sharptongue crow on her shoulder

Tin cup in her hand."

We whisper-sang it together.

"You think it's really hers?" I asked. He picked the cup out of the net and turned it over in his hands. Every dent and bang was greeny black, and there was a tiny crab inside.

It sure looked old, but once a thing's been asleep in salty water for a while, it gets hard to tell its true age.

"Look," Small Bill said, showing me the bottom of the cup. There was a bird stamped in it, a bird with hunched shoulders, perching on a key—a crow. Tingles of excitement bubbled up from the bottom of me to the top. It had to be hers.

"'Drink the cup of fortune that you make for yourself.' The grown-ups are always saying that. Sabelle Morning's motto. Maybe it means we can find a way to get you to see Jiminy," Small Bill suggested.

"You think?"

"C'mon, you guys!" called Clara. "We're going to the garden floats next!"

"Okay, okay!" we called back, and quickly poured the keeper fish from the net into our bucket and dumped the rest.

"Let's not tell anyone else about the cup just yet, okay?" I begged. Small Bill nodded.

Sometimes you gotta keep some things private for a while. Like Kaya's letters. Small Bill's the only person outside my family I've told about them.

It was only when we were checking the garden floats that the thought hit me, *Is the cup the Seafather talking? Maybe Small Bill's right: it's best for him to talk with the voice of the sea. When you're hungry, he sends you fish, and when you're losing hope, he sends you a cup.*

We were late getting back. The tide had already set our houses down, and we had to drag the dinghies over the mud the last little bit.

The parents had relit the fires from yesterday, right on the mud, only instead of cooking up seagift stew, like they were yesterday, they were mainly canning the extra, to take to sell in Sandy Neck and other towns. But Mrs. Tiptoe and Skinnylegs' stepmom Silent Soriya were reheating a portion for everybody to share, and when they saw we'd come back with fresh fish plus vegetables, they called us over so we could add what we had to the pots. Clara's twin brothers were playing with Skinnylegs' little sister Anna, and Mrs. Tiptoe and Silent Soriya were letting them all take turns stirring, even though they can barely reach over the top. Brightly Tiptoe, who's a bit bigger than the twins, was sticking bits of driftwood into the fire and watching the flames turn colors. Lindie Ovey and her friends had gone to the other garden floats and gotten mint, and Cody and Jenya were pouring cups of mint water for everyone from the Oveys' rain barrel.

"You're gonna empty your barrel," Clara said, peering into it. Her voice echoed.

"It'll rain again soon enough," said Jenya. "Our dad's been listening to the weather channel. Hurricane Gaspard's gonna miss us, but there'll be thunderstorms. Maybe tomorrow. What do you think, Granddad?"

Jenya and Small Bill's grandfather is also Clara's grandfather, because Mr. Tiptoe and Mrs. Ovey are brother and sister, and Snowy Tiptoe is their father.

Thing I wonder: What did everybody call Snowy Tiptoe before his hair turned white?

Snowy smiled in my direction and said, "Why not ask the girl who knows when the Seafather's herding fish our way? She'll be able to tell you. Right Em?"

That made me feel sunshiny bright.

When someone puts sunny words on you like that, the thing to do is pass the sunshine on, so I said,

"Seafather sends them to us cause he misses his smallest mermaid," and I gave Tammy a nudge. "Don't go back to the merlands just yet, okay? The longer you stay, the more seagifts we'll get."

I thought Tammy might fall over for grinning so much.

"Okay," she said.

Ma was over with Dad and Uncle Near and Auntie Chicoree, helping with the canning, and I caught her looking my way and smiling.

That had to be one of the perfect moments, right then.

August 10 (Em's diary, second entry)

And now Ma and Dad are arguing again. It started out with Ma saying something that sounded like a good thing, something like, "Now see, Brett's idea of canning the stew and selling it is a good one. Don't see why Deena and the rest won't consider selling those sun capes and straw hats. Those are real handicrafts. If we sold those—"

And Dad laughed and said, "Can you imagine some dry-lander wearing one? It'd be like putting fins on a cat," but Ma came back with, "There's plenty of people could use them on dry land. And dry-land folks fish, too, you know." And then Dad just said, "They're for people in Mermaid's Hands. They're part of Mermaid's Hands. We don't sell parts of ourselves." And if it was me arguing with Dad, I would of known to shut up then, cause his voice had gone from laughing to hard, and who keeps arguing when someone says we don't sell parts of ourselves?

Ma does. She said, "You know Mermaid's Hands needs more money than we can get just selling fish we don't need and jars of seagift stew. It ain't just us needing money for the doctor, it's for things everybody needs."

And from there it turned into one of their favorite fights, with Dad saying how Mermaid's Hands has always managed in the past and always will, and why can't Ma like it as it is, and Ma getting going about all the things wrong with it.

"Must be true love, the way y'all fight so hard," Gran said, and sometimes a line like that'll get them to calm down, but not tonight. I hate falling asleep with them fighting. I'm going to write to Kaya.

August 10 (Em to Kaya)

Dear Kaya,

We went to the post office today, and your letter was waiting for me, but there was a new lady working there, and she gave me a hard time. Dry-land people do that sometimes. There's one librarian who says things like, "Don't come in here with your muddy bare feet," or if I pick up a book she'll say, "Do you have clean hands?" So this post office lady said, "This can't be really for you, a letter from overseas." "That's my name," I said, pointing. "You better give her her letter," my dad said. "I hear it's a federal offense to tamper with the mail." And the lady rolled her eyes and grumbled stuff about offenses and lazy and criminals.

But she gave me the letter.

It makes me pretty mad to think that your government has you locked up over the Ruby Lake and pretends it's an honor. How could anyone believe that? I wouldn't believe it if I lived in your mountains. I'd hate your government.

You asked if I believed in the Seafather. I was thinking about it all day, and about your dream. I never had a dream like you had. I haven't ever seen any of the merpeople or heard the Seafather talk in words, at least, not words that people use. But I believe in the sea. I couldn't not *believe in the sea. Nobody could. It's all around us. And I can feel it* noticing *us, and it can't be just water and silt and gulfweed and fish that notice us, can it? So that must be the Seafather. Who else could send seagifts, or hurricanes?*

Yesterday we had a dawn of seagifts. The Seafather sends them once a year, always in the summer, before hurricane season. All kinds of fish come swimming right up to Mermaids Hands, right up to shore, even, so many of them, so thick, that if you kneel down in the water, they press all around you, bumping your legs, sliding past each other. They come in on a dawn tide and go out before the tide is high. The dry-land people come to collect them too, but we always get more because we're here to meet them. We have a game we play when it's a dawn of seagifts, me, and Small Bill and my sister Tammy and Clara Tiptoe and Skinnylegs and Wade. We swim around, and half of us are fish and the other half are catchers. When I'm a fish, no one can catch me except Small Bill, and when I'm a catcher, I can catch everyone but him and sometimes Skinnylegs. Everyone can catch Tammy, so she always asks to play dolphins instead. That's okay; it's fun to play dolphins, too. We do dolphin dives and try to catch fish in our mouths.

It smelled good all that afternoon because everyone was cooking stew on the mudflats after the tide went out. Today they canned some of it, and some of the dads are going to sell it to some of the restaurants inland a bit.

Ma said we should thank God for the bounty of the sea, but Mrs. Ovey said we should thank the Seafather. Ma said, the Seafather won't protect you when it comes hurricane season, and Mrs. Ovey said, nor God neither, and the Seafather at least don't make promises. The sea makes no promises and tells no lies. The sea is always true.

I think the Lady of the Ruby Lake must love you the way the Seafather loves us. It's not a very gentle kind of love. The sea is always true but not very gentle. And how could the Lady of the Ruby

Lake be gentle if she lives in a volcano? But you said her sparks call the rain and make the plants grow for you—like the Seafather sending fish, for us. Maybe she felt lonely and ignored for a while, but now that you've cheered her up with the fire festival, maybe she'll find a way to help you.

Your friend,

Em

Chapter 5. A Festival for the Lady

(From the W— State Security Service's files on the insurgency: August 20 editorial in the online English-language edition of the Palem *Courier*)

More Trouble from the Mountains?

Back in January, we watched uneasily as the agitators in the mountains staged an illegal demonstration, fanning old cultural resentments in an apparent attempt to resurrect a defunct separatist movement. We applauded the government's handling of the situation: there were no mass arrests, no crackdowns on general rights. Only the ringleaders were detained, and special efforts were made to acknowledge and respect the mountain minority's religious sensibilities, with honors being paid to the apparent leader of the mountain minority's volcano worshipers. But despite initial signs that the disturbances had settled down, unrest in the mountain region now appears to be gaining momentum once again.

Trem Gana, member of Parliament for the western mountain district, insists that the activists do not speak for the majority of mountain dwellers. "It's just a few troublemakers. The vast majority of the mountain people are as patriotic and as dedicated to the well-being of the nation as any lowlander. People here have complaints—as do people on the coast, as do people anywhere—but they don't try to solve their problems by undermining the country."

"It's a concern," says Resh Woor, chief of operations at Emerald Diversified Casting Foundry, a coastal company that is known for its willingness to hire migrants from the mountains. "It took a while to get local people to warm up to the idea of working side by side with the mountain folk. It can be difficult to understand their accent, and some people feel uncomfortable because—well, it can be hard getting used to people who are so different from the the ones you've grown up with. But the mountain folk I've known have all been very cooperative and hard-working. People just need to get over their prejudices.

"These threats of violence, though, they're another matter. It's hard enough for our country to make a go of it when we live in the shadow of powerhouses like Indonesia and Malaysia. We can't let ourselves be undermined from within. If the trouble keeps up, people are going to start to look at the migrants as potential enemies. I can't understand why some of the folks up in the mountains want to ruin things for everyone else. It's not just lowlanders, it's their own people they're hurting, too."

It is a question we are all asking. Can mountain dwellers be persuaded that it is better for all of us, whether on the coast, the lowland interior, or the mountains, to support the national polity? If not, it may be in the best interests of the state to act quickly and firmly rather than to continue to try to engage with those who, far from working for the good of nation, wish to separate from it.

Comments

1. You won't find a paved road anywhere in the mountain districts, and half the schools are open-air affairs. And they want to go it alone? I'd like to see them try.

2. What do you expect they are all backward up there.

3. @1 @2 The best way to integrate our society is to spend money in the mountain region. If the schools and infrastructure there are

substandard, they should be improved. Prosperity = loyalty.

4. @3 That would just be throwing money away. The mountain districts will never amount to anything. Better investments would be to reorganize the shipping lanes in Palem Bay and improve the rail line to Gapsin, Manah, and Rai.

5. @4 Too right. It takes far too long to get from Rai to Palem.

6. @3 You want to reward agitators and rebels by building them roads and schools? Every region will rebel then.

August 23 (Kaya's memoir)

Just finished rereading Em's most recent letter. What a comfort her letters are, especially when Mother has only bad news about things at home, and no news at all of Ramiratam and the others. Em is outraged on my behalf. Is it wrong to find that heartwarming? And yet when I think about my situation, and about Mother left on her own, and even more when I think about Ramiratam and the rest, I feel only self-doubt and remorse. Was there any way I could have kept my promise to the Lady without causing all this?

But isn't the government to blame, too? Hasn't it been wrong all along, the way we in the mountains have been treated?

But that's politics. So am I lying to myself, then, and to the State Security Service, when I say there were no political motives in what we did?

I don't know. I just don't know.

I am sure my intentions were innocent when I first suggested the festival to Dinasha, and when she said I should speak to Rami, my reservations had nothing to do with politics.

"But you have to talk to him," she argued. "Why wouldn't you? You two always with your heads together, all through primary school. I thought for sure when you got back from America he'd be the first person you'd get in touch with—after me, of course! You mean you haven't spoken with him at all?" Lines of concern made a rift between her eyebrows.

"He never answered any of the letters I sent from St. Margaret's, so I thought maybe … I didn't want to make a pest of myself. And then later, while I was in America, I thought he might even have married. You did. It seems like everyone has. What's he doing now? Did I see him at the primary school? Does he teach there now?"

"Only just filling in, if one of the teachers is ill. He's not on staff there. He hired on to help with the construction of the generating plant at the falls, when they were building that, last year and the year before, and since then he's been helping Mr. Tirabran keep his buses running."

Construction work? Bus maintenance?

"But those are—but he was top of the class. He should be …" I couldn't finish. *He should be teaching. Or he should be an engineer, designing the generating plant, not pouring the concrete.* That's what I was thinking.

"He's the same Rami he ever was, regardless of his job," Dinasha said. "You're not too high and mighty to meet with him, I hope, now that your colleagues are all lowlanders." She softened her words with a smile, as if to say she was merely teasing, but they still stung.

"Of course not! I'm still the same me, too, you know! It's not about prestige or, or social standing. It just doesn't seem right, that's all. He always had such a knack for schoolwork. Remember the song he made up about the articles of the constitution? I can still remember Mr. Apar's glowering face—he couldn't figure out why we were all humming when he tested us on it. Really Rami should have had a scholarship to Palem Boys, like Nawalam."

Old hesitance kept me from saying more on that topic, and suddenly a terrible thought struck me. What if Rami hadn't received any scholarship at all, not even to one of the mountain district secondary schools? What if he hadn't been able to continue his education past primary school?

"He did go on to secondary school, didn't he?" I asked, feeling faint.

"He did, but … Oh Kaya, you've been away a long time. Rami's situation is complicated. It might be hard for you to understand. But talk to him. I think he'll love the idea of the festival."

How alone I felt then. I could bear feeling that way at St. Margaret's; I knew I was an outsider there. And the same during my first months in America. But to come home and be an outsider? To be told I don't understand my childhood friend's situation?

I could feel my jaw tighten. There was no point in being aggrieved: The only solution was to get to know my home and friends again. If I cared about Rami, I could take the time to learn how things were for him, and why. Sharing my idea with him could be a first step.

I found him at Mr. Tirabran's, his head at the level of my feet as he worked on the underside of one of the old buses from within some kind of trench dug for that purpose. Two little boys were crouched down on the damp earth beside him. I thought at first he must be giving them a lesson in bus anatomy, but then I heard his voice over the drum of the rain on the steel roof.

"—easier than some of the lower tables actually, because look, as the number on the left goes up, the number on the right goes down, and they always add up to nine. Two nines are eighteen, three nines are twenty-seven, four nines are thirty-six. See the pattern? A one and an eight becomes a two and a seven and then a three and a six. So what comes next? What are five nines?"

"One and eight … two and seven … three and six … four and

five. Forty-five! Five nines are forty-five!" said one of the boys.

"You're lucky," I said to them, closing my umbrella. "Getting private lessons from the best teacher in the mountains."

The two boys jumped up in surprise, one nearly falling backward into the trench, but Rami steadied him, then looked up at me—and smiled.

"Kayamanira. I heard you were back. Dinasha said you might stop by." He hopped up out of the trench. Flew out, it seemed like. He was taller than I remembered him, and he'd filled out a bit, though he was still slight compared to Nawalam.

"How have you been? And who's this fine creature?"

Such warmth in his voice! So he didn't resent or despise me for going to the capital for high school? And then on to America? But then why no word from him during those years?

Sumi was perched on my shoulder, giving him her sideways glance. I stroked her head, keeping my eyes on her glossy feathers rather than Ramiratam's face.

"It's Sumi."

"Crows are the Lady's birds. Dinasha said you had a dream about the Lady. And now, with Sumi—" he paused, and each part of me grew warm by turns as his gaze traveled "—well, you look the part."

"Dinasha told you about the dream?"

"Just that you had one, and that it put an idea in your head, something about a celebration."

"She told you practically everything!"

"She seemed to think you might not come and tell me yourself," Rami said.

The taller of the two boys Rami was tutoring extended a tentative hand, and Sumi hopped from my shoulder to his wrist. The boy grinned and held up his arm.

"I'm sending, sending, sending the Lady's birds

To find, find, find what you have hid

They'll seize, seize, seize your every secret

And pierce, pierce, pierce your many lies.

They'll leave, leave, leave a burning ember

In the place, place, place of your coward heart

And fan, fan, fan the Lady's fires

To flame, flame, flame in your fevered eyes," he sang, and his friend joined in.

"Children still sing that song?" I asked, and the boy holding Sumi nodded.

"When we play hunters or hide-and-seek," said the smaller one.

I laughed.

"When I was your size, the big sisters and brothers used to sing it if they thought their sweetheart was losing interest in them," I said.

"Sweetheart," snickered the little one, hiding his face against his friend's shoulder. That one stifled a laugh but permitted himself a grin. Sumi hopped back to my shoulder.

"Do you know other songs about the Lady and the Ruby Lake? Do you know 'Ruby waters, ruby waters, make the corn grow high'?"

The taller boy nodded. "But mama sings it 'make the coffee ripen.'" The little one whispered something in his ear.

"He says he likes the one about hunting the moon, the one where the Lady gives the hunter a spear with a flaming spearhead."

"My granddad has a spear," the little one piped up. "From the olden days. It's hanging on a wall in our house."

"Have your parents or grandparents ever told you about the fire festival that we used to have? At the beginning of the rainy season? We'd call the rains with fire, and parents would use brooms and spears to carry the fire back home—flaming spears, just like in the song, and flaming brooms. Those fiery brooms were to sweep away small evils, and the flaming spears were to drive off bigger ones.

"That was the first time I ever saw you—do you remember?" I added, glancing at Rami. "You were riding on someone's shoulders, at the front of the procession. There were so many flaming spears! It was a river of fire, and bobbing along in that river, with his head among the stars, a little boy no bigger than I was."

"My father's shoulders," Rami said, nodding. "There was so much noise all around, everyone chanting and singing, but I could hear someone small, someone my size, calling 'sweep the sky, sweep the sky!' I looked down and saw you holding up a tiny broom torch."

"Did you go down to the Ruby Lake to get the fire?" asked the smaller boy, interrupting our reminiscences.

"Oh no—you can't go into the crater. The descent is too steep, and you'd be roasted alive before you got near enough to the lake to take fire from it. No, we'd just light bonfires all along the rim of the crater, so it danced with flames. Then we'd dip the spears and brooms into those fires."

"The crater dancing with flames … I'd like to see that," breathed the bigger boy.

"Would you? Would you like to coat a spear in salu pitch, so it takes a flame, and then carry it through the cornfields and past the papaya trees? Do you think your friends would like to sing some of those old songs, and get dressed up, and dance? Right up at the edge of the crater, one of these nights?"

"Yes!" the little one said, and "Can we?" the bigger one asked.

"So this is your idea? To hold the fire festival?" Rami asked.

I nodded, and told him what the Lady had said, in my dream.

"It's illegal, you know," he said. "And it's a little late to welcome in the rainy season."

"But the constitution promises freedom of religion. And they only made the festival illegal because of the separatists. If it's just a religious celebration, a cultural celebration, with no politics mixed in…"

I didn't finish the sentence. The cloudburst was trailing off too, just individual metallic notes on the roof now, and I could sense, rather than see, the two boys shifting from foot to foot, trying to decide whether they should stay or go. Rami's face was hard to read.

"You don't think they'll be suspicious if you hold it in the middle of the rainy season instead of at the beginning?"

Mist was rising up from the puddles in the ruts in the road now, as the sun came out, and I could see her again so vividly in my memory, the Lady, a old woman with thin white hair escaping from a knot at the back of her head and a red and black checked shawl pulled tight around narrow shoulders. I could hear again the reproach in her voice, just before she turned and walked away into drifts of white, like those wreathing the mountainside just then.

"I know it should happen before the rains come, but it can't be helped. I had the dream *now.* And I promised."

"So … we'd do it for the Lady's sake," Rami said. "Not for

politics. Not for an autonomous state. Not even to summon rain or to drive away bad spirits. Just for the Lady."

"That's right. As a true celebration, to show her we remember her."

Rami was silent.

"It-it would also be for us, though," I added, struggling to make my idea of the festival blossom in his mind. "It would be a joyful thing. It would give everyone a chance to put down work for a few hours and be part of the world of old stories and legends. These children should have that chance, the way we did, and the way people always used to. And they'll enjoy it just as much now as they would if we held it in October—right?" I appealed to the boys. The smaller one nodded vigorously, and the bigger one started to, but then stopped and looked up at Rami, as if for permission.

He took a deep breath.

"All right. Yes, let's do it."

I was so happy, I forgot myself completely and wrapped Rami in a hug, American style.

"Thank you! Thank you." I couldn't stop smiling.

"No—thank *you*," he said, and he was smiling too, as bright and warm as the freshly washed sunlight streaming down, and as I pulled away, he gave my hands a squeeze. "Thank *you*," he said again, then let them go.

Our first intimacy. Not like in childhood, when we could sit side by side, push and shove, even link arms, and it meant nothing.

And our last intimacy. If I had known, if I could go back—

But I didn't, and I can't.

August 24 (Kaya's memoir)

Em assumes our festival cheered the Lady. I wonder. Was it what she hoped for? When we were planning, it was hard to keep her in mind. Everyone wanted slightly different things from the festival.

Nawalam, interested in politics and hoping to be the first mountain native to represent our people in parliament, wanted a pageant in which he could play a leading role.

"Remember the banners on the spears?" he said, at our first meeting. "The black, red, and green ones? We should have some of those. Mirasan, you could make something like that, couldn't you? You and your friends?"

"I don't really remember them, but if you drew me something..."

Mirasan was his wife. She was a few years younger than we were, probably only a toddler the year of the last festival. But Rami was shaking his head.

"Those weren't banners; they were flags. It was the flag the separatists designed, for an independent state. We can't have anything like that, nothing with those colors."

"A flag? Really? I didn't realize … but all right, if you say so," Nawalam said. "How about just streamers, then? Streamers attached to the spears?"

"I don't think we can even have the spears," Rami said.

"But we have to have spears," I protested. "They're part of the festival. How else are we supposed to drive away big evils?"

"That's the problem: 'driving away big evils' can be interpreted as a call to arms. And a procession of flaming spears never seems peaceful."

"I understand that," I said, "but how many changes can we make to the festival without destroying something essential?"

"We'll still have the brooms, even if we give up the spears," said Dinasha. "If we're singing the old songs, and if there's the procession, with dancing, the children will still have the real flavor of it." That's what was most important for Dinasha: giving the children the experience we had had when we were little. She'd already spoken to the gym teacher at the regional secondary school about teaching the dances to the girls and boys there.

"Our own songs, that's what counts," said Jeteman, Dinasha's husband. It was startling, hearing his voice: it was rare for him to speak. He was always quiet back in primary school, too.

"You all learned the national language without too many scars on your shoulders, but it isn't that way for everyone," he continued. "It burns me up, hearing about the agents from Highland Coffee or Sunrise Fruit coming round and raising their voices and waving their hands in the faces of farmers twenty-five years their senior, just because the farmers stumble over words. The farmers complain about it to me, since I'm the head of the growers' cooperative, but what can I do? And don't get me started on State Security officers, or district officials. So much rudeness." He turned to me. "You don't feel it, working with all those lowlanders at the research station?"

"I do feel it, a little," I admitted. "Some of the other researchers act like I'm just an intern, and one always makes me repeat myself."

Jeteman laughed and shook his head. "And yet you sound just like one of them, when I hear you speaking to them," he said—and I felt ashamed of my facility. "Singing in our own language, raising our voices up at night, together, in our own tongue—it'll feel so good!" he finished. We were quiet a moment. Maybe the others were remembering, imagining, as I was.

"Rami, you think you can get Grandmother Jemenli to bless the arrow that goes into the flames?" Nawalam asked. Grandmother Jemenli was an old charm maker everyone respected whom I remembered only vaguely from childhood. She lived alone in a forested part of the mountains and rarely came into town.

"No! We can't get anyone like her involved," Rami said sharply. "None of the old activists."

"You're oversensitive," Nawalam said, with that teasing smile I remembered from primary school.

"Nawalam, leave it," said Dinasha, but her warning was lost in Rami's quick reply.

"I'm not oversensitive! What we're doing, we want it to be nonpolitical? Then we can't bring any of those people in. It's dangerous for us. And, and—I know it's not what we expect, but suppose for a moment that we do end up having some trouble with the government. If that happens, then being involved would be dangerous for them, too. The government might forgive us—we're new, we're young. But it won't forgive them. They have a history of being troublemakers."

"Maybe *you* shouldn't be involved, then," Nawalam said, still the ghost of a smile on his lips, but aggression in his voice.

"What are you talking about?" I asked, but Nawalam and Rami weren't listening.

"Are you worried?" Rami shot back, locking eyes with Nawalam.

"Not at all. And you shouldn't be either. Don't let yourself be ruled by the past."

"It's Rami's parents." Dinasha's cheek touched mine as she whispered the information into my ear. "They were leaders in the separatist movement. They were execu-"

She didn't finish, because Rami was speaking, and his voice threatened violence, though all he said was "You have no idea what you're talking about," and that in quiet tones. It was how his words trembled with anger that made us all sit still.

They were execu-

I put my hands to my ears, even though Dinasha had leaned away and no one was speaking, but I couldn't stifle my thoughts.

"I have a idea about the brooms and spears," said Mirasan presently, breaking the silence. "What if we use plain torches, but painted with a design to represent either a broom or a spear?"

"Yes, and we could get the children to do the painting," Dinasha said, nodding. "They'll love the torches as much as real spears and brooms, if they get to paint them themselves. And Kaya, you should bless the arrow, don't you think?"

"You think so? Even though I've been away for so long? It feels … presumptuous."

"You're the one who had the vision. If it wasn't for that, we wouldn't be planning the festival at all."

Just a dream. It was just a dream, part of me wanted to say. But dream, vision, whatever it was, what Dinasha said was true. If I saw the blessing as a responsibility and not as an honor, I could accept the task.

"All right. Yes, I'll do the blessing."

And so our planning continued, as if Nawalam and Rami hadn't nearly come to blows.

Rami walked me home that night. We shared one umbrella, just like sweethearts. The scent from evening cooking fires lingered in the air, intimate and comforting.

"I didn't know about your parents until tonight," I said. "Dinasha told me."

"I never wanted anyone to know, back when we were in primary school," he said.

"You must hate the government," I murmured. But it wasn't really the government I was thinking about. It was Nawalam and I, going off to school in Palem, and Nawalam angling for parliament. How could Rami stand *us*?

"I do hate it," he said, so quietly, so fervently.

A dog barked at us from beneath a nearby house, as if protesting Rami's declaration.

"Did you want this festival to be more than it is?" I asked. I had assumed that Rami's questions and warnings were to guide us away from politics, but had he maybe intended them as challenges? *It's illegal*, he had said to me, when I first mentioned the festival to him. Had he hoped I'd say *I don't care*?

Rami shook his head.

"No. We don't have the strength to oppose the government. They have manpower and weaponry on their side. It would just end in lives lost and more repression."

The resignation in his voice depressed me. But then he added,

"I liked what you said: that this could be a joyful thing. If it can be just that, then that's enough. That's a gift. And …" he hesitated, then plunged ahead. "You'll take me for superstitious, but—Well …

we have no power, but the Lady does. I don't mean power to magic us an autonomous state," he added quickly. "But maybe just to remind us who we are. Restore our pride in that. And from there?" He shrugged. "Who knows?"

(From the W— State Security Service's files on the insurgency: email records)

From: Capt. Aran
Subject: "Voice from the Lotus" a go
Date: August 24
To: Lt. Sana, Lt. Den

We've decided on operation "Voice from the Lotus." Interrogations of Prisoner 116's co-conspirators indicate that she's the least political of the group and will be eager to prevent unnecessary violence. I'm sure you can persuade her of the wisdom of this course of action. Succeed, and we're all heroes. Fail, and we have a police action to look forward to.

(From the W— State Security Service's files on the insurgency: email records)

From: Capt. Aran
Subject: Re: Re: "Voice from the Lotus" a go
Date: August 25
To: Lt. Sana, Lt. Den

Any more queries on procedure or requests for clarification will be taken as insubordination. Just do what it takes to make "Voice from the Lotus" a success.

August 25 (Kaya's memoir)

In my memory, the rest of the planning for the festival was given over to dealing with a constant tumult of clamoring questions. Who will bring brush and firewood for the bonfires at the rim of the Ruby Lake? Who can provide pitch for the torches? Can we practice dances with the younger children on the grounds of the primary schools? Can we ask families to welcome people from the eastern mountain district into their homes, so the people from the east don't have to travel on the day of the festival? What route shall the procession take?

And as we planned and worked, we had to be so careful with our words. They had to be mild, bland, unassuming—and yet pregnant with possibilities for those who were listening. We wanted words that would speak volumes to those who wanted to join us without alarming those who didn't, and most of all, we wanted to avoid antagonizing the regional government. It's supposed to represent us, but it's composed of lowlanders.

"Mr. Gana's got wind of what we're planning," said Nawalam, just a week before the festival.

"Our member of parliament?" said Dinasha, making a face.

"What did he say?" I asked.

"That he hoped we weren't planning some tribal rally up by the Ruby Lake—I think that's how he put it. 'Doesn't seem like a wise career move,' he said to me. Nawalam used the national tongue to quote Mr. Gana. His accent was perfect; if you closed your eyes, you'd have thought it was someone from the streets of Palem talking. It made me recall Jeteman's remark to me: *you sound just like one of them.*

“I told him it was a cultural awareness festival, and he should come along and bring his friends,” Nawalam continued, reverting to the mountain tongue.

“Good,” I said, nodding. “Lowlanders should feel welcome. Did you know they honor the Lady too? Some of them, anyway.” I told them about the fisherman I had met when I found Sumi.

“You were smart to invite Mr. Gana,” I added. “It shows we have nothing to hide. Maybe we should be inviting journalists, too.”

“If Mr. Gana does turn up, and if this festival helps me unseat him next election, then I’ll offer him a place on my staff as a gesture of good will,” Nawalam said, leaning back on his hands, away from the red cloth on which our empty coffee cups sat. Mirasan refilled them with rich honey coffee. Nawalam sipped his and flashed his wife an appreciative grin.

“Why wait for the election? Maybe we can persuade him to resign at the festival,” said Mirasan, returning his smile. “I hear he’s not comfortable among crowds of mountain people.”

“Make sure he only speaks to you in the mountain tongue,” Jeteman said, “and with proper deference.”

We all laughed, but I could see uneasiness in Nawalam’s eyes, and it dawned on me that if Nawalam did get elected, he wouldn’t necessarily try to change the language laws. Nawalam’s primary concern was Nawalam.

The evening of the festival, as everyone was gathering for the procession, Mr. Gana did actually show up, to plead with us to call the whole thing off. But even if we had wanted to, how could we, at that point? The crowd pressed round as eagerly as swarming bees, bodies jostling one another, sweaty from the fields and the cardamom plantations, and on top of odors of hard work was the sharp scent of the pitch on the torches, not yet lit. We couldn't disappoint them. But oh the wretchedness in Mr. Gana's voice as he spoke to Nawalam! The handkerchief he mopped his forehead with was soaking.

"Mr. Gana cares about what happens to us," I said to Rami, moved.

"He's frightened at the thought of what might happen to *him*, if there's trouble here," Rami replied, jaw set.

"We're holding the festival," Nawalam insisted. "The Lady spoke to Kayamanira in a dream and asked for this." He turned to me. "Isn't that right?"

"It is," I said, my voice not much more than a whisper. I cleared my throat. "It is," I said again, this time in a loud, clear voice, and to my astonishment, a cheer went up.

And so we left Mr. Gana behind. We climbed the barren sides of the Ruby Lake, lit the bonfires, set red flames and sprays of sparks swaying and reaching, like dancing arms. I spoke the necessary words, took an arrow fletched with crows' feathers, slit my palm with its tip, and bloodied it. Then Nawalam shot it into the Ruby Lake. Dinasha, Rami, Mirasan, and Jeteman lit the first torches and put them in the hands of those closest to us.

We heard helicopters overhead, and I think we sensed what was coming, but still the ripple of lit torches widened as people passed the fire one to the next. We chanted the customary words, then shifted to song, and the girls and boys from the regional high school stamped their feet and started to dance, and the younger children who had watched their big brothers and sisters practicing for weeks joined in, and the parents and grandparents and aunts and uncles who could still remember the steps did too, and we danced back down the gravel and scree and into the world of greenery, ready to bless and shield the first fields.

Where the path to the rim of the crater joins the road, though, State Security Service vehicles had formed a barricade, and men were fanned out from the vehicles, weapons drawn. Warning shots were fired and a voice over a megaphone called out our names and told us to surrender, because we were under arrest.

I won't write more just now. I don't like recalling those next hours and days. If I start to, the memories spring to life too real, too vivid. My heart races, and I tremble.

Chapter 6. Jiminy

August 30 (Em's diary)

Dad brought home a letter from Clear Springs Prison today. It said Jiminy got hurt in some fight and was in the infirmary a few days. Dad told Ma when he handed her the letter. Then he went right back out, off with Uncle Near in his sailing skiff. Ma read the letter, but not out loud, even though Gran and me were right there too. When she was finished, she folded it up and stuck it in her pocket without saying a thing, and then she fetched her bag of old clothes and started cutting up a pair of Jiminy's jeans for patches for mine and Tammy's. Cutting up his clothes! I know Dad can't forgive Jiminy, but I don't understand about Ma. Don't she know that's bad magic?

I've been setting out Sabelle Morning's cup every night so it can catch the dawn light, for Jiminy, but that's not good enough. I need to go see him.

Thinking about Jiminy makes me think of my pen pal, since she's in prison too. Jiminy has to stay in prison for five years. I wonder how long Kaya has to stay in that house hanging over the Ruby Lake. If the government is pretending it's an honor, then does that mean she won't ever be able to leave?

And however long she's stuck there, she can't have no visitors, not unless they come riding in by helicopter. Somehow that makes me want to visit Jiminy even more. Nobody who's able to have visitors should be left all alone.

September 3 (Em's diary)

I woke up extra early this morning, thinking about Jiminy, and couldn't fall back asleep. I checked on Sabelle Morning's cup and asked the Seafather for good luck. I made me and Tammy lunches and convinced Tammy that we should go by the Oveys first, before stopping at the Tiptoes for Clara, instead of the other way round.

"Small Bill probably won't even be up yet," she grumbled. "He probably ain't even coming."

Small Bill does skip school a lot. Ma never lets me or Tammy skip, unless we're sick, but the mothers and fathers who grew up in Mermaid's Hands don't fuss about going to school the way Ma does.

The water was not quite knee high as we waded over. We had our shoes tied together by their laces and slung around our necks so we didn't have to try to fit them in our backpacks. Tammy was making hers bang together as she walked and singing something to herself.

"Look, it's fairy-wing color," I said, pointing out at the open bay. It was, too: all pink, tinged with gold, with sparkles on the top of each ripple and swell.

"I wish it would stick, but it never does," Tammy murmured, sprinkling a few drops on her T-shirt. Of course they just made wet blotches.

"You looking for Small Bill?" It was Lindie Ovey, at the window of the Oveys' kitchen. She's between Small Bill and Jenya in age, but she always fishes and swims with her big sister and the other older kids.

"Is he up?" I asked.

“I’m here!” he said, sticking his head into the window next to Lindie. Then he clambered onto the sill and slipped down onto the veranda.

“There’s a door, you know!” Lindie said.

“But this is faster!” he called back, splashing into the water.

“Don’t you have any books or papers to bring to school today?” Tammy asked him, her hands on her hips and her voice scoldy, a mini-version of Ma. “And what about a lunch? You better get it, or you’ll be hungry.”

“Yes ma’am,” said Small Bill, grinning. He’s such a good sport. He always goes along with Tammy’s bossing. He’d make a good big brother.

“Here you go, showoff,” said Lindie, dropping Small Bill his backpack out the window. He caught it.

“You want to walk with us too?” I asked Lindie, afraid that maybe this one time she might say yes, but she shook her head.

“Nuh-uh, y’all are gonna get there way too early,” she said. “I’m waiting for Daisy and Fairchance.”

“Why *did* you come so early?” Small Bill asked me, after we’d put a little distance between us and his house.

I told him about the letter from the prison. His grin faded.

“I took the envelope it came in,” I said. “It has the address of the prison on it.” I pulled it out of my pocket to show him. “After school I’m going to the library and find out how to get there. You can do it on the computer. Tell it where you are and where you want to go, and it’ll give you directions. Want to come?”

Small Bill doesn’t know about all the stuff you can do in the library. I don’t think he’s been there since we went with our school class to get library cards, back when we were Tammy's age, but he said yes. Just dry-land luck that it was the mean librarian at the checkout desk today instead of the nice one. She frowned when me and him and Tammy came in and frowned even harder when I signed up for the computer.

"You sure you know how to use that?" she asked.

"Yes, ma'am. The other librarian showed me," I said.

"Game sites and chat sites are blocked, you know," she said.

"I'm going to make a map," I said.

She followed us to the computer work station and stood by, watching. There was no way I was going to take out that prison envelope with her hovering there, so I typed in Aunt Brenda's address instead, and the address of our school, and a blue line appeared on the screen—a route between those two places. Still she wouldn't leave. I tried to think of another dry-land place I could ask the computer to find. While I was still thinking, the phone rang at the checkout desk, and the librarian had to go answer it—though she kept looking at us over her shoulder, like she was afraid we might break the computer if she didn't keep her eye on us.

I put in the prison's address, and a long, long line appeared, from Sandy Neck west and north, across two state lines and over to where the prison is. I copied the route onto the back of the letter, along with the name of each town the blue line went through. The librarian made us show her our backpacks before she let us leave. It's a good thing our pens and pencils didn't match the library's ones, or she'd probably of said we swiped them.

"I hate that place," said Small Bill.

"The other librarian's different," I said. "She helped me find

Kaya's country on a map, and she showed me how to find pictures of it."

Outside, the hot, damp air pressed against our arms and legs as close as the sea does, when we're swimming. Up here, we're air fish. I swung my arms a little, to make a bit of breeze.

"Can we get a Coke?" Tammy asked as we passed the gas station, where a guy was unloading a pallet of Coke from a giant Coca-Cola trailer truck.

I told her I didn't have no money, but she opened up her butterfly change purse to show me two dollar bills.

"Aunt Brenda gave me money, last time we visited," she said.

Aunt Brenda gave her the change purse too, last Christmas. Aunt Brenda and Uncle Lew always fuss over Tammy, what with her being sickly and also looking a lot like Ma's side of the family. Me and Jiminy take after Dad and Gran, but Tammy's practically as pale as Mr. Winterhull.

"Well okay, then, if that's what you want to spend it on," I said. "Want me to buy it for you?"

She shook her head.

"I want to do it myself!" And she marched into the gas station store like Sabelle Morning off to face the revenue agents.

The man who's normally behind the counter was out front chatting with the Coke delivery man. First they talked about car racing, and then about fixing up cars, and then about road conditions, and where the delivery guy was going next.

"Creole Creek," he said, "then Antioch, 'n after that—"

"Hey, ain't those places on your map?" asked Small Bill. "He must be taking the same road."

He was right. Those were the names of the first two towns on my list.

The delivery guy wheeled his handcart into the gas station store, leaving the half-empty pallet beside the open rear of the trailer. I peeked in. Along one wall were pallets loaded with crates of Coke, and along the other were stacks of empty pallets and crates. It would be so easy to hide in there.

I could feel my heartbeat speeding up. *Calm down, heart.* I took a couple of deep breaths.

Sabelle Morning would do it. She'd do it in an instant, to rescue one of her crew. She's practically made of bravery. And Vaillant too. His name means brave, and there wasn't a monster on sea or land he wouldn't face down. And what about Kaya. She don't even have a choice about being brave. She has to be, whether she likes it or not.

I can be brave too. I clenched my teeth, to keep the bravery in, and climbed into the trailer.

"Em! What're you doing?" Small Bill shot a glance at the door of the gas station store, but the delivery man was still inside.

"I'm gonna ride to see Jiminy. I'll go as far as Antioch and get out there, and then I'll … I'll find another ride." I was trying to shove one of the loaded pallets a little ways away from the wall of the trailer, to make a hiding spot, but it was too heavy.

"Help me?"

Small Bill grimaced, but he followed me into the trailer. "You don't want to do this," Small Bill said, even as he helped me with my pushing. "You'll end up stranded in deep dry land.

"I ain't afraid of dry land," I said, rubbing the palms of my hands from my eyebrows to my scalp to push the sweat away from my eyes.

The door of the gas station store clanged shut after Tammy, who emerged holding a can of Coke.

"Tammy!" I whisper-shouted.

Her eyes got wide when she realized where I was calling from, and she shook her head, but I beckoned hard, and Small Bill leaned out of the end of the truck to give her a hand up.

"I don't like it in here," she said in a quavering voice, eyes on the stacked pallets and dark walls of the trailer. "Why are we in here?"

"I'm going to see Jiminy. You heard what Dad said yesterday. He got beat up. He needs us. Want to come?"

"No! And I don't want you to go either. You'll get in trouble! Please can we get down and go home?" She was silhouetted against the bright square of afternoon light at the open end of the trailer, standing between the full pallets on our side and the empty ones on the far wall, when somebody called.

"Tammy! What're you doing in there? Where's your sister? Come out of there!"

It was Cody, in the Mermaid's Hands truck—Mr. Tiptoe's truck—that we all use. He'd just pulled in at the pumps.

Of course it would be right then that the delivery man came out, and of course he saw Tammy.

"What the? Get out of there!"

His language got a lot more colorful as he strode over.

Me and Small Bill slid out from behind the pallet, and the three of us climbed down. The delivery man was pointing his finger at us, jab jab, like a stick, and saying things like theft and vandalism and police, and I felt panic rising up in me, because it looked like Tammy was right, and my bright idea was going to get us all in big trouble. Big unfair trouble! We weren't stealing nothing or breaking nothing!

"Whoa, slow down," Cody said, shutting the door of Mr. Tiptoe's truck and walking over as loose and easy as could be, his whole body saying, *everything's fine, everything's fine, there's no problem here.* The delivery man looked like he was getting ready to give Cody an earful, but Cody spoke first—to Tammy.

"You making mischief again?" he said, smiling, like the two of them had a secret joke. Tammy looked confused. She never makes mischief. Her lips were trembling: I could tell she was about to say *No it wasn't me*, but—Cody's smile. It was begging a return smile from her.

"I apologize for all this, sir," said Cody, "but I'm sure my little neighbor here just got some wild idea in her head about exploring, and then the bigger two went along with it. Nobody can say no to that face!"

To Tammy he said, "You planning a stowaway adventure? Think how worried your parents would be! And Mr. Coca-Cola here would've had a heart attack next time he opened up the doors of his truck."

Tammy looked at him in wonder. She's used to being delicate Tammy, and Tammy-who-needs-to-rest, and remember-to-wait-for-Tammy, and sometimes Tammy-the-mermaid, but Cody was giving her a whole different kind of story. Small Bill's mouth was quirking upward at the thought of Tammy the mastermind. Even the delivery man was smiling a little.

That Cody's pretty smart. Once he got Mr. Coca-Cola looking at tiny, cute Tammy, with her good hair and big eyes and freckles, how could the man stay mad? Cody talked to him a few more minutes, asking him about where he was from and if he had any kids, and got him telling stories about his four-year-old son, and by the end him and Cody were practically best buddies.

Mr. Coca-Cola closed up the back of the trailer, and me and Small Bill and Tammy piled into the Mermaid's Hands truck, which Cody drove to the Sandy Neck town parking lot, where it stays. Cody had been on a shopping run for Mermaid's Hands, buying T-shirts for everyone. Mrs. Tiptoe and Mrs. Ovey will sort out who needs what and pass them round. They usually dye the ones for us kids, tan and pink, from Spanish moss and poke berries. It's like we're all part of the same club, the Mermaid's Hands club.

"It's handy I ran into you," he said. "You can help me carry them back." So we each took an armful of T-shirts.

"Why in the world were you up in that truck?" Cody asked presently, as we squelched across the mudflats. He frowned at me and Small Bill. "You two should know better." Then, frowning deeper, "You weren't trying to run away, were you?"

"Run away to dry land? Not ever!" Small Bill said, practically shuddering.

"I was thinking more of Em," he said.

What the heck? Why me? Like I would run away from Mermaid's Hands!

Is it because of Ma? Does he see her keeping to herself and clinging to some dry-land ways and maybe think I'm that way too? *I'm the one who knows when the fish are coming,* I wanted to shout. *Just ask Snowy.*

"No!" I said. "I was—"

I couldn't tell him. I couldn't say I was trying to visit Jiminy, because what if Jiminy's the reason he thinks I might want to run away? Some people think bad things are catching. Your brother steals stuff, so maybe you might could be a runaway.

"—just … wanting an adventure, I guess?" I finished. It was a weak story. "I wanted to see … I wanted …"

But I couldn't say about wanting to be brave either.

"Didn't you ever just want to see something new?" I asked. "It don't have to be because you want to run away. You know what I mean? Like you coming to Mermaid's Hands."

"If I grew up in Mermaid's Hands, I'd never look elsewhere," he said with feeling. "You've got a thousand lifetimes of worlds to explore right here." He nodded out at the horizon and the fringed edges of Foul Point over on our left. There was a whir of wings out that way as a handful of pelicans took flight.

Small Bill nodded emphatically. "That's the truth."

I ground my heels into the mud in irritation. *I'm pretty sure I love Mermaid's Hands as much as y'all do, even if I ain't* testifying *to it,* I thought. But at least Small Bill didn't tell about Jiminy. That's something.

"There's some good things on dry land too," Tammy remarked. I could practically see her remembering all our cousins' old toys in Aunt Brenda's house.

Visiting dry-land relatives. Maybe Cody thinks that makes us not quite real seachildren, too. Most folks who get sung into Mermaid's Hands leave dry land behind them. In fact, I can't think of any other kid in Mermaid's Hands who spends much time on dry land, outside of school. *Maybe we really* aren't *quite real seachildren.* The thought made me want to punch somebody.

But then Cody surprised me.

“You bet there are good things on dry land. Ice cream’s pretty good. And Coke’s pretty good,” said Cody. “Can I have a sip?”

Tammy grinned and nodded. She stayed grinning as he took a swig from the can, appreciated it loudly and dramatically, and gave it back to her.

“Delicious! Yep, ice cream and Coke. That’s two good things that dry land has.”

Tammy giggled, and I smiled a little too. That Cody! He really does know just the right thing to say.

September 4 (Em's diary)

I am in big trouble. I don't know what I'm going to do next, so I might as well just sit here and write this until they kick me out.

This morning, Gran was getting ready to go out with Auntie Chicoree and Granny Ikaho to cut cordgrass for repairing the thatch part of the roof.

"Everybody's up on their roofs these days," I said. "Clara said her ma and dad replaced all their thatch, and yesterday I saw Mr. Winterhull hammering down nails on their kitchen roof."

"Next storm's brewing out in the Caribbean," Gran said. "What letter are we up to now? H? This one's a dawdler, so it's getting big. Seems likely to come our way, so we're making sure we're snug."

"Can I help?"

"Course you can, once you get back from school. I'm not climbing up there."

"Can I stay home and help?"

Gran put down the twine she was rolling and fixed me with a raised-eyebrow look.

"Whyever would you ask to do that? You like school, don't you? Getting essays in books and things?"

She meant my essay in the *Kids Speak* book. Ma and Dad and Gran still think it's a big deal.

"Everybody in class got their essay in that book," I muttered.

"What's that now?"

"You'd let Wade come along, if you were at Auntie Chicoree's, and Wade asked," I said, louder. Tropical Storm Unfair was gaining strength inside me.

"Auntie Chicoree's not as fussy about school as your mama is."

"School ain't optional, contrary to what some folks seem to think," Ma said, handing me and Tammy our lunches. "And not everything that's useful to know can be learned on the water."

Hurricane Unfair, with sustained winds of 110 miles a hour, just about knocked me down at that point. Thanks to Ma, someone like Cody takes me for a runaway, and thanks to Ma, I don't even get the chance any other seachild would get to prove my loyalty to Mermaid's Hands.

"Make sure you scrape those," Ma added as I stacked Tammy's unfinished bowl of fried jumblefish and pickleweed in mine. And there above the bait bin, peeking out from among the bills which Ma keeps propped between the thyme and the jar of pennies on the windowsill, was the letter from the prison. I slid it free and read it.

"Ma, it says multiple fractures! It says clavicle, scapula, and ribs. What bones are clavicle and scapula? And it says lacerations and loss of blood. It sounds real bad! We should go see him!"

"That wasn't addressed to you; you shouldn't read other people's mail!" Ma said, snatching the letter out of my hand.

"But are we going to go see him?"

Ma squinched her forehead between her two hands.

"Sometime, maybe, Em. Not today or tomorrow; we have other things to worry about just now. You get yourself on to school."

I imagined Jiminy laid up in a hospital bed with broken bones. But just for a few days, the letter said. What then, back in a cell? Still hurting? And nothing but silence from the folks that are supposed to care about him.

Before the morning announcements came on at school, I went up to Ms. Tennant's desk, because I know she keeps a dictionary on it, next to the attendance book, and I wanted to find out which bones Jiminy broke. There were a bunch of folders on top of it, though, and Ms. Tennant came into the classroom just as I was setting them to one side to get at the dictionary.

"What do you think you're doing there! Get your hands away from my purse!"

I didn't even see her stupid purse there, and I said so, which got me sent to the principal's office. Mr. Barnes told me stealing is a crime and talking back is rude and I needed to return anything I took and apologize to Ms. Tennant.

"I'm sorry," I said to Ms. Tennant, who was standing there with her arms crossed and her stingy lips shaved down to just an angry line. I fixed my eyes on her shoes because I was seething mad, and I was afraid I might burn holes in her face if I looked her in the eye. "I didn't take nothing, though. I just wanted to check the dictionary."

Mr. Dubois came into Mr. Barnes's office just then. Mr. Dubois is the other seventh grade teacher. Jiminy had him, when Jiminy was my age.

"Checking the dictionary—I approve," he said with a smile. "What were you looking up?"

Ms. Tennant would never ask that. She would of just accused me of looking for dirty words. But Mr. Dubois sounded like he really wanted to know. Like he was actually interested.

"'Clavicle,' and 'scapula,'" I told him. "I wanted to find out what bones they are."

"And did you?"

"No, because …" I clamped my mouth shut. I'd just get in bigger trouble if I complained about Ms. Tennant.

Ms. Tennant rolled her eyes. “She’s making it up.”

“Why do you say that? It sounds to me more like she’s interested in bones. Curious about anatomy?” Mr. Dubois asked me.

“She was going through my purse.”

“I was not!”

“Was there anything missing from the purse?” Mr. Dubois asked.

Mr. Barnes looked irritated and started to say that he was handling the situation. Ms. Tennant looked like she’d just stepped on an eel. She said she hadn’t yet had a chance to check and she wasn’t exactly sure how much money was in her wallet anyway. When she said that, Mr. Dubois laughed.

“Well I don’t see as how you can go accusing people of stealing when you don’t even know for sure that anything’s missing.”

Then the bell rang, and Tucker Brady came in to do the announcements, and Mr. Barnes said it seemed the misunderstanding was cleared up, but looked at me sternly and said a few more words about backtalking and not rummaging around on Ms. Tennant’s desk without asking.

“You can use one of the dictionaries in my room, if you want,” Mr. Dubois said as we got to the classrooms, but Ms. Tennant bristled and said that wouldn’t be necessary.

So I found out that Jiminy fractured his collar bone and shoulder blade as well as his ribs. People get bruised and broken if they’re out at sea during a storm, but how does one person break another that way?

Maybe it was more than one person. Maybe they ganged up on

him. Poor Jiminy. Do you feel forgotten, there in Clear Springs? Do you think no one cares what happens to you?

I haven't forgotten you. I care.

I was talking to him in my head like that after school as me and Small Bill and Tammy walked home.

"Hey! Hey Em, you listening?" Small Bill said, coming round to stand in front of me. I nearly walked right into him, I was so lost in thought.

"You been visiting the Seafather at night or something? You need to shake the water out of your ears when you come back up," he said.

"Sorry."

Up at the corner was the gas station, with the state highway snaking away north. Go on it eighty miles, and then take another highway west if you want to get to Clear Springs.

Small Bill and Tammy were talking about Hurricane Helga, how the news had been saying it's stalled out over the Gulf, but Snowy reported the sharks are already heading out into the deep water, away from shore, which means it's on its way.

I frowned, because if the storm was coming soon, then there wouldn't be a chance for me to find my way up to Clear Springs.

"Let's cool off," Tammy said, nodding at the door of the gas station store.

"You used up your money yesterday," I pointed out.

"We can just sit on the bench," she said.

We do that sometimes. They don't like you hanging around in the store if you're not buying anything, but if you sit on the bench right outside the door, you can get a big whoof of cool air any time anyone goes in or out.

"You still fuming about Ms. Tennant?" Small Bill asked as we flopped down on the bench. Tammy leaned forward, scanning the ground for bottle caps.

"Oh her. She can go sink. No, it's Jiminy, still. I was thinking about trying to get to Clear Springs."

A girl with a short ponytail and a T-shirt that said "Lookin' for trouble?" across the chest shot me a funny look—like maybe *she* was looking for trouble—as she went into the store. We all leaned toward the breath of air-conditioned coolness.

"I was wondering if there was any way for me to make it up there before the hurricane comes. If it's sitting out at sea, that's one thing, but if the fish are already on the move …"

"Go after. It's not like he's going anywhere. He'll be glad for visitors any time."

For the second time that day, I forced myself to keep my mouth shut, so as not to say something I'd regret.

It's not like he's going anywhere.

Like Jiminy's on a shelf. Like we can care about him some other time. Small Bill's my best friend, so I know he didn't mean it that way. It still hurts, though, and if I feel that way, just being Jiminy's sister, how does Jiminy feel?

I told Small Bill what I'd found out about Jiminy's injuries.

"That's why I want to go see him *now,*" I said. "If there can please just be enough time to get to Clear Springs and back before the storm comes."

There was another big puff of cool air as the girl in the t-shirt came back out with a big bottle of Diet Coke, a half-gallon of milk, and a pack of cigarettes.

She glanced down at us—at me.

"You fixing to go to Clear Springs, Louisiana?" she asked. Small Bill and I glanced at each other, and even Tammy frowned. Since when do strangers come up and ask you your plans?

"Is it the prison? You know someone inside?"

I guess I must of looked pretty surprised, because the girl laughed.

"Why else would anyone go to Clear Springs? Vacation? Ain't nothing in that town but the prison and farms. My old boyfriend was there for a while. I ran away from home to go see him. At the time, I wasn't too much older than you are now." She put a foot up on the end of the bench, balanced the bag with the milk and Coke in it on her knee, and tore the plastic off the pack of cigarettes.

"Who is it? Your dad?" She lit the cigarette.

"My brother," I said. Small Bill and Tammy were looking at me like, *why're you telling her this?* but I was thinking, *she has a car.*

"I don't miss Louisiana none," she said. "I like Mississippi better. And Alabama's not bad either, of course," she added quickly. Like I care about Alabama or Mississippi or any other state!

She inhaled, and the end of the cigarette got bright. "I'll take you as far as Clarksville, if you want a ride," she said.

My thoughts came down in an avalanche on top of any words I might of had to reply. *Clarksville—that's halfway! But how do I get the rest of the way there? I shouldn't try. Not now. I need to stay at home, help look after Tammy. Tammy needs me. But Jiminy does too. Gran said the Seafather would find a way to save Jiminy—and ain't this a way? But what about Hurricane Helga? But a better chance might not come. No plan can be perfect.*

"So, do you?" the girl asked, exhaling smoke.

You can't see the sea from the gas station, so I looked to the sky for guidance. It had the thick, gray look of the innards of an old mattress. The air was stifling still, like the sky was holding it back, waiting for my answer.

"I have to do it," I said to Tammy and Small Bill. I hadn't been sure until I said it. Saying it made me sure.

Small Bill's face was so serious, you might of thought he was angry, but he nodded. "'A cup of fortune,'" he said.

"Come back before Helga," Tammy whispered.

"I'll try," I said, giving her hand a squeeze.

"Thanks," I said to the girl. "Yeah, I'd like a lift."

"Great. I'm Hayley. What's your name?" I told her, then waved goodbye to Small Bill and Tammy and followed her over to her car.

She liked her music pretty loud, so it was hard to hear everything she was saying, but all the same, I caught a fair amount about her old boyfriend, and how her and her mom hadn't always seen eye to eye, though they got along now, and about running away and seeing Patrick and promising she'd marry him, even though she was only sixteen at the time. Being in prison had changed Patrick for the worse, she said ("That's why it's good you're visiting—I should of visited more," she told me), and anyway, in the meantime her and Nate had kind of started seeing each other, and then Patrick got involved with some real bad people—

Then the music stopped for an emergency broadcast, a funny, fake voice, like a robot, saying,

"HURRICANE HELGA NOW MOVING NORTH-

NORTHWESTWARD TOWARD THE NORTHERN GULF COAST...HELGA IS NOW AN EXTREMELY DANGEROUS CATEGORY 4 HURRICANE ON THE SAFFIR-SIMPSON HURRICANE SCALE"

and

"A HURRICANE WARNING IS NOW IN EFFECT FOR THE NORTH CENTRAL GULF COAST FROM MORGAN CITY LOUISIANA EASTWARD TO PENSACOLA FLORIDA."

and

"A HURRICANE WARNING MEANS THAT HURRICANE CONDITIONS ARE EXPECTED WITHIN THE WARNING AREA WITHIN THE NEXT 24 HOURS. PREPARATIONS TO PROTECT LIFE AND PROPERTY SHOULD BE RUSHED TO COMPLETION."

And then a regular announcer came on and said the governor was ordering an evacuation of the coast.

My stomach tried to curl itself into a little ball, like it could hide from the news.

"I need to go back," I blurted out. *Sorry, Jiminy. I do care, I do. But you're pretty much a grown-up, and Tammy's just a kid.*

"Are you crazy? With the storm coming? No way. You heard the report. It ain't safe. They're probably gonna close the road, anyway. Ride along with me as far as Clarksville. You can call your sister from there if you want, find out where your folks are evacuating to."

I didn't want to try to explain about Mermaid's Hands, and how we always ride these things out. All I could think about was how it was a race now between me and Helga, who could get to Mermaid's Hands first.

"No, I really gotta go back," I said.

Hayley slowed down and pulled off the road by a small building with a big sign: Casey's Hungry Man Coffee and Cornbread.

"I can let you out here, if you really want," she said, looking doubtful. "We haven't been on the road that long. Maybe you can hitch a ride part of the way back. Here." She shifted in her seat so she could get her hand into her cutoffs. She pulled out a couple of dollar bills, all creased and soft from being in her pocket. "Get yourself something to drink before you head home."

"Thanks. Hey, do you think—" I caught myself.

"Do I think what?"

"Clarksville's really far away from Clear Springs … You never just go there, do you?"

"Drive all that way? Uh-uh. I told you, there's nothing there but the prison."

Of course she wouldn't. I didn't mean to let tears come, and I really didn't mean for Hayley to see them, but it was too late. She bit her lip.

"Hey now, hey. Don't cry. You were thinking I could visit your brother for you? That ain't how it works. A stranger can't just up and visit him. He has to put people on a list and things."

I nodded, but I couldn't meet her eye. It was quiet in the car for a minute.

"Tell you what. Maybe I could phone the people there, if you want," she said. "Tell them Jiminy's little sister's trying to be in touch."

I looked up. "Will you? Can you tell him his family hopes he heals up soon? Can you tell him his sister hasn't forgotten about him?"

Hayley tucked some stray hairs behind her ear. "Yeah, okay," she said softly. "What's his full name?"

I wiped my eyes.

"Baptiste. Jiminy Baptiste."

"Okay, Jiminy Baptiste. I'll remember that."

"Thank you," I said.

I got out of her car, and she drove off. The sky wasn't holding its breath any more: there was a panting sort of breeze all around, and the grass was flattening under it, but the dust was rising up. I started running back the way we'd come, but I stopped after a few hundred feet. Behind me, the sign for Casey's Hungry Man Coffee and Cornbread still loomed tall. Up ahead, nothing familiar. We'd only been driving about twenty minutes, half an hour tops, but Hayley'd been going fast. I couldn't beat Helga home by running. Hayley was right: I was going to have to try hitching a ride. I crossed over to the other side and started walking backward, but not much was coming by. One big truck, going fast. A pickup with two guys in it, laughing loud and swerving for the fun of it. I shrank way back from the side of the road and tried to be invisible, but they caught sight of me, screeched to a stop, then put the pickup in reverse.

"That a kid or a stray dog back there? Hey kid, hop in, we'll throw you a bone or two! Hey, she's running away—You know how to call a dog to heel?" And they were whistling and catcalling, but I was pounding back toward Casey's Hungry Man Coffee and Cornbread, running so hard it felt like lightning in my lungs when I breathed in. *Stupid, stupid, stupid,* my feet said to me each time they hit the gravel.

But at least the creeps in the pickup didn't chase after me. I was jelly-legged by the time I got to Casey's, and feeling like I'd better sit a spell and think, so I used Hayley's money to buy a Coke, and I started writing this on the paper placemat, hoping I could work out what to do next.

But now I've finished my Coke, and I still don't know my next move. And it ain't like Helga's sitting somewhere biting her nails and wondering what to do. I guess better just start walking again and hope somebody safe to ride with comes by before they close the roads.

September 4 (Em's diary, second entry)

I'm home now. It's real late, but I have to write this all down.

I got a lift from one lady as far as her turnoff, and when she dropped me off, she asked if I wanted to use her phone to call anyone, but I don't know what Mr. Tiptoe's number is, so I said no, I was nearly home. I didn't want her to worry. After that it started raining, fine as mist, but coming fast, in ripples like wind through sheets hung out to dry. Traffic going north was getting real heavy, but hardly anything was going south, and what there was was going real fast. I kept on getting splashed, but I didn't care. Just keep going, keep going, I was telling myself. And then I heard a bunch of honking, and I could tell from the shape behind the headlights that it was another pickup, and I felt a spike of panic, because I was too beat to run away again. Then I heard a voice say "Em! Emlee, get yourself over here!" It was Dad and Mr. Tiptoe, in the Mermaid's Hands truck. Turns out they'd been driving up and down all the roads hereabouts, looking for me.

When we got home, Tammy confessed.

"I told. I'm sorry." She hung her head and wouldn't look at me.

"'sokay. I'm glad you did. It was stupid, what I did," I said.

Sometimes all my ideas seem stupid.

"I'm just sorry I made trouble for everybody."

Gran came up from behind and gave me a surprise hug.

"It wasn't no trouble. We can't have any little minnows going missing. And you ain't stupid. You're a loyal sister. And so's Tammy." She beckoned for Tammy and Tammy squirmed into the hug too. From over the top of Tammy's head, I could see Ma glance at Dad, but he wasn't letting his thoughts or feelings show in his face.

"Em. Come here. I have something for you," he said. "Another letter from that friend of yours overseas."

I opened it and read it. Now I feel scared and sick again, but for Kaya. I'm pasting the letter in here, because I'm keeping my diary with me even if the Seafather decides to take all of Mermaid's Hands down to the merlands. Here's what Kaya wrote:

August 28

Dear Em,

I've walked the perimeter of this floating prison three times, trying to calm down, but my hands are still shaking, so please forgive the poor handwriting. I had planned to write one sort of letter to you, but what happened just now has sent those thoughts flying away.

I don't receive any news of the outside world unless the government brings it to me, which it did today, wrapped in accusations and threats. It seems the spirit of unrest is bubbling up among my people once again. Some of the old activists, who have lived quietly all these years, have been demanding to know why my friends in prison have not been brought to trial, and why, if the government is sincere in its claims to honor me, no one has been permitted to see me. They have been asking their friends and neighbors, Are we going to be content forever to accept whatever laws and judgments the coastal government presses on us? And more and more people are answering no.

And so today two officers from the State Security Service paid me a special visit—apparently the matter was too urgent to wait for the weekly supply helicopter. They said that I must tell everyone to cease and desist, to stand down and return to work, to fulfill their responsibilities as citizens—they gave me a long script.

"You need me to actually say these things?" I asked. "Why not just claim that I did—who can contradict you?" One of them looked like he might hit me at that point, but the other stopped him. People are waiting for a message from me, he said. The government wants to film me conveying that message. The government's message.

"I'll do no such thing," I told them. I said it without thinking, I was so angry. The officers seemed barely able to believe it. The violent one asked if I had forgotten how very precarious my situation was. The more reasonable one said I should think of the consequences of my decision for everyone else.

"No one's died—yet," he said. "Do you want deaths on your conscience?"

*"*My *conscience? Not yours?" I said.*

Then the bully of the pair lunged forward and kicked over the low table where I write and eat, spilling everything to the floor. In one step he was standing right over me. I had no time to flinch or shield myself: that same boot struck me right in the chest and I fell back on the floor. It hurt terribly! I couldn't breathe for a moment, and I couldn't see anything, just red darkness, but I could hear the bully knocking down the stack of books I keep beside the table and scattering and flinging around the few loose items in the room. When my sight and breath returned, I saw the other officer gathering up my books and papers. He said they were confiscating them as I needed time to think things over without distractions.

Do you keep a diary or journal, Em? I was keeping one, these past few weeks. I was writing up my memories in a notebook. I was recording my inmost thoughts and feelings. Private things. And now the State Security Service has it. I feel more exposed than I would if they had taken my clothes.

As they were climbing into the helicopter to leave, the bully said, "I'm not sure we can spare a helicopter next week, so bear that in mind when you get this week's delivery," and the other one said, "I hope you'll consider your options carefully."

My options. I never intended to launch a rebellion. I don't want to be responsible for people dying! But does that mean I must tell people to acquiesce to injustice?

I remember, in your last letter, you said you thought our festival must have made the Lady of the Ruby Lake happy. I am much less sure. You said the Lady's love could not be gentle. I find myself wishing for more evidence of that love, even ungentle. I feel only her absence.

Well, I must close now. My head and chest and back ache; I need to rest. I would like to dream of your mudflats and your seagifts. Such abundance!

Your friend,
Kaya

P.S. My dear Em, a very strange thing happened just now. I lay down to rest, as I said I would, and I had a dream, about you! A young girl was walking out of the ocean toward me, and in the dream I was certain it was you. Now I wish I could see a photo of you. In my dream, you had thick, dark hair that curled around your face, and wide, dark eyes. You had something in your hands. I asked what, and you smiled and showed me—night crawlers. "Are we going fishing?" I asked, and you said, "Do you know what these are?" I cupped my hands, and you emptied yours, but it wasn't worms that I caught, it was butterflies. They flew away from me up into the trees, and suddenly the trees were full of blossoms. I laughed, and looked over at you, and when I did, I noticed steam rising from where you had walked through the water. And I realized that somehow you were the Lady of the Ruby Lake. I didn't know what to say. "Did you-did you like the festival?" I finally managed to stammer, but you just grinned and said, "Thank you for being my friend."

This dream frightens and excites me. Maybe the Lady really can be a friend to me, and through me, to all the mountain people. Distant, like you're distant, but real, like you're real.

I gotta write her back right away. And then, when this storm's past, I'll send it.

Chapter 7. Helga

September 4 (Em to Kaya)

Dear Kaya,

I'm scared for you! If a helicopter can't come to you, how will you get food? They have to send a helicopter, don't they? They can't let you starve, can they? The prison Jiminy is in is pretty rough but at least all the inmates get food.

I wish I could get to the library. They have computers there that they let anyone use, if you sign up on a sheet at the checkout desk, and they have three different paper newspapers, too. If I could go to the library, maybe I could find out news about you. But I can't go right now, because Hurricane Helga's coming. Most of the dry-landers who live on the coast are evacuating—the governor ordered it. Ma wants us to, too—she wants us to go stay with Aunt Brenda inland, but no seachild ever runs away from the sea. Fish don't move inland, Dad always says, they nestle close to each other on the bottom. Ma just gives him a look when he says that. Once she said that a seachild will drown just as surely as a dry-lander if you put him down beneath the waves. That was maybe their worst fight ever.

"Seachildren don't drown. They go home," Dad told her.

"Home? To the mud and the dark, to lie down with eels and toadfish? Not me. If that's a seachild's home, then I ain't no seachild," Ma said.

Ma might as well of thrown a knife at Dad, from the look on his face. Then he narrowed his eyes and said, "But they *are," pointing to me and Tammy. Threw that knife right back at Ma.*

It was the only time Ma ever said she wasn't a seachild, but none of us have ever forgotten it.

I can't believe you dreamed of me as the Lady of the Ruby Lake. Me! If I was as wild as a volcano, people would have to watch out. I like that idea. Nobody bosses around a volcano. Someone should remind those government people in your country that you can't tell a volcano what to do.

Thinking about the Lady of the Ruby Lake makes me feel braver about Hurricane Helga. A hurricane is a pretty wild thing, but if anything can stand up to a hurricane, it's a volcano.

When you get this letter, please write back right away so that I know you're okay. I'll write you, too, after the hurricane, so you won't have to worry about me.

Thinking of you,

Em

(September 5 AP Newswire)

Hurricane Helga's Impact Less Than Feared

Hurricane Helga made landfall east of New Orleans in the predawn hours today as a Category 2 storm, substantially weakened from the potentially catastrophic Category 4 storm it had been a mere 12 hours earlier. Some 500,000 homes on the northern Gulf Coast lost power in the wake of the storm, and storm surge damage is significant in some Mississippi and Alabama coastal communities, but initial assessments indicate that overall destruction is less than was initially predicted. Seven fatalities have been reported so far, though that number may rise, as there have been several reports of persons unaccounted for.

"We're all glad this wasn't a Katrina," said Jared Rodney, a FEMA spokesperson. "We've improved a lot from those days. Coastal evacuations for all four affected states went smoothly. You always get some people who stay behind, and that's where you tend to get loss of life. But most people are sensible."

Residents in most areas are expected to be able to return home tomorrow.

September 6 (Em to Kaya)

Dear Kaya,

I'm writing to you from the basement of Jordan's Waters Fellowship Church. Everyone from Mermaid's Hands is camped out here, and there are people from Sandy Neck here, too—the ones who didn't evacuate. Hurricane Helga sent us here. The news is saying that it wasn't such a big-deal hurricane after all, but to people in Mermaid's Hands and Sandy Neck it was.

The hurricane came in the night, which made it extra scary, because we couldn't see anything. And it was so loud. The storm was howling, like it was in terrible pain and had to get rid of all that pain by pouring it out on us. Gran kept her arms wrapped around Tammy and me in the bedroom, and we locked arms around her. Ma was with Dad in the kitchen, helping him with the signal lantern. All the Mermaid's Hands families always signal each other during any storm. Each house has its own signal, and the grown-ups flash them so everyone know everyone's okay. I once asked Dad if they ever signal other stuff, and he said, "Sure, we tell jokes: 'I ain't afraid of you,' the boy said to the hurricane. 'Oh yeah? Look me in the eye and tell me that.'"

He says things like that to make me laugh. "Laughing makes you braver," he says.

There wasn't no need for signaling this time, though, because Helga was making high mountains and deep valleys in the water, and all our houses were slipping into the valleys and knocking up against each other. If the bedroom window shutter hadn't been locked shut, and if Gran and Tammy and me hadn't been tight in each other's arms, we could've just reached out the window and touched the Tiptoes' house.

We keep tires all around our houses' support rafts for bumpers, but even with the tires, you could hear the wood cracking as the Fisherkins crashed into the Oveys, and the Tiptoes crashed into us. The Tiptoes' house broke right through into our bedroom and poured wind and rain and Clara and Brightly and the twins right in on top of me and Tammy, and then our house listed toward theirs, and the rain was pummeling us, and I thought we'd be beaten to death by it if we didn't drown.

The twins were sobbing, and Clara and Brightly and Tammy too, but I was too terrified to cry. We were all slipping down toward the big hole in the bedroom wall. It's a good thing all the broken beams and walls and thatch from the Tiptoes' house were still in a big heap in the hole, because they kept us from being pulled right out. I could see a quilt caught in the smash-up. The wind wanted to tear it free, but it was stuck and rippling and snapping like a ship's flag.

Sometime later the wind went from howling to just blowing and the rain went from beating to just pattering down, and I could hear Ma and Dad and Mr. and Mrs. Tiptoe calling out to each other, and then Ma climbed in from the kitchen and told us to come along because Dad and Mr. Tiptoe were bringing dinghies around. Gran had a twin on each knee and was telling them, don't be scared. Don't be scared. Brightly had his arms tight around Clara's waist and wouldn't let go—they walked together like one person, climbing over the mess and out to the open air.

And here we are now, because all the houses are smashed or broken somehow, and no one yet knows what the mudflats look like now because no one's been back. And all the parents have worried faces because in other hurricanes maybe one house would be smashed, and everyone would help rebuild it with the salvage and sea flotsam the storm left behind, but all the houses, from nothing? That's a harder thing. And I heard one of the dads saying that maybe we won't even be allowed to move back, because even though we've lived there forever, we're still just squatters and maybe now the state will decide they don't want us out on the mudflats anymore.

Can they decide that? That sounds like something your government would do—not let people live where they've always lived.

And another bad thing, a real bad thing. People died: two of the Fearings, Granny Fearing and Indigo. And Mr. Ovey.

When the Fisherkins' house crashed into the Oveys, Auntie Chicoree and baby Dawn-day and Wade all went into the water. Mrs. Ovey grabbed Wade, and Uncle Near helped Auntie Chicoree, but then Dawn-day slipped out of Auntie Chicoree's arms. Mr. Ovey dove in and got her and reached her up to Auntie Chicoree, but then he was pulled away and under, himself. Wade saw him bob back up once, just like a cormorant, but then the mountain waves hid him from sight.

Jenya and Lindie have been crying, but not Mrs. Ovey or Small Bill. Cody's like a mother tern with chicks: he's got Jenya under one wing and Lindie under the other. Mrs. Ovey's sitting with Small Bill in front of her. She's wrapped both arms around him, and he's letting her hold him like that.

The church people gave us kids chocolate milk in little plastic bottles, and packages of cheese crackers. I gave my package to Small Bill.

"My dad grew gills," Small Bill said. "He can't come back now. Once you have gills, you can't live up above the water."

I nodded. I could feel tears rising up in my eyes, but I blinked them back.

"I won't ever worry about being called underwater now," Small Bill said. "Because Dad'll be there."

Ma doesn't usually talk much to Mrs. Ovey, but she joined everyone gathered round. She told Mrs. Ovey that Mr. Ovey was a real hero. "You married a fine man." That made Mrs. Ovey smile.

"I did, I surely did," she said, in a tired, faraway voice.

I'm putting my Aunt Brenda's address at the bottom of this letter. We have to go live with her for a little while, until the grown-ups figure out what's happening next. I wanted to stay with Dad and the others, but Ma said we can't live on the charity of Jordan's Waters Fellowship Church when we have family that'll take us, and Dad actually agreed with her.

I asked Ma if I could go to the library at Aunt Brenda's. I told her I needed to get on the computer and find out whether there was a rebellion in your country and whether you're okay. Ma got cross with me and told me to save my worry for people closer to home. And then, I don't know why, but I started bawling, even though I didn't cry all through the hurricane or after. I said but maybe you don't have any food or even water, and I didn't even know if you were alive.

Gran gave me a hug and said, "Didn't you say your friend has a volcano to look after her?" But it didn't make me feel much better, because volcanoes are even less gentle than the sea, and if the Ruby Lake goes wild, growing gills won't help you.

Please write and tell me you are okay.

Love,

Em

September 7 (from the Mobile *Press-Register*)

Should Sandy Neck's offshore neighbor rebuild?
By Justin Landau

If you were to take a scenic drive through all the seaside and bayou towns along the Gulf Coast, you couldn't be faulted if you overlooked the small community of Sandy Neck, let alone Mermaid's Hands, which is the fanciful name given to a collection of ramshackle houses that locals say have stood out on the mudflats for as long as anyone can remember. But attention turned to Sandy Neck earlier this week when Hurricane Helga swept through, uprooting trees, washing out roads, and destroying property. Three of the storm's seven fatalities were residents of Sandy Neck—or more precisely, of Mermaid's Hands.

This unnecessary tragedy has prompted both local and state authorities to ask whether Mermaid's Hands should rebuild. Some are asking if the settlement was ever legal in the first place.

"We're having town counsel look into the legal issues," said Sandy Neck's Mayor Dick Hemingway. "Nobody's got title to that land—water it is, really, when the tide's in—which means it's under state jurisdiction, I believe.

The state permits certain activity in coastal waters, but I'm pretty sure maintaining a small village isn't one."

"The people in Mermaid's Hands go shrimping in restricted areas," complained Trent Moore, a Sandy Neck fisherman. "I don't care if they're not trawling. It's still illegal. They seem to think they can fish just anywhere."

Brett Tiptoe, a resident of Mermaid's Hands, insisted that the community doesn't engage in commercial fishing. "We just fish for ourselves. Maybe sometimes, if we catch extra, we sell it, but that's all. We get the permits we need to get. We've been here since before Sandy Neck incorporated," he added. "We just want to rebuild, like everyone else."

September 8 (Em's diary)

When Dad dropped us at Aunt Brenda and Uncle Lew's house, Aunt Brenda barely had two words for him. I think what she said was, "You won't be coming in, I assume," but maybe she didn't mean it as unfriendly as it came out.

Dad went back because him and some of the other grown-ups have to protect whatever's left of Mermaid's Hands while we try to figure out a way to rebuild. If we're allowed to. The people in Sandy Neck, or the state, or the Army Corps of Engineers—whoever gets to decide stuff—they better tell us we can. They just better.

I told Dad again that I wanted to go with him, but he said no.

"Not now, Minnow Em. Soon."

That's what he said. Then he kissed me and Tammy on the top of the head and Ma on the cheek, nodded at Aunt Brenda, and left.

Once he was gone, Aunt Brenda had lots of hugs for the rest of us. She was full of it-must-have-been-terrible and you-poor-things and wait-till-Lew-sees-ya'll. (Uncle Lew is on the road right now). To Ma she said how we'll probably have flashbacks and nightmares and how it's a good thing we're someplace safe and stable. Then she asked Mandy to take me and Tammy upstairs, and she wrapped an arm around Ma's shoulder and led her into the kitchen, saying I-don't-know-how-you've-managed and you're-a-saint-you-know-that.

Me and Tammy are sleeping in Jenny and Mandy's room with Mandy. Tammy gets Jenny's bed and I have an air mattress on the floor. (Tammy can have Jenny's bed because Jenny's all grown up now and lives in Memphis.) Ma's in Connor's room. (He's pretty much a grown-up too: he joined the army and is away at basic training.)

Mandy showed us where we could put our things and then showed us the phone Uncle Lew and Aunt Brenda gave her last month, when she got her license. It's way fancier than Mr. Tiptoe's phone, and it has a little ballet-slipper charm dangling from it because Mandy likes ballet. She started to show us the different ringtones she has for her different friends, but then Aunt Brenda called upstairs that it was almost time for rehearsal and maybe me and Tammy would like to go along.

"Our church youth group is acting out Jesus's parables, only set in modern day," Mandy explained. I wasn't sure what she was talking about, but I nodded anyway.

"Mandy and her friends are doing the story of the Prodigal Son, only in their version, it's the Prodigal Daughter," Aunt Brenda said. "Girl leaves home to go live in a godless way, but she returns in the end." Here Aunt Brenda gave Ma a significant look. Ma rolled her eyes.

"Honestly, Bren," she said.

That's how much Mermaid's Hands gets under Aunt Brenda's skin: it don't matter that Ma says prayers each night and won't ever mention the Seafather. If you ask Aunt Brenda, just living in Mermaid's Hands means living in a godless way.

"You'll like the youth group," Aunt Brenda assured us. "They're all great kids, and Pastor John is a wonderful man. He's heard so much about you! I'm so glad you'll be here for a while. Drive safe, Mandy!"

In Mandy's skit, after the Prodigal Daughter leaves home, she spends every night partying with her friends. She smokes and drinks and takes drugs and buys lots of clothes and makeup and jewelry, until all her money runs out. Then her friends all disappear, and she has no place to stay, and she starts feeling sorry about the way she's been living, but she thinks her parents will never forgive her. But they *do* forgive her—they forgive her enough to throw a big party for her to welcome her home.

I know the skit made Aunt Brenda think about Ma, but I was thinking about Jiminy. I was thinking how great it would be if he could come back like that, and if Ma and Dad were like the parents in the story, so happy to have him home that they'd have a party for him.

Too bad you can't come home from prison once you're sorry for what you've done.

These days, thinking of prison makes me think of Kaya, too. I looked in Aunt Brenda and Uncle Lew's newspaper, but there weren't any stories there about the country of W—. Their newspaper mainly has nearby news, with a few paragraphs on the third page about stuff going on in the other parts of the country and the rest of the world.

They have a computer, but Mandy's only allowed to use it for homework, so I didn't feel like I could ask to use it to try to find out about Kaya. I hope she has food. I wonder if she gave in and decided to read that thing they want her to read.

I just thought: If police in Kaya's country can make her say things she don't believe, can they do that here, too? Could they make Jiminy say yes, he stole from those people in the casino, even if he didn't?

September 9 (Em's diary)

Aunt Brenda's taking Ma to the school offices here to sign me and Tammy up for school. We have to go from tomorrow, they're saying. How long are we staying here? It's meant to be temporary! Going to school in a place means you're living there. I was feeling pretty stormy about it this morning.

Tammy wasn't. She was too excited about the ballet costume Mandy gave her—one of Mandy's old ones from when she was Tammy's age. We were supposed to be getting dressed so we could go with Ma and Aunt Brenda and see the school, but Tammy put on the costume instead. The top part is white velvet, with ruby-colored sequins down the front in a V. The skirt is layers of floaty material in shades of green, with here and there some white, and there are tiny, puffy sleeves just at the shoulders, in matching green and white.

"Mandy said it was for a Christmas recital," said Tammy. She was twisting around to try to see her back in the long mirror on Mandy's door. "See? It's Christmas colors."

"Or ruby-throat colors," I said. "You look like a ruby-throated hummingbird."

"Really?" Her voice and face were sunshine-water-sparkle bright. "I'm going to show Ma!" She thundered down the stairs the way no hummingbird ever did. I pulled on a Mermaid's Hands T-shirt and followed her down.

"I'm a hummingbird," Tammy was saying. "See? Ma, do I look like a hummingbird?"

"Tammy, put some proper—" Ma began, but Aunt Brenda interrupted her.

"Ain't you the sweetest thing! She's adorable, Josie; let her enjoy the costume. It's been so long since my girls were anything like that small!"

"I wish I could be sung into a hummingbird line—is there a hummingbird line, Em?" Tammy asked, flying forward on tiptoes, then backward, arms out.

"Not in Mermaid's Hands, I don't believe," I said, flinching inside at the face Aunt Brenda made when she heard that name. "Anyway, you already got two lines to choose from, red-winged blackbird and Vaillant's ..." I trailed off. I wanted to add *You wouldn't want to fly away from those lines, would you?*—but I couldn't, not with Aunt Brenda in the room, not seeing as how she thinks it was running away for Ma to go to Mermaid's Hands in the first place.

"Maybe—" I was going to say *Maybe you can start a whole new genealogy. The sea hummingbirds, who have scales instead of feathers, and both lungs and gills,* but Aunt Brenda interrupted me.

"You've got a real-life bloodline right here with us Parkers," she said crisply. "No made-up stories, just real people. No, no arguing; I don't want to hear it. You do look a picture, though. Maybe if we can get your mother set up with a job, you can have ballet lessons. Wouldn't that be nice?"

Tammy looked from Aunt Brenda to Ma to me, like she was trying to find the right answer. Ma gave a tiny, tight smile and looked away. Those sea hummingbirds I made up started making trouble in my stomach, and I felt a powerful longing for Dad.

"You better put on some real clothes, if we're going with Ma and Aunt Brenda," I said. "I'll follow you up."

Question I have: Do people change, depending on whether they're on dry land or in the water? Because at home, Ma's always arguing so loudly with Dad, and always has her opinions and her say, but here, she's so quiet. Is it because Aunt Brenda's her big sister? (Am I that bossy with Tammy?) Or is it because we're guests? Or is it because she agrees with what Aunt Brenda's saying?

September 10 (Em's diary)

Today on the second page of Aunt Brenda and Uncle Lew's newspaper, there were photographs from down by the coast, of hurricane damage, and one had the title "Showdown in Sandy Bay." I recognized Dad and Mrs. Ovey and Snowy and some others: they were standing on the wreck of the Winterhulls' house—just half a house, really. That's all that's left. The tide was in, so it was floating. All around, where the other houses should be, were just splintery floating piles of broken-up boards and corrugated tin and thatch, mixed together like a giant stew. In the picture you could also see a bunch of boats, swarming round like a shiver of sharks, and you could tell that the men in the boats were arguing with Dad and the others on the veranda of the Winterhulls' house.

"Locals and clean-up crews face off near Sandy Bay," the caption said, and then "Workers hired by the state to clear away dangerous debris, which presents a hazard to marine traffic, meet resistance from locals." But nothing more. Nothing about who won. Did the cleanup crews go away? Or is Mermaid's Hands gone now?

I showed Ma, but she just patted me on the shoulder and said, "Your daddy and the others can't rebuild out of those broken bits and pieces anyway. They need it cleared away so there's room to start fresh. Don't worry. So long as people are in the Winterhulls' house, nobody's gonna clear it away."

Ma doesn't care. She's already applied for three jobs here. I don't think Tammy cares much, either. After just one day at school, she's already talking about new friends. I asked her if she missed Clara, and she looked surprised and sad and said, "Yeah, I do miss her." I felt as rotten as a waterlogged plank for wrecking her good mood—except, except, except, is it right to be in a good mood when Mr. Ovey's gone below forever, and maybe our home has, too?

You know what else? I decided to try out my idea about Jiminy on Ma. I cornered her after dinner, when Aunt Brenda had gone in to work and Mandy was at a volleyball game, and asked her whether maybe it could be that Jiminy was innocent—that they just forced him to say he was guilty when really he wasn't. Her face got sad in almost the exact same way as Tammy's did, and she said, "He had the cash and jewelry on him when they arrested him." She paused a moment. "And he had a gun," she said. That part she said in a real quiet voice.

I remember when I was little and Tammy was even littler, how Jiminy would swim with us on his back and let us jump from his shoulders into the water. But that was a long time ago. When he got to high school, he started arguing with Ma and Dad a lot and doing stupid things. Like, one time he took the dinghy out fishing and left it grounded by Foul Point at low tide. How could he take it out and not come home with it? Things like that: careless. He still was always fun with me and Tammy, though. He once brought home a magnet from inside a computer and showed us how it would gather up all of Tammy's bottle caps.

I never stopped to think about where or how he got the magnet.

Then he left school and said he was going to get a job on an oil rig. That's not so strange—lots of people go away from Mermaid's Hands to work for a while—but he only came back to visit once, and was sea urchin prickly and super jumpy. Then we got a postcard from him from New Orleans, saying he was switching jobs, but he didn't say to what. And then he got arrested.

All this time, I've been imagining good-guy Jiminy, laughing Jiminy. Big-brother Jiminy. But people can change. Look how different Ma is here from the way she is in Mermaid's Hands. Maybe Jiminy ain't like Sabelle Morning or like Kaya. Maybe he's just somebody who threatens folks with a gun and steals their stuff.

Right now, I hate everything.

Chapter 8. Hurricane Heart, Fire Heart

(From the W— State Security Service's files on the insurgency: email records)

From: Lt. Den
Subject: Update
Date: September 2
To: Capt. Aran
Cc: Lt. Sana (attachment)

The attached document summarizes the writings we confiscated from Prisoner 116. Briefly, her research work is nothing more than that—investigation of the potential of some naturalized shrub to replenish the soil. However, she also began a memoir, which is useful for our purposes in three ways.

1. It reinforces our impressions about Prisoner 117's political ambitions. It's still hard to say whether these make him more of a threat or whether they offer us leverage. Promise of amnesty might induce him to turn on the others.

2. It gives us new insights into Prisoner 118. We already knew about 118's past, but from the memoir it would appear that 116 is fond of him in a special way, which is helpful to know.

3. It confirms what the people at St. Margaret's said about 116's friendship with Tema Baii, the daughter of Ty Chell (CEO, Pearl Fin Consolidated Fisheries). I'm very sure Baii can be persuaded to put pressure on 116 to go along with "Voice from the Lotus."

116 has also been corresponding with someone in America, apparently a child. At first we suspected this to be a cover for some sort of covert communications with mountain insurgents, but 116's mother has, in fact, been posting letters out of the country, and none of the others admit to any knowledge of the exchange. Furthermore, our contacts in the mountains say that the separatist movement remains parochial; most of the locals can barely speak the national language, let alone English. There's always the risk that the correspondence is an attempt to stir up international sympathies, in which case it would be good to put a stop to it. That is Sana's recommendation. I am inclined to let it continue and see if there's a way to wring some benefit out of it for our purposes.

September 2 (Kaya's journal)

Having come to rely on writing as a form of release, I find I can't stop, not even with the risks being as great as they are. If I don't put the buzz and jangle of my thoughts down on paper, they will surely drive me mad. Writing quiets my mind for a while.

Here, between the lines of text in *Trees of Insular Southeast Asia,* I can write safely, I think. I'm lucky those thugs overlooked it when they took away my other books. I doubt they will ever bother to flip through its pages, and if they do, they'll take my scratchings for marginal notes, not worth their time to translate into the bloody national language.

Still, I'll be careful. I won't write about certain things. Or people. If my heart gets too full, I'll just … I don't know. Sing my thoughts out to the Lady, maybe.

(From the W— State Security Service's files on the insurgency: email records)

From: Tema Baii

Subject: Re: Re: State Security Service visit

Date: September 3

To: Hetan Baii

Yes of course I'll write the damn letter! It's just the whole thing is so upsetting, you know? I'd been thinking of writing her anyway, to ask what in heaven's name she thinks she's doing, but there's something about a team of goons arriving at the house and *demanding* that I do it, with all kinds of threats implied, that gets my back up.

At least they didn't come to the office. I don't want to become known as the reporter with ties to the insurgency!

But I can't help thinking. It was in January that we reported on a half-dozen mountain agitators being arrested for inciting riots—that's eight months ago now. They have Kaya in that bizarre temple, but what about the others? We haven't seen or heard anything about them. What's going on? A little bit more openness on the government's part might help dispel people's anxieties.

Anyway, I'm trying to organize what I'm going to say to Kaya. I hope I can persuade her to cool things down.

Tema Baii

Correspondent, Prosperity Television

September 3 (Kaya's journal)

For three nights now, when I've gone out to stand by the guard rail and look at the stars, I've seen something, a bright pinprick of light, right at the rim of the Ruby Lake. Maybe a small fire? Not a bonfire, maybe not much more than a torch flame, but bright in the darkness. The first time it shone for almost an hour before disappearing. Yesterday it appeared in another place along the rim, and I had its company for about half an hour, maybe, before it flickered out. Tonight it was only minutes.

Is it friends? Mother said the State Security Service barricaded the path to the Ruby Lake even before they built this "lotus" for me; no one's been allowed near. But are they finding a way up? I feel so grateful for the company, but I worry about the risks the people are taking in lighting them.

September 4 (Tema to Kaya)

Dear Kaya,

It's been some time since I last wrote to you. I meant to write sooner, but I misplaced your address, and now, of course, you are no longer at home. I would say I hope you are well, but the circumstances being what they are, I can't really imagine that you are well. In fact, I feel obliged to ask: Are you crazy?

What in the world are you doing? And why? When I first heard your name among those arrested back in January, I was sure it must be some other Kayamanira, not you. But then they said you had attended St. Margaret's and had a degree from an American university, and I knew it had to be you.

I know mountain traditions and customs and all that culture stuff means a lot to you—I remember you sometimes bringing it up when we were at school. That's great. I like the traditions from my grandfather's village, too. But don't you see how these things can be twisted around—are being twisted around? It's one thing to like old dances and songs and so on, and it's another thing to use them to stir up people's resentments and dissatisfactions. Doesn't that seem like the worst sort of corruption, to corrupt a tradition? You and I both know it would be a disaster for the mountain region and for W— as a whole if the mountain districts tried to separate. You do know that, right? I think you do.

I can imagine you pining after old festivals and organizing one. You probably didn't realize or couldn't believe that it would get co-opted by agitators, but there's a history of that happening. That's why the law is the way it is.

Do you have access to newspapers or television in that temple thing you're in? Are you following the news? All those work and school boycotts in the mountains, during August? They only confirm lowland stereotypes of mountain people as undisciplined and irresponsible. They see people throwing rocks at the regional government buildings and they just say, "Well what do you expect? It's the mountain districts." And now the parliament is considering ending the scholarships for mountain schoolchildren, as a punitive measure. I think it's a terrible idea, but you can understand their logic. Why waste money on people who are just going to use the education they receive to make trouble? I hate to say it, but currently you're who they point to as an example of what can go wrong. "Invest all that in her education, and she still reverts to some kind of shamanic priestess what-have-you."

And things are getting worse. Did you hear about the tires being slashed on that mountain MP's car? And about the fire at the hotel in Palem? People are saying that mountain activists set that fire. That's just hysteria; no one in the mountains claimed responsibility for it, but that's how people in the capital are feeling! They're ready to blame every bad thing that happens on mountain separatists.

Members of the State Security Service came to see me. They said they thought you could stop all this, and they asked me to try to persuade you to. I worry they may be attributing too much power to you, but for goodness sake, if they're right, please do. I know you care about a better future for everybody in our country. You've seen what happens in the countries round about us when there's division and agitation. Lives are lost, economies stagnate, governments become more authoritarian. I know you don't want that. If W— does better, we all do better. If W— plunges into civil unrest, we'll all do much, much worse. Please, do what you can to stop the protests and the demonstrations—for everyone's sake.

I care about you, Kaya. I don't like thinking of you sitting above that lava lake, even if it's supposed to be an honor. Maybe if all this mess gets sorted out, you can go back to a more normal life.

Your friend,

Tema

September 5 (Kaya's journal)

A helicopter came today, which I wasn't expecting. It was those two officers from the State Security Service. After last time, I quailed when I saw them, especially the bully, but they didn't say one word, just handed me a long brown envelope and left again. Inside the envelope were newspaper clippings about what's been happening in the mountains. There was also a letter from Tema.

The news stories … there's so much anger in them. It's only a matter of time before someone is killed, and then what will happen? Will the government send troops into the mountains?

And Tema's letter. What hit me hardest is what she writes about the scholarships … I think of the boys Rami was helping with their multiplication tables the day I first talked to him about the festival. Will those boys be barred from scholarships, because of what we've done? It will set the mountain region back a whole generation. So few can afford secondary school, let alone university, without scholarship money.

I feel so ashamed. I've stolen from children. I've been given everything, but it wasn't enough to have my own future, I had to steal theirs as well.

But there's a little, hot, angry ember in me that says why? Why must I shoulder responsibility for the government's punishing measures? Yes, I'm responsible for the festival; I won't shrink from that, but am I to blame if the government goes to extremes?

It's heavy-handed punishments that make people rebel, not festivals.

But we can't win against the government. Rami said so, and he knows. So what can I do? What are my options? That's what I'm supposed to be thinking about.

Tema's right. I have to try to cool everyone's hot tempers—mine first. The alternative is too horrible. I'll take another look at that statement they gave me to read. Maybe I can do some creative editing. Add a few words, something to prick the hearts of the lowlanders a little and make them feel for all of us up here.

September 5 (Kaya's journal, second entry)

There were three fires on the rim of the Ruby Lake tonight. The first only shone for a moment, then it was gone. But just as it disappeared, I noticed a second, further along the rim, and then I turned round and saw a third. Then those both vanished, too.

The State Security Service must be putting them out—no doubt arresting whomever they find nearby. But people keep lighting new ones, even knowing that they'll likely be caught and punished for it.

When we were planning the fire festival, we tried so hard to play it safe. I thought we *were* safe. Would I have been so bold if I knew we'd be arrested?

These people, lighting fires for me to see … they are much braver than I am.

September 5 (Kaya's journal, third entry)

Not for me. I've had it wrong, these past days. It's for something bigger than just me. Bigger than just the festival. It's for mountain autonomy. The fires are for freedom.

September 6 (Kaya's journal)

No supplies. I suppose the authorities wanted to make good on their threat. I don't mind about the food and water; I can make what I have stretch for another week, I'm pretty sure. It's their exercise of power that burns. It's knowing that when the men from the State Security Service finally return, and I tell them yes, I'll make a statement, they'll smile and believe it's because they compelled it.

September 8 (Kaya's journal)

What a thoughtful friend Sumi is! She's brought me a ripe Malay apple. Oh that scent! One of my favorites. I cut it up and shared it with her.

September 8 (Kaya's journal, second entry)

Black ants are swarming the spots on the floor where Sumi let bits of apple fall from her beak. Where did these ants come from? Did they travel from the rim of the crater along the chains that support this floating lotus? Or did they arrive with some box of supplies the helicopter left?

They say black ants are children of the Ruby Lake, immune to fire. When you clean house, you mustn't swat them or stamp on them. You must always sweep them gently away. I won't sweep these ones away, though. It's good to have friends near, even tiny ones.

September 10 (Kaya's journal)

The winds are high, but not so high as to make the roof tiles on the house whistle, and yet the platform is trembling like a dog in a thunderstorm. And I, in this little house, am a flea on that dog!

And now rain? Surprising, a storm like this in the dry season, but good: if the wind lets up, I'll set out the water tank and refill it some.

* * *

Success! Thank you, rainstorm. Look how I'm provided for: first Sumi brings me fruit, now you bring me water. And oh rainstorm, it was good to feel your touch on my forehead, shoulders, and arms and to hear the hiss of your kiss on the face of the Ruby Lake.

The Ruby Lake seemed brighter now—washed by the rain?—And more full. But that's not possible. Rain can't swell the Ruby Lake; it's filled from below, not above.

September 11 (Kaya's journal)

Another three fires on the rim of the Ruby Lake tonight. They barely appeared before they were gone again. I thought I heard shots fired. Please let me be wrong. It makes me sick to think on it. I just want to scream *Stop, stop*—to everyone. To the separatists, *Is this act of defiance worth losing your lives for?* To the State Security Service, *Must you become murderers?*

But now I'm remembering that last fire festival before the ban, back when I was four years old. In my mind's eye, I can see Rami's smiling face, see him bobbing along on his father's shoulders amid a thicket of flaming spears. And where is his father now, and where is his mother? The State Security Service already are murderers. And must I now make myself their tool? I'd rather dip a cup in the Ruby Lake and drink it. But if I refuse, then I may as well serve the self-same drink to the very people I want to protect. They'll die just as surely.

September 12 (Kaya's journal)

I couldn't fall asleep last night for the longest time, I was so troubled and trapped by my thoughts. After tossing and turning on my sleeping mat for what seemed like more dark hours than can fit into a night, I finally jumped up in frustration and went out onto the platform. At least, I thought I was awake, but I must have been dreaming at that point, because the Lady was waiting for me there. She was not a child anymore. She seemed a bride, all dressed up in wedding finery, with her lips painted bright red and her eyes underlined in red, too.

"Let's play a game," she said to me, glancing at me obliquely from downcast eyes. "You talk to me like I'm your beloved, and I'll answer."

"I don't have a beloved," I protested.

"You don't?" Now her gaze was direct. Ramiratam filled my mind, and tears rose in my eyes.

"Rami, we've—I've—done a terrible thing," I cried. "I promised you and the Lady and everyone else a joyful celebration, and instead what I've caused is detentions and riots and now maybe deaths. And it seems that the only way to reel time back is to cooperate with the killers."

"Why would you want to reel time back?" There was challenge in the Lady's tone. Was that what Rami would ask me?

"But you said … We can't win. And there's so much to lose. I wanted to make people happy, make the Lady happy, not …" My eyes slid to the blood-red channels moving through the thin black scabs that form on top of the Ruby Lake. Fresh injuries. The Ruby

Lake never heals.

Red on black, like wounds from a switch on a child's back. Only a handful of children each year get scholarships, but everyone gets switched from time to time. Is that what I'm so afraid of mountain children losing? A tiny chance for a scholarship—and a certainty of aching shoulders?

A fountain of lava spurted up from between the scabs.

"I love uprisings," the Lady said.

"What about you, Rami?" I asked, trying to find him again in the Lady's eyes.

"What do I love?"

It was his voice, not hers. I don't know if I heard it in the air or in my heart, but my heart *felt* the words with a pang.

"No, I meant—"

"You, Kayamanira. I love you."

And then I woke up.

And what have I done now, writing it all down? I must scratch this all out, or tear out this page and drown it in the Ruby Lake. But I can't bear to, not just yet.

September 13 (Kaya to Em)

My dear Em,

Both your letters arrived; they came together today with the supply helicopter. I was very sorry to read that the hurricane stole away Mr. Ovey and destroyed your village. It's a hard thing, when our lives are tied to someone like the Seafather or the Lady of the Ruby Lake. The closer they get to us, with all their power, the more dangerous it is for us. And yet you all were there to greet the Seafather's storm when it came in, despite the danger. You have hurricane hearts! I admire that way of living.

As you can see from this letter, I am still alive and well. The State Security Service did skip one delivery of supplies, but I knew they wouldn't let me waste away—not when they want me to make a statement telling everyone in the mountains to stop their protests and accept life on lowland terms.

My opinion on that, well, I shall not write it here. It's enough to say that I am going to do as they ask. A government can be as powerful as a hurricane, and it's one thing to greet a storm, but another to fight it. Try and fight it, and it's likely to smash you into splinters. I don't want that for my neighbors and others in the mountains.

Today, when the helicopter came, the Bully and Friendlier (as I think of my two keepers from the State Security Service) were much more sober than I was expecting. I was prepared for loud demands for my decision as soon as they disembarked, but instead they seemed almost distracted.

More surprising was the pilot. Even after the blades of the helicopter stopped spinning, he stayed in the cabin, staring at me through the window, until the Bully ordered him to start unloading, and then he kept stealing glances at me as he worked. Finally, after everything was unloaded, he turned to me and asked, "Do you really speak for the volcanoes?" But the Bully snapped at him to return to the helicopter before I had a chance to ask him what he meant or give any kind of answer.

Then Friendlier asked me if I had felt the earthquake two days earlier. That was the day of a rainstorm. I had been surprised by how the platform of my prison had rocked and shaken in the wind—but it hadn't been the wind at all. "It wasn't a very powerful earthquake," Friendlier said, "but it opened up a volcanic fissure about thirty kilometers north of here, in Taneh District, that released a nasty cloud of superheated sulfur dioxide. Torched the hillside and left it littered with dead wildlife. Another two kilometers to the west, and it would have hit the town of Rai. As it was, there were only two human casualties—hikers."

Friendlier raised an eyebrow. "Eruptions are to be expected on a volcanic island, but it seems that credulous people like our good pilot, here"—he nodded at the helicopter—"just can't resist reading events as supernatural support for you troublemakers up in the mountains. Educated people know better, of course. You know better. Don't you."

A wave of dizziness came over me just then, maybe from my restricted diet these past days, or maybe because I was thinking of what the Lady's friendship might really mean. I made the mistake of telling them something the Lady said to me in a dream: "The Lady loves uprisings."

Before I could turn away, the Bully struck me with his open hand, on my face. I staggered back, and my own hand flew up to cradle my cheek, but the Bully grabbed hold of it and yanked it down.

"Oh she does, does she?" he said. "Then I guess she doesn't love people much, because the punishment that'll rain down on these mountains if there's an uprising will make people wish they'd never been born." Then he flung away my hand.

"That's not what you want, is it," said Friendlier.

I shook my head.

"So you'll help diffuse tensions by letting us record a statement from you, for television."

I nodded and said, "But I want to use my own words."

"You'll use the statement we gave you," said the Bully.

"I'll say what's in the statement. But I want to choose the words myself."

"You get too creative with your words, and your friends in prison will pay the price."

I nodded again. My mouth felt so dry, it was hard to speak. "And foreign journalists. There have to be foreign journalists present."

"Fine," said Friendlier. "We'll find a foreign journalist or two. But they'll be coming with nothing more than notepads. No recording devices, no cameras."

They left after that. They'll be back soon, though, and I'll get to speak to the world. I know they will edit out whatever I say that they don't like, but if there's a foreign journalist present, then there's a chance that what I really say will be reported, somewhere. Please look for the story, Em, because I have an idea, a plan for helping you and Mermaid's Hands. I can do next to nothing for the people who need my support here, but with a heart of ruby fire, I can perhaps make a difference for Mermaid's Hands, at least.

My thoughts are with you,

Kaya

September 13 (Kaya's journal)

Em and her people have hurricane hearts. And me? I must cultivate a heart of ruby fire from now on. The power of ruby fire is different from hurricane power. Everyone can see a hurricane coming, and so they shake with fear. The ruby fire no one can see coming until it arrives—and so they shake with fear.

"Separatist leader urges a conciliatory approach, expresses concern for minority cultures worldwide"

September 17 (Reuters) – One of the instigators of the most recent flare-up of minority separatist agitation in the island nation of W– issued a plea for restraint from her unusual temple prison suspended above "the Ruby Lake," a lava lake in the crater of Abenanyi, a volcano in the country's mountainous central region.

In an apparent effort to cool down inflammatory rhetoric and rapidly escalating demonstrations, Kayamanira Matarayi, a botanist with a degree from Cornell University's Department of Crop and Soil Sciences, said that the mountain minority region could no more separate itself from the lowland-based national government than the mountains could separate themselves from the coast. She followed that statement, however, with a plea for greater autonomy for the mountain region, including recognition of the minority language as an official language in minority-dominated areas and a lifting of the ban on the practice of the traditional mountain religion. In the postcolonial era, the populous coastal plains of W— have largely secularized, but folk beliefs persist strongly among the mountain minorities.

Matarayi called on governments everywhere to preserve the rights of minority cultures in their midst, highlighting the case of a tiny community in the Gulf Coastal region of the United States displaced by Hurricane Helga. "The people of Mermaid's Hands have lived for generations not by the sea but in it. Now the state wants to forbid them to rebuild their homes. This is how cultures are lost."

A highly edited version of Matarayi's remarks, containing only the call for restraint, aired on W—'s television networks this evening. The Cambridge (MA)-based organization Minorities Mobilize expressed interest in taking up the cause of the community of Mermaid's Hands and also in following developments in W—. "W— has sacrificed minority rights on the altar of national progress," said a spokesperson for the nonprofit. "It's something we see all the time, unfortunately."

A spokesperson for Human Rights Watch Asia expressed concern over the condition of Matarayi's detainment. "Imprisonment over an active volcano amounts to a constant threat of death; it's psychological torture." The government of W— has insisted that house arrest in the "Lotus on the Ruby Lake" is a mark of respect for Matarayi, based on her special relationship with the Lady of the Ruby Lake, a deity who is the focus of veneration among Matarayi's people.

Chapter 9. Phone Calls

September 11 (Em's diary)

Up here in Mandy's room, I can barely hear Ma and Aunt Brenda talking. It's not like at home, where each and every thing Ma and Dad say when they're arguing flows right into our ears, whether we like it or not. I know they're talking about Jiminy, though, because of him calling here. I was the one who answered the phone. It was close to suppertime, but only me and Tammy were in the house, because Mandy had ballet and Ma and Aunt Brenda were at the supermarket. Me and Tammy were mixing up some chocolate milk, making little whirlpools in the glasses as the syrup turned the milk from white to brown, when the call came.

Aunt Brenda's house phone ringing is like a baby starting up crying. Just like with a baby, you can hope maybe somebody else will pick it up, or maybe it'll just stop crying on its own, but its wailing gets to you. Picking up a phone is more scary than picking up a baby, though, because a baby's always just a baby, but with a phone, you never know what voice you'll hear on the other end. I've only answered Aunt Brenda's house phone twice before. Once it was Uncle Lew, calling from the road. He has a gruff, deep voice. The other time it was a lady from the school office who wanted to know why we didn't fill out the free lunch form. She had a too-sweet voice. Talking to her made me feel sticky.

This time, it was a voice like a television announcer that started up before I could even say hello, and it talked without hearing me—a recording. And in the middle of the recording came Jiminy's voice, just the tiniest sliver of it, just saying his name, and then it was back to the recording. It went like this:

"Hello. This is a collect call from *Jiminy* and Clear Springs State Prison. To accept this call press 3. To decline press 9 or hang up."

I pressed 3.

"Jiminy … are you there?" My heart was pounding harder than when I got sent to the principal's, harder than when the Coca-Cola man was yelling at us.

"Em? Is that you?" His faraway voice took on light and color. "So y'all really are staying at Aunt Brenda's. I saw on the news about the hurricane, and I though you might. Wasn't looking forward to getting Aunt Brenda or Uncle Lew on the phone though … I'm glad you're the one that picked up."

"Jiminy …" I didn't know which thing to start with. *Jiminy, Mermaid's Hands is all gone and might not come back. Jiminy, Tammy's taking to this town like a fish to water—no, like a hummingbird to flowers—and Ma's looking for work here, but I don't want this to be our new home.* But I pushed those ones down, because I remembered about his clavicle, scapula, and ribs. He'd still be wrapped in bandages and wincing each time he took a deep breath. "How are you healing up?" I asked, but he spoke at the same time:

"They told me somebody called from outside and said you tried to come see me. By yourself. On the day the hurricane hit. Is that true?"

"Yeah it is, but—"

"Ha! Sweet. Dad and Ma must've been freaking out. Nice to know I'm not the only one in the family with some spirit," he said.

"Yeah, but I had to turn around." At least six flavors of regret on my tongue as I said that.

"S'okay. You've got more brains than me about making choices," he said—and why did that make me feel bad? "You're still friends with Jenya's little brother, right? Small Bill? He's a good kid. You gotta pick your friends carefully." There was an edge to those words, and I wanted to ask him what he meant, but just then Ma and Aunt Brenda walked in the front door, loaded down with plastic shopping bags full of groceries.

"Who's that on the phone?" Aunt Brenda asked.

"It's Jiminy," I said.

"Calling here?" Aunt Brenda frowned. Ma's lips twitched. She let the grocery bags slide off her arms and hurried to my side.

"Let me talk to him," she said.

"Em, you still there?" Jiminy was asking, anxious.

"It's Ma," I said, handing the phone to her.

"Those calls cost a fortune, Josie," Aunt Brenda said. "I really don't think Lew's gonna be happy having him—"

Ma wasn't listening, though. She even had a finger pressed in her free ear to muffle Aunt Brenda. She slid open the glass door into Aunt Brenda's backyard, stepped out, and slid it shut behind her.

She came in a couple minutes later.

"Is he still there?" I asked, reaching for the phone, but Ma shook her head and put it back in its cradle. Aunt Brenda had her arms crossed and was giving Ma a look.

"I'll pay for the call," Ma said.

Aunt Brenda raised an eyebrow.

"I'll pick up hours at Taunton's until something better comes along. I don't mind farm work." Ma lifted her chin just so. She reminded me of me.

"Can I make some more chocolate milk?" Tammy asked, in a small voice.

"Not now," said Ma. "Em, take your sister upstairs."

So here we are, upstairs. And now Ma and Aunt Brenda have moved into the living room, and I can hear some of what they're saying:

"... our house and our rules, Jo. Repentance first, then forgiveness. He's gotta show that he's making an effort to mend his ways—they have programs, you know, in some of the prisons—maybe if he gets involved in one of those. But didn't you say it was brawling sent him to the infirmary? That doesn't sound like a change of heart. It's not something I want Mandy exposed to, and honestly, you should consider the effect on Em and Tammy. I ain't saying it'll always be so, but right now he's a bad influence."

"Listen to yourself, Bren. Makes me recall why I left home."

"Mmmhmm, and how did that work out for you?"

Ma's not answering, and Tammy, sitting next to me on the bed and listening in too, is all big eyes and hunched shoulders. Maybe it's time for me to take her for a little walk. I'll write more later.

September 13 (Em's diary)

Aunt Brenda laid down the law yesterday at suppertime. "Mandy," she said, "If ever you answer the phone and it's a collect call, you give it to me or your father or Aunt Josie, understand? Don't you accept any collect calls on your own. And if there's no grown-up around, just hang up. Em and Tammy, that goes for you too."

"'K, will do," said Mandy, reaching for the lemonade. "Want a top-up?" she asked me, after filling her own glass. I don't think Aunt Brenda's new phone rule made even the tiniest splash in Mandy's thoughts.

"Em? Tammy? Do you understand the rule?"

"No thanks," I said. I was answering Mandy, but I half meant my reply for Aunt Brenda too, and I think she knew it, because her eyes widened and her mouth squinched up. I waited the barest half-grain of a second more before saying "Yes, I do, Aunt Brenda." Tammy chimed in with a solemn me-too, nodding.

Ma had talked to me alone earlier in the day, so I knew it was coming.

"I know you heard me arguing with Aunt Brenda yesterday," she had said. "But I expect you to abide by any rules she makes regarding Jiminy and the telephone, you hear?"

"But she don't want to let him call here at all!"

"No buts. She has her reasons."

"Her reasons stink! She's just stingy and, and prissy! And mean!"

"Mind your tongue!" Ma had flashed back. "Don't you dare speak about her that way! Last I checked none of your cousins were behind bars. She must be doing something right." That last part Ma had said more to herself than me, still with heat in her voice, but as if it was her own self the flames were for.

"She tried to be both mother and sister for me, after your grandmother—your other grandmother, my mother—died. That can't have been easy. And she even stood up for me to your grandfather when I announced I was getting married, even though she didn't think much of the idea herself. All the evil things coming out of your grandfather's mouth that day, the old racist—she wouldn't tolerate them. So anyway. We're both going to respect her rules."

We're both, Ma had said, like maybe it's hard for her, too.

"But what about Jiminy?"

"I was thinking, when I've earned a little money, maybe I can get us a cell phone. Then he can call that number."

So that's why I said yes to Aunt Brenda without any fuss or argument, yesterday. And now I've already broken the rule.

It was just like last time, no one here but me and Tammy, and the phone call came in, and I couldn't press 9, I just couldn't. Jiminy asked for Ma. He sounded jumpy.

"She's not around, and Jiminy, me and Tammy aren't allowed to take your calls no more, Aunt Brenda said. Only her and Uncle Lew and Ma."

Jiminy called Aunt Brenda a rhymes-with-witch, which is language Ma never likes to hear.

"Ma said she'd get a cell phone though, maybe, soon, and then you can call that," I told him. But it felt weak.

"Yeah, okay. Jesus. I dunno. I guess I was just hoping … It's terrible here, Em. They won't leave me alone."

A big cold wave of dread crashed over me. “Who won’t? Is it more fights? But you’re still not better from the last one.”

“Tell me about it!” he said, with a short almost-laugh.

“Is it because you’re a seachild?” I asked, and then he laughed for real.

“Aww, Em, nobody cares about that, except as how coming from Mermaid’s Hands makes me one dumbshi … uh, one dumbass,” he corrected, as if he could see me squirming at the words he was using. “Too stupid not to beat up, I guess.” He paused. “Looks like some of my friends—the guys I thought were my friends—they think it’s my fault they’re in here.”

“But it’s not, right? You didn’t rat them out, did you?” It was bad enough that Jiminy had to be a thief, but so was Sabelle Morning a thief, if you look at things the way Ma and Aunt Brenda do. But Sabelle Morning was never a rat.

“I didn’t mean to! I was trying *not* to—I took the fall for them! ‘Here, you take the gun. You never been arrested; if they catch you, they’ll go easy on you,’ they said, and ran, and it was just me that got caught. I was terrified. None of them came to see me at the police station or before sentencing … I guess they had to lay low, but it felt real cold.

“But I didn’t turn on them! Even when the police said that the lady picked me out of the line—which I still don’t understand, because I don’t look nothing like Ace—and they were charging me with armed robbery, I just said, okay, yes, it was me. But maybe they had their doubts, cause they kept pressing me with questions. ‘You’re loyal; you’re a good friend, aren’t you,’ they said. ‘You’d never give up Ace or Sandman or Dusty or Weathervane, would you?' And I was like, 'Weathervane, what's he got to do with anything?' and then they go, 'Oh, so Weathervane wasn't involved? But the others, they were all there, weren't they.' That's how they do it. Talking to them is like wandering into soft mud. Every word you say just gets you deeper and deeper in the muck. Next thing I know, the word going round is that it's because of me that Ace and Sandman were arrested."

My thoughts were dragonflying this way and that. Jiminy maybe picked some bad friends, but he tried to protect them. He was loyal. My eyes felt tear-stingy.

"Wish you could of fallen in with someone like Sabelle Morning," I said. "She'd of come in with guns blazing to rescue you."

"Huh, Sabelle Morning." He made another not-laugh sound. "You still listening to those stories? Still treasure hunting? Yeah, Ace and them ain't nothing like Sabelle Morning. Ace's cousin told me when Ace gets ahold of me, he's gonna break my neck. Ace was like a brother before, and now he wants to kill me."

"I'm a sister for you," I said, "a real one, not just a like-a-sister." I wanted to tell him about Sabelle Morning's cup and speaking his name to the sea, but it isn't much to offer, not in the shadow of guys who want to break your neck.

"I know you are, Em. I'm counting on that. I want you to see if you can get Ma to—"

I heard a car pull up in the driveway. "I gotta go. Someone's come home."

"K." There was a click, and then the hum that the phone makes when no one's calling.

Outside, a car door shut, and then the engine started up again. Out the front window, I could see somebody driving away and Ma walking up the driveway, looking tired. I opened the door for her just as she was reaching for the handle.

"Em. What's wrong?" Her eyes narrowed. "Did you or Tammy break something?"

"No! It's…"

Tammy appeared.

"Ma!" She gave Ma a hug, and the hard lines of Ma's eyes and mouth softened a little.

"Maybe mix Ma a chocolate milk," I suggested. Tammy nodded and ran to the kitchen.

"Go on then," Ma prompted, sitting down on the couch with a sigh. "What's got you so fidgety?"

"It's Jiminy." I took a breath, then said, as fast as I could, "He called again, and I know I ain't supposed to accept a call, and I won't again, but he said—" and then I told her the rest of it. She looked set to interrupt me when I said the part about taking the call, but by the end she was just listening, and even after I finished, she didn't speak. I waited. She put green-stained hands over her face and said, voice muffled, "How did that boy get himself into so much trouble?"

"Will you get a cell phone soon?"

Ma ran her fingers along her eyebrows. Tammy brought in a tall glass of chocolate milk.

"I made it real dark," she said.

"Thanks, love." Ma took a sip. "It's delicious."

"Ma, will you?" I pressed.

"Yeah. Yeah, soon." She didn't meet my eye but her voice

sounded firm.

"I'm sorry about accepting the call," I said. "I told Jiminy I couldn't do it again." Ma reached up and gave my hand a squeeze.

"Don't you worry. Sometimes you have to break rules. I'll explain to Aunt Brenda."

"Ma?" Another thought had occurred to me.

"Yes?"

"Will you try to get word to Dad? About Jiminy?"

Back went her hands over her face.

"Yes, I suppose," she said at last.

"And Ma?"

She looked up at me, eyebrows raised. *What more?* they asked. I wanted to tell her about Jiminy being a loyal friend, just to the wrong people, but Ma looked so worn out, I decided to save it for another time.

September 15 (Small Bill to Em)

Em I know you are not gone for good you will be coming back one day but I wish it was sooner. I wonder did you happen to save Sa Bell Morning's cup when Helga came. Most likely not but if you did you should set it out to catch the morning light because even on dry land that charm will work. Ma didn't say so but ~~its true~~. I ~~know~~ think it's true. I been saying your name and Tammy's to the tide. I even been saying your mother's because maybe she might want to come back too.

Your friend Small Bill

September 16 (Em's diary)

As everyone was trickling in for homeroom this morning, the teacher called me over. Ms. Hughes, her name is. "You're from Sandy Neck, aren't you?" she asked. "What do your parents think of this whole Mermaid's Hands thing? Have they been following it on the news?" She folded a newspaper over and pointed to a headline, "Local Reaction to Mermaid's Hands Decision."

"I'm from Mermaid's Hands, not Sandy Neck," I said. A couple of the other kids looked up when I said that. "You mean, how do they feel about rebuilding? They want us to be able to rebuild," I said. *That headline said Decision,* I was thinking. *Have they made a decision?* More kids were listening in now. I could feel prickles of sweat forming on my hairline and under my arms.

"You're actually from Mermaid's Hands itself? The place in the water?" Ms Hughes asked, disbelieving.

"Yeah. What was the decision?" I scanned the words underneath the headline—*ordered … vacate … demolish … protest*—I jerked my head back. I felt dizzy. The sweat was running down my side now. My mouth felt tacky, and I struggled to swallow.

"I'm sorry … I didn't imagine … I'm sorry to bring it up," Ms. Hughes said, her pale pink skin going red in the cheeks.

I forced my eyes back to the paper, where they landed on "seeking a stay on the demolition of the one remaining structure pending an appeal to the courts."

"Is it true y'all don't have birth certificates?" one of the kids said. I realized most of the classroom had gathered in a half-circle around me and Ms. Hughes.

"Sam, maybe now's not the time," Ms. Hughes said, pulling open a desk drawer, jamming the newspaper in, then letting the drawer slide closed.

"Yeah, I heard that too," said another kid. "It's like half of them don't even exist, as far as the government's concerned. "There's only like fifty of you anyway, right?" he said, staring at me with new curiosity.

"Sixty-six," I said. Sixty-five, if you don't count Jiminy, but I'm always gonna count Jiminy. But then there's Mr. Ovey, and Granny Fearing, and Indigo gone now. "I mean, sixty-three," I said.

The kid dropped his eyes. "Sorry," he muttered.

I was pondering what the first kid meant by birth certificates. What is a birth certificate? A prize you get for being born? Maybe they give you one if you're born on dry land. I should ask Ma.

"Y'all should move somewhere safer now," one of the girls said, but another said, "I'd like to live on the water. Like a houseboat." Then another kid said he'd once taken a Cajun riverboat tour in Louisiana where they guaranteed you'd get to see alligators. Then Ms. Hughes told everyone to settle down and go back to their seats.

"I had no idea you're actually from Mermaid's Hands," she said to me as I started for my desk. It looked like maybe she was going to say sorry yet again, but she didn't.

I couldn't concentrate for the rest of the day, just kept going over impossible things in my head. Does Ma know? Have she and Dad talked? Ma was going to talk to Dad about Jiminy. Did he tell her about this? What's going to happen now?

Are we stuck on dry land forever? Can we go somewhere else, on the water? I remembered my message in the bottle. *Sometimes I wish I could unrope our house and see where it might float to.* But my wish didn't make this happen. It couldn't. Right?

Ma didn't get home until after the rest of us had eaten. Me and Mandy were doing homework on the living room floor, with *American Idol* on in the background. Aunt Brenda was watching too. She says she don't care much for the show, but Mandy says she always watches. Tammy was upstairs getting ready for bed. I waited until Ma came in to join us to ask her if she'd heard the news from home.

"What news?" she said, settling down with a sigh at the other end of the couch from Aunt Brenda.

So she didn't know. I told her about the decision.

"Is that so," Ma said, lackluster and tired. "That's like the government, ain't it. People live in a place for forever, and then suddenly they get told they can't. Well, they'll work out something, I suppose." She let her eyes close.

"Not *they, we*! *We* have to work something out. Have you talked to Dad yet?"

"Let your mother rest, Em. She's had a long day," Aunt Brenda said. "Y'all can stay here as long as you need."

"But it's not *home,*" I muttered, looking down. The carpet under my knees was the same color as the sand on the shore at Sandy Neck. From the corner of my eye, I saw Mandy raise her head up from her calculator.

"Are you talking about going home?" Tammy asked, coming downstairs in the long t-shirt she wore for sleeping. She still had a smudge of toothpaste in the corner of her mouth, but she wiped it with her hand.

“We can’t go home,” I said. “They won’t let us rebuild our houses. They’re saying even the Winterhulls’ house has to come down, that made it through the storm.”

Mom’s eyes flew open and she sat up straight.

“Em for goodness sake hold your tongue! What good does it do to upset your sister?” Tammy did have a strangled, wide-eyed expression, like she sometimes gets when she has an attack of coughing. But she didn’t cough.

“Where will we live, then?” she whispered.

“Stay here with us and be my ballet mascot,” said Mandy, reaching out to poke Tammy’s ankle, and she managed to tickle a grin onto Tammy’s face, but it faded fast.

“I liked visiting your ballet class today. I like being here. But seachildren can’t stay forever on dry land.” Tammy was speaking to Mandy, but her eyes were locked on mine, and I could feel her asking me *What’ll we do? Where’ll we go?*

“That’s foolishness,” said Aunt Brenda. “You’re a little girl with delicate lungs, not a fish. You’ll be much better off in a regular house and visiting the beach from time to time, like the rest of us do.”

And meanwhile I’m thinking about that kid in school who said that the government thinks half of us don’t even exist, and I’m remembering about Vaillant pledging allegiance to the sea, and I’m wondering if that’s what we ought to be doing, and if the Seafather would give us gills and take us home below. Only somehow it makes me frightened to think about that, because once you go below, you can never come up above again.

“Can we at least go home before they tear down the Winterhulls’ house?" I asked.

"Em!" Ma held out I-have-nothing-to-give-you hands. "How am I supposed get you anywhere, without a car? Hmm? We'll wait for your father to be in touch. If he can use Mr. Tiptoe's truck, I'm sure he'll come and get you."

"If he can't, then we'll walk!" I said.

"Am I hearing your oldest's attitude in this one?" Aunt Brenda asked Ma, waving an arm at me, Exhibit A. "What did I tell you: bad influence." To me she said, "You behave yourself. You think your mother needs anything more to worry about? You go along up to bed with your sister."

I was writing this in bed, by the nightlight, thinking Tammy was already asleep, but then her voice came floating over.

"Em?"

"Yeah?

"You think Dad will come and get us?"

I wanted to say, *No matter. We really will walk home, if he can't.* But then I thought about Aunt Brenda giving Ma a hard time about me, and Ma being so tired from working at that farm, and I just wasn't sure anymore. And what if we walked and walked and were too late? So all I said was, "Yeah, I think he will," even though I ain't one bit sure. There's only one truck for everybody in Mermaid's Hands. Maybe they have other things they need to use it for.

Instead of a truck, I wish it was a sailing scow, like Sabelle Morning had, with an armed crew on board, that could run aground right by the Winterhulls' house and protect it. Then I wouldn't even mind if they couldn't come and get us.

September 17 (Em to Small Bill)

Dear Small Bill,

Thanks for your letter. ~~*I don't have Sabelle Morning's cup. It's lost with everything else. Not that it did much good really.*~~ *I don't have Sabelle Morning's cup. Anyway Aunt Brenda would never let me do nothing like set out a cup to catch the dawn light because she thinks that stuff is devilish.*

I want to come home but I just heard yesterday that Mermaid's Hands can't rebuild. What does your ma say? What's Mr. Tiptoe say? ~~*Do you listen for your dad beneath the waves? What does he say? You must miss him something fierce.*~~

Maybe we should just take to the water like Sabelle Morning.

I'm thinking of you. I hope you're doing all right, and your ma and Lindie and Jenya. Wish I was sitting near you in the Winterhulls' house.

Your friend,

Em

September 18 (Em's diary)

Ma's side of the conversation, on the phone just now:

"Hello? Oh. Trace. It's good you called. The girls were—Yes, Em told me, which is why—What? Come again?"

When she said Dad's name, I stopped labeling countries on the empty map of Europe we got for homework in social studies and Tammy stopped putting her spelling words in the blanks in the raccoon story on her worksheet. In the kitchen, the sound of dishes sliding into place, one on top of the next in the cupboards, stopped, which means Aunt Brenda was listening in, too.

It figures that just when we all start listening, it goes quiet on Ma's side. Dad must have lots to say. I wish my hearing was good enough to pull his voice out of the phone and into my ears. Then Ma spoke again:

"Well don't that beat everything. That's … that's hard to believe, is what it is. But good! Good. We'll watch on Friday. Yeah, I'll tell them that, too." Then she laughed. It's been so long since I heard Ma laugh! "Yeah, I suppose," she said, her voice still full of sunshine. I couldn't hear what she said next, and when I was able to catch her words again, all the brightness had already drained away. "I don't know about that," she said. "It's not that simple. Look, we'll talk more when you come. All right. Uh huh, you too. Bye now."

When we heard the click of the phone going back into its cradle, me and Tammy raced downstairs. Aunt Brenda came in from the kitchen, and we all pounced on Ma.

"What did Dad say? What's hard to believe? What's happening Friday?" I asked.

"Is Daddy coming here?" Tammy asked. "Is he gonna take us home?"

Aunt Brenda just looked at Ma with raised eyebrows: a question face.

"He says they got permission to rebuild Mermaid's Hands after all. Said a group of people from some culture organization or some such came by, and then after that a news crew, all before Brett even got word from the authorities. The folks from the culture organization intend on staying a while and asking questions about life in Mermaid's Hands. Following folks around with movie cameras. Can you imagine that?"

She'd started out talking to Aunt Brenda, but she turned to us at the end, a smile creeping back onto her face.

"Can you imagine?" she repeated, hiding her smile with her hand, "Someone following you around all day, filming you?"

Mandy and Uncle Lew got back just then.

"What's that? Who's following who around?" Uncle Lew asked, frowning.

"Are you talking about reality TV?" Mandy asked.

So Ma explained again, and Uncle Lew just snorted and went into the kitchen. I heard the fridge door open.

"You're gonna let him take the girls back with him during the rebuilding?" Aunt Brenda asked. "Where y'all going to sleep? In that one half-broken-down house? Don't you think it would be better to wait a little longer? What'll the girls do for school? Is the one in Sandy Neck back up and running? And what about your job?"

"I'm barely making anything at Taunton's. Anyway, the decision's not just up to me," Ma said, meeting nobody's eye, not

Aunt Brenda's, not mine or Tammy's.

"Sure it is. You're the grown-up. You're the *responsible* grown-up. You really want to go back to all that now?"

"Leave it be, Bren," Uncle Lew called from the kitchen. "Some people don't learn from mistakes."

I felt my fists clenching for Ma's sake—and for Dad's—but took a breath and let my hands fall open.

"Is Daddy coming here?" Tammy asked again, standing between Ma and Aunt Brenda and taking Ma by the hands. "Is he coming Friday?"

"No, he's not sure just yet when he'll come, but Friday there's going to be a special segment on the news about Mermaid's Hands. Maybe we can watch it." Ma looked sidelong at Aunt Brenda.

"I want to see," said Mandy. "I always wondered about where y'all lived, houseboats and such. We should visit!" That last suggestion was made to Aunt Brenda, who pursed her lips.

"Some of us need to work at proper jobs to pay for the roof over our heads and clothes and doctors and whatnot," she said, "and can't be taking trips and vacations whenever we please."

"Yeah, but we do take vacations sometimes, and Aunt Josie and Em and Tammy are family. We visit Uncle Mike and Aunt Bonny and Cal and Megan. How come we never—"

"Enough, Mandy."

Then Mandy invited me and Tammy to watch her practice ballet, and now Mandy's brushing Tammy's hair.

And I'm writing this and thinking, we're gonna get to go home. Mermaid's Hands won't just disappear. Is it somehow the Seafather's doing?

September 20 (Em's diary)

It was weird to see everybody on TV. I guess they're all back there, except for Granny Ikaho, who had to go to the hospital, and Silent Soriya and Skinnylegs' little sister Anna, who stayed on with a Jordan's Waters family because of Anna getting her leg broken in the storm.

The Winterhulls' half-of-a-house is one big bedroom for everyone, but there are no mattresses or quilts in there. Instead it's filled up with sleeping bags, pressed together like fish spawn so everyone fits. Where'd the sleeping bags come from? The Jordan's Waters people or some other group must of donated them.

They showed a bunch of the parents outside, rebuilding the part of the support raft that broke off, and the reporter asked them how they knew how to build the houses, and you could see that it must of felt strange to have the cameras there, and the reporter, because Mr. Winterhull wrinkled his brow like he was thinking hard, and Mrs. Ovey had an overcast face, and Auntie Chicoree and Uncle Near wouldn't even look at the camera—they kept their eyes on what they were nailing.

"We just know," said Mr. Tiptoe with a shrug. "Storms come most every year. Houses take damage most every year. You learn a bit at a time, one year to the next."

"And the building materials? Does it cost a lot to rebuild?" You couldn't see who asked the question. It must of been somebody behind a camera.

Snowy spoke up to answer that one.

"We always used to salvage the broken-up bits the storm left.

Don't quite see why the state had to clear away the wreckage this time. We would've used that stuff. It would've been cleaned up, just slowly. Folks on dry land sure are impatient.

"So what are you doing now? Buying supplies?"

Snowy pursed his lips. "Some buying," he said. "And some salvaging, farther out and around." Mr. Tiptoe shot Snowy a warning look, but Snowy didn't say more than that.

"And the donations? Are they a help?"

Snowy gave a single nod. "They surely are a help," he said, keeping dignity in his voice and looking slantaway from the camera.

Then the cameras moved over to kids, first Fairchance Fearing and Pearlheart Dunne, who showed some nets, dip nets and throwing nets. The reporter got all excited about the shell weights on the throwing nets, because, he said, Indians long ago used shells for weights in just the same way. He didn't say anything about the pattern, though: two oyster shells, then a wedge clam, then two more oyster shells, then another clam: white, white, brown, white, white, brown—like that. Fairchance and the other older kids always do that pattern. Me and Small Bill and our crowd like doing two-two better: oyster, oyster, clam, clam: white, white, brown, brown. I wished I could jump into the TV and tell the reporter that—I felt so wriggly, stuck here just watching.

Then, "Hey, it's Clara," Tammy said, scooting closer to the TV. Clara was wading thigh deep, pulling along the Tiptoes' dinghy, which had Brightly and the twins in it. Skinnylegs was there too, in the Winterhulls' dinghy, over by where the garden floats used to be. Skinnylegs was squinting, even with one hand shading his eyes, and the camera came in close, so you could see the hairs on his arm, paler than his skin, as he pointed to a floating, broken chunk of raft still bristling with green, and to a new raft, under construction.

"They were my stepmother's idea," he said.

That must be why they got Skinnylegs to tell about them. I can just about remember before Silent Soriya came, when we almost never had dry-land vegetables, just things that grow swaying beneath the waves, like rainbow frill, or that watch over the tides, like pickleweed. But Silent Soriya showed us how they grew things on rafts in the floating village she came from, halfway round the world, and everyone liked the idea.

"There they go," said Tammy, as the twins and Brightly tumbled out of the dinghy and into the water, starting up a game of stingray-lie-down. Clara slipped under too and came up in the upper right-hand corner of the TV screen. "You can stay under a long time!" exclaimed the bodiless voice behind the camera. Clara pushed her hair out of her eyes and grinned, and Tammy and I exchanged looks, because even Tammy can stay under longer than Clara, and Tammy's famous for her weak lungs.

Then the camera was back at the Winterhulls' house, and they'd gotten a whole crowd outside, and it was later in the day—or maybe they filmed it on a different day—because the tide was in, and Mr. Winterhull and some others were sitting in fishing skiffs and wearing sun capes, and the littler kids were splashing and hollering in the background, and the reporter was saying stuff about way of life and so on, and I caught sight of Small Bill, over on the left, leaning against Mrs. Ovey and looking straight at the camera—at me. I missed him so bad at that moment. I hope Dad comes for us soon.

September 24 (Em to Kaya)

Dear Kaya,

You saved Mermaid's Hands! I knew it had to be some kind of miracle, but I thought it was the Seafather—but really it was you!

I didn't find out for sure until after we got home. It was like this: Dad came for us on Monday, late, after Ma got back from Taunton's. Uncle Lew and Aunt Brenda could barely manage a hello between them, but Ma smiled and let him hug her and even put her arms around his neck. I couldn't believe it—it's been forever since they got all kissyface in public. But when Dad said, "Ready to go?" Ma's smile faded. "Walk with me a little," she said, pulling him back over the threshold and into the cloud of moths and mosquitoes by the porch light.

"Get your stuff together, girls," we heard Dad say, even though Uncle Lew shut the door on his words, muttering about not paying to cool the whole neighborhood. Tammy and I crept upstairs to grab our clothes. Mandy was sitting on her bed.

"So I guess you're going," she said. I nodded. Tammy jumped onto the bed and wrapped Mandy in a hug from behind.

"We'll miss you, though," she said.

"Mom wanted me to make sure y'all know you can stay if you want," Mandy said, craning her neck round so she was nose to nose with Tammy. Tammy dropped her eyes.

"But I know you want to get home," Mandy added quickly. "Anyway, we'll hang out when you come to visit Aunt Josie."

Tammy shot me an anxious look. "Ma's not coming back with us?"

"First I heard about it," I said. One part of me was thinking, I should've guessed, *but another part was thinking,* How can she want to stay with Aunt Brenda and that crummy job?

"Aunt Josie hasn't told you? That's messed up. I thought- Mom said- You know, maybe I got it wrong ... I'm sorry. Just forget what I said." Mandy went on like that a little, trying to bury what she first said in a whole pile of apologies.

"It's okay," Tammy said, twirling a strand of Mandy's hair around her index finger. She let it go, but it fell back straight as ever. Tammy climbed off Mandy's bed and slipped herself into my lap.

"You think Ma's really not coming home?" she asked me.

Downstairs the front door opened again, and I could hear Ma and Dad's voices.

"Let's ask her," I said.

It sure was frosty downstairs. Ma and Dad were standing near but apart from each other, like there was a pillow of air between them that they couldn't push through. Aunt Brenda was standing next to Uncle Lew, arms crossed, and Uncle Lew had his hands on his hips. Both were shooting death-ray looks at Dad.

"That's right, I'm staying here for now," Ma said, when Tammy asked. Out of everybody, it was me Ma fixed her eyes on.

"Em, you wanted Jiminy to have a number he could call, right? To help him? But to get a cell phone takes money, and money takes a job. I'm not earning if I'm back at Mermaid's Hands."

"That's not why you're staying away," Dad said, his voice light and calm, but you could feel the anger singeing the edges of it.

"If that's the excuse she has to use to be free of you—" began Aunt Brenda.

"It's not an excuse!" flared Ma. "You're as bad as Trace. I know my mind. Don't go looking for different reasons!"

"I told you, I can arrange with Brett—" Dad began, but Ma shook her head.

"No. I ain't asking nothing from any of them for Jiminy. Or from you either, Bren. I have an interview in town the day after tomorrow. Once I get a better job and start earning a little better money, I can move out and find a place of my own."

"Ain't you coming home ever?" Tammy asked, in a thin voice.

"Tammy should stay here with you; better for her health," murmured Aunt Brenda, but neither Tammy nor Ma seemed to hear her. Tammy was waiting on Ma's answer.

Nobody can get to Ma like Tammy. Tammy's her baby, the delicate one. I guess it must of been hard for Ma to summon up an answer, because she was quiet a moment, pressing her lips together so hard all the color disappeared from them. Then she breathed in deep, lifted her eyebrows, and said,

"You don't need to worry about that. You concentrate on school and helping Dad and Gran and the others, and we'll see each other before you even miss me." She smiled a tight Aunt-Brenda's-house smile. Tammy didn't smile back, but she didn't press Ma further, and she didn't cry. She just gave Ma a silent hug, then walked over to Dad.

Me, I don't think I've ever felt so complicated. I still feel complicated about it. I want to be angry at Ma for not coming home, but how can I be, when she's working to help Jiminy? And I don't want to be angry at Dad, because it's not like Ma staying with Aunt Brenda is his fault, or like Jiminy being in prison is his fault, but ...

Dad can pull all sizes of fish out of the water and into the skiff when he goes out with Uncle Near, so why can't he pull Ma and Jiminy back home?

"How'd that boy end up to be so much trouble?" Dad said, to himself really, as we bounced along in the Mermaid's Hands truck, heading back to Sandy Neck. Ma asked almost the exact same thing, but the way Dad said it was more blameful.

"He was a loyal friend," I said, hoping maybe to get Dad to see at least a smidge of good in Jiminy.

Dad glanced my way, and the truck swerved a little.

"Where was that loyalty earlier?—What about his family and his line? What about Vaillant's pledge to the sea?"

What could I say?

"He's as sour on Mermaid's Hands as your mother," Dad said. All the fire was gone from his voice. He sounded worn out and sad.

I remembered Jiminy saying that being from Mermaid's Hands just made people think he was dumb. Or was it that he thought he was dumb, being from Mermaid's Hands? I can't tell. Both thoughts made me gloomy—Dad's sadness was soaking into me.

"I love Mermaid's Hands," I announced.

"Me too," said Tammy. She'd been leaning on my shoulder, and I thought she'd fallen asleep, but she sat up to say that.

Dad smiled. "Course you do!" And then, "And thanks to those dry-landers from the culture organization, there'll keep on being a Mermaid's Hands to love." He shook his head and laughed. "Too bad I couldn't fetch you home earlier, when they were following everyone around with cameras and questions. There wasn't a thing they didn't want to poke their noses into—you could've told them about knowing when the Seafather's going to send seagifts, Em. They would've loved that." He hesitated a little. "It got wearing, having them hovering around like hungry gulls all the time, but we all agreed it's a small price to pay for what they done for us."

"Why'd they do it?" I asked. "I didn't think anybody outside of Sandy Neck even knew about Mermaid's Hands. Not till Helga, anyway."

Dad shrugged. "Not sure."

By now we were in Sandy Neck, coming up to the town parking lot. The huge limb of the live oak tree that came down by the entrance was still lying there, across half a dozen parking spaces, but you could see that someone had started chainsawing it into chunks.

"They kept talking about way of life and preserving endangered cultures," Dad said. "Endangered. Like we're manatees or something. You feel endangered, Tams?"

Tammy shook her head.

"That's my girl."

"But do you think they just noticed us from the news?" I asked.

"I suppose—no wait, it wasn't just the news. It was a speech. The lady who talked to Brett and Deena and me that first day said something about a speech someone gave, overseas, mentioning Mermaid's Hands." He frowned. "That just makes it stranger, though, if you think about it."

And that's when I started thinking it had to be you, Kaya. You know about Mermaid's Hands and its troubles, because I wrote about them in my letter. And you said in your letter that the government wanted you to make a speech. I nearly burst out with my theory then and there, to Dad and Tammy, but I was afraid if I said the words, I'd make it turn not true. I decided to check first, and today, that's what I did. I used Mr. Dubois's computer, since the library's still closed because of Helga pushing a tree through its roof.

I searched on "Kayamanira" and "W—" and "speech," and I found it, on lots of different sites—you saying we have a special culture, just like your people in the mountains. A special culture. That's why the cameras and reporters came, and that's why we're getting to rebuild. Because of you!

And I just had another thought. I said it was you, not the Seafather, but I think really maybe it was you and *the Seafather. He carried my message to you, so we could start writing each other. It's like he was pushing us to be friends. Maybe the Lady of the Ruby Lake helped somehow, too, what do you think?*

I'm going to mail this tomorrow. Now that we're back home, you don't need to send letters to Aunt Brenda's address anymore. Maybe you already sent one, but don't worry, I'm going to find a way to call there to check, so I won't miss it if you did.

Thanks for rescuing our home, Kaya! It feels so good to be back in the arms of the sea again. My feet have missed the silt and sand so bad! I wish there was some way I could be as good a friend to you as you've been to me.

Love from your friend,

Em

September 26 (Em to Kaya)

Dear Kaya,

I had to write you another letter. This is the fourth one I've written you and you haven't written back yet. Are you ever going to write again? I'm worried about you. I decided I can't bother Ma about whether any letters from you have arrived at Aunt Brenda's. She'll send them to me if any come. I just have to be patient, but I stink at being patient.

Today during lunch hour I went to Mr. Dubois's room and asked if I could use his computer again. I thought I'd just check to see if there were any other new stories about your country. Maybe one would mention you, I thought.

I wish I hadn't looked. The story at the top of the list had the headline "Tensions Increase on the Island Nation of W—." It sounded pretty bad. People in the mountains attacked a bus from the capital, it said, and set it on fire, and in the capital a mob beat up two men from the mountains and left them to die by the factory where they worked.

And then the article said that one of the "imprisoned insurgents" confessed to plotting to overthrow the government. Not you—it was another name. I can't remember it now, but it must be one of your friends, right?

But it's not true, right? I don't believe it. You told me you just wanted to have a festival for the Lady of the Ruby Lake ... Your friends couldn't of been planning a rebellion behind your back, could they? You have to be careful about who you pick for friends, my brother says. He should know. He confessed to something he didn't do to try to protect his friends, but they turned on him. Do you think your friend confessed to protect you? But that doesn't make sense, because confessing just makes you all *look bad. Maybe your government is just lying, and he didn't really confess at all.*

And there was another story from W—, about an earthquake. It said the earthquake opened cracks in the ground, and poisonous steam came out. It made me think that nothing at all is safe in your country right now. I wish I could bring you to Mermaid's Hands.

Love,

Em

September 28 (Em's diary)

A letter from Kaya at last! September 13th, it says on it. It did go to Aunt Brenda's, but Ma sent it here, like I knew she would. She says she has an idea of how to help us in Mermaid's Hands—I know what THAT was. And it worked! I love you, Kaya. But then there's the other parts of her letter, the parts about the Bully and punishment raining down on the mountains if there's an uprising. All that stuff I read in Mr. Dubois's room, about tensions increasing and the bus being attacked, does that count as an uprising? I bet it does. Thinking about it makes me feel like I've swallowed a bowl of fishhooks. I thought getting a letter from Kaya would make me feel less worried, but instead I feel more worried.

Chapter 10. Visions

September 19 (Kaya's journal)

Something new: thick clouds of steam rising from somewhere in the bowl of the Ruby Lake, and sulfur fumes. Three days ago it was mere wisps, and I took them for ordinary mist; today I can see nothing beyond the edges of the platform, nor even one end of it if I stand at the other. Not the rim of the crater, not the Ruby Lake, barely even the sky. If it's like this tomorrow, I don't see how the supply helicopter can possibly come. How could it see to land? I shall have to be careful with my supplies again. I suppose I should be grateful to have postponed hearing what the Bully and Friendlier have to say about the additions and adjustments I made to their script. They certainly didn't look pleased on the day.

What is Sumi fussing about, out there? I must go see.

September 19 (Kaya's journal, second entry)

All right. I have stoked the brazier. I have made tea. I will drink it and calm down. I am not hallucinating. I am not having visions. It's just imagination.

Sumi was wheeling around in great loops above the platform, and then down into the steam cloud, calling in her hoarse voice. When she vanished from sight down there, my heart cracked. *Please don't disappear. Don't leave me alone here with only the black ants for company*, I was thinking. Then, even before my mind understood what my eyes were seeing, my sad, cracked heart started up a war drum beat. In the clouds that blurred the far end of the platform was a figure: a man? The Bully, or Friendlier? Impossible; they can't just appear here. Rami? Even more impossible. I started down the platform, the war drum pounding away in my chest, but stopped halfway, feeling sick from the smell of rotten eggs and the clinging heat.

I squatted down and let my head droop between my knees, hoping the nausea would pass, but raised it when I heard Sumi cawing—thank you, friend, for not abandoning me—and saw the figure had come closer. A young fieldworker, he seemed to be, a ragged, sunfaded shirt hanging from his lean frame, a shortcloth round his waist, and another cloth wrapped round his head for sun protection. Black, red, and green. Not any old cloth: a flag, a separatist flag.

We did end up having streamers at our festival, but only red ones. We were careful to avoid the separatist colors. Certainly we had no flags. There have been no flags out in the open since that other festival, years ago, when we were all small children.

"They're making these again," he said, unwrapping the flag from his head and holding it up. There was a red-brown stain running the width of it, and, I realized, a matching gash on the man's head and down his left cheek by the ear.

"Are you a ghost?" I managed to ask.

"Look around you. Do you sense the power, beneath your feet? You mustn't cower. Remember your heart of ruby fire. You must be fierce."

I blinked and squinted, trying to resolve the features of the young man's face, but he had changed; he was not *he* any longer, but *she,* a woman, clutching her ragged shirt closed in her fist, and I recognized Grandmother Jemenli. In the same moment I remembered as a child climbing the ladder and pushing aside the curtain to enter Grandmother Jemenli's tiny mountainside house. I remembered kneeling beside my mother there, taking small sips of honey coffee while she and my mother exchanged formal words. My mother slid a neatly folded length of orange-and-gold checked cloth across to Grandmother Jemenli, who pushed a small green bundle—charms, for me, wrapped in a leaf—to my mother. Bored, I let my eyes wander round the room. They rested briefly on a memorial photo in a teak frame: a serious-faced, thin young man. The fieldworker—Grandmother Jemenli's son? To child me, it had been just another unknown grown-up. Grown me bowed my head.

"You must be fierce." This time, the words were breathed right in my ear. No, they came up through my feet; the platform was vibrating with them. I pulled myself to my feet. No one else was on the platform now.

"I can be fierce! I will be fierce!" I shouted, startling Sumi, who had perched on the railing. She flew up, protesting, and disappeared into a billow of heated mist. My arms, legs, and face were slick with sweat, my longcloth and shirt clung to my limbs. Can I be fierce even while being steamed like a sago dumpling?

Yes, sure. Let me be heated until I glow as red as the Ruby Lake. Let me be an ember that lights a fire.

September 20 (Kaya's journal)

The steam clouds have subsided somewhat today; I can see the cracks they're coming from, not on the Ruby Lake's surface, but along the sides of the crater, a bit higher up.

The Ruby Lake is swelling, too. I'm sure of it. The curled golden rock I called the salamander has disappeared into the lava, which is lapping the knees of the four hunched boulders I think of as the old grandfathers. The Lady really is coming, but how soon?

I don't care when. I have a heart of ruby fire. I will be fierce.

I hear a helicopter. Time to face the Bully and Friendlier.

September 20 (Kaya's journal, second entry)

Beside the helicopter, Friendlier seemed browbeaten, harassed; the Bully, on the other hand, was practically feverish with excitement—as if the two had been arguing on the way over and the Bully had prevailed. I felt a pang of concern for Friendlier, though I suppose it was for myself as well. I'd rather have Friendlier winning arguments than the Bully.

Friendlier handed me a letter from Mother (nothing from Em this time) and a copy of the Palem *Courier* and took the letters I wrote last week, one for Mother, one for Em.

"No more of that from now on," the Bully said, emphasizing *that* with a jut of the chin toward the letter in my hand.

"No letters?" I asked. I hadn't realized how much I depended on that thin lifeline until that moment, facing the prospect of losing it.

"What did you expect, after what you did with the speech?" Friendlier shook his head. "I said you were reasonable. I vouched for you."

"I didn't break trust! I did what you asked."

"You had a moment in the spotlight and you used it as a call to arms."

"How can you say that? You were here; you heard what I said. Language rights. Religious freedom. That's not a call to arms."

"'Greater autonomy' is," said the Bully, his teeth and tongue seeming to disdain the words.

"I hope you're happy with the fruits of your actions," Friendlier continued, eyes falling on the newspaper.

The photo on the front showed some kind of accident, a burnt-out wreck of a bus. "Terrorism!" the headline shouted. Underneath, in smaller print, was a promise to keep the roads through the mountains open and safe. My heart constricted. Attack a bus? Had the separatists done this? Why?

I looked at the photo again. I know the interdistrict buses; I bumped and jounced in them down to the coast and back again each term, when I was at St. Margaret's. This wasn't one of those buses. Half soot blackened but still visible on the front was the jasmine-flower-and-shield medallion of the State Security Service. My cheeks warmed, and I felt a harsh joy I've never felt before.

"Self-defense, not terrorism." I tapped the medallion in the photo.

"It wasn't a combat vehicle!" Friendlier said. "There were civilians on board!"

"Her kind don't respect those distinctions," said the Bully, disgusted. To me he said, "You can respect this, though: You can't win. Destroy a bus? We can impound every vehicle in the mountain region and have them all scrapped. Ambush one of us? We can take out twenty of you. A hundred of you."

Threats, always threats. The heat in me grew stronger.

"Your friend confessed, you know," the Bully continued. "Your sweetheart, the separatists' brat. Signed a statement. Early this morning, it was. He admitted to manipulating you and the others to rekindle old fires. I have a copy here. Look." He held out a paper with a list of charges. Rami's signature was at the bottom.

A wave of nausea, worse than last night's, swept over me. Grandmother Jemenli's son, with his wounds and bloody flag, filled my mind—but wearing Rami's face. What must they have done to

Rami to make him sign such a thing? The whole world was spinning; the platform was tilting, trying to send us all to the Lady … Friendlier caught my arm and steadied me.

"This confession is false," I said, each word like glue, sticking my tongue to the roof of my mouth. "Rami never …" I couldn't look at Friendlier or the Bully. I set my eyes on the Ruby Lake.

"You know he hated the government. You wrote as much in your memoir." Friendlier's voice. Quiet. Firm.

My head shot up. Had my words doomed Rami? Friendlier was watching me intently. The Bully stood two steps back, arms folded, radiating impatience.

Is there any way for me to save him?

There was no way to ask that question; all words fell to ash before I could speak them. But perhaps Friendlier is a mind reader, because he held out a recorder and said, "You can still help him. Order a stop to all this, in no uncertain terms. A good-faith gesture like that could mean clemency for your friend."

Could mean. Not *will* mean. *If I do exactly as they ask, will they make me a promise, and keep it? Do I really have the power to issue the command they're asking for? If I order, will people listen?* I thought of the pinpricks of light I've seen at the rim of the Ruby Lake's crater, the fires people have lit. *Do I have the right to command those fires to be snuffed out?*

"Speak in the name of the Lady," Friendlier said, a curl to his lip as he made the suggestion, almost as if he were inviting me to share a joke. Mocking the very idea of the Lady.

They can afford to mock. They know right now I'm ready to do anything to save Rami. But does he want to be saved, at such a cost?

Did he risk everything, suffer everything, to be told to accept the rule of his tormentors? And what about everyone else? Rami would never buy his life at the price of everyone's hopes.

The wind was turning; the scent of sulfur was strong in the air.

"I can't do that," I said. "I told you before: the Lady loves uprisings. Can't you tell? She herself is uprising."

Friendlier flung down the recorder, which bounced twice on the platform. He turned away, paced toward the helicopter, then back.

"You don't believe that nonsense. You're an educated woman, a scientist," he growled.

I realized—remembered again—at that moment: they are both enemies. Friendlier as much as the Bully. Enemies, and liars. I must not forget it.

"It's over, Den," the Bully said. "Leave it to me now." And to me, "We'll let your friend know that you agreed to his death—we'll tell all of them. How being a priestess went to your head."

"It's not about me! Or Rami. It's about them." I nodded to the world beyond the Ruby Lake. Grandmother Jemenli and the others in the mountains. "You know who's destroying W—? Not me. Not Rami. Not our people. It's your masters. The gold-stars and shiny-boots in the State Security Service, the parliament, the prime minister—all of them. They're the ones gambling with our nation." I looked past the Bully and Friendlier to the pilot—it's always the same man who flies them here—who was hanging back by the helicopter cabin door.

"*You* know, don't you. Tell your family and your neighbors how the State Security Service is putting our country at—"

"Enough of that!" said the Bully, he of the quick hand, but this time I was ready, arm raised to block his blow. For a couple of heartbeats no one spoke. The ocean rumblings of the Ruby Lake filled all our ears.

"Your days are numbered," the Bully said, lowering his hand and stepping back.

"Do you have anything extra you'd like to add to this, since it's your last communication?" Friendlier held up my letters to my mother and Em.

"It won't be my last," I said, but I said it in the mountain tongue. Why should I use their words? Let them learn ours.

They left then.

"See how fierce I was?" I said, but it came out a quavery whisper. Sumi gave a creaky-hinge assent and rubbed her beak against the damp hair at the base of my neck.

I was fierce, but now I feel like weeping. All possible futures are misery and darkness now. I feel like weeping, but no tears come.

September 21 (Kaya to her mother)

Dear Mother,

I worry about what the State Security Service people may say to you about me. You mustn't believe what they tell you; they are liars whose single goal is to end all resistance in the mountains by whatever means. They will not bring your letters to me any longer, or mine to you, so I am trying something new. I'm fastening this to Sumi's leg and telling her to fly home. Will she do it? Crows are smart. You said once that she visits you sometimes. I hope she will. If she does, give her something tasty to eat and then write me a quick note and send her back.

If she will be a messenger, then we can communicate much faster and more securely than we did before.

My heart twists like wrung-out washing when I think of you, anxious and alone, and maybe badgered by the State Security Service. Please put on a smiling face for them, sigh and shake your head about me and say (which is probably true) that you don't know how I became the bad daughter that I am. Say nothing political. But when you speak to friends in town, and to neighbors and to my uncle and cousins, tell them the Lady is with us. Tell them the Ruby Lake is uprising too—but not to worry about me. There's no need to fear for me. I'll explain more once I know I can rely on Sumi to carry the messages.

The State Security Service men showed me a confession with Rami's signature on it. I hope it was a forgery, designed to manipulate me, but if it's real, and if they decide to make an example of him, if—

I don't want to even say it.

If they take his life, then please make sure to bring incense and salt to his grandparents. Please see that they have everything they need. Tell them if I ever find a way to come to them, I'll serve them like a granddaughter.

Your loving daughter,
Kayamanira

September 21 (Kaya's mother to Kaya)

My dear girl,

There is more than a crow's usual intelligence in your Sumi! I gave her some bits of salt fish.

We can see the clouds from the Ruby Lake. We know what it means. Days, weeks—we don't know when its fires will spill out, but we know it will not be long. I have gone to Mr. Gana's local office, to appeal for your transfer to somewhere safer, but he is in Palem and his staff are not sympathetic.

I am so worried for you. You are not sounding like yourself. If anything should happen to you, I don't know how I will survive it. Of course I will do as you ask with regard to Ramiritam's grandparents. I'll light incense here as well. May the Lady save him. And you.

Sumi is a strong bird; I am tying a little net bag to her other foot, with three bites of papaya in it for you, and sending her on her way with two kisses on her glossy head, one for her and one for you.

I do not need to say be brave. You are very brave.

Always with love,

Your mother

September 22 (Kaya to her mother)

Dear Mother,

Sumi is the Lady's bird through and through! The papaya was delicious. It took the taste of sulfur from my mouth for a few moments—that alone was a blessing.

I realize I must sound strange now, but my existence now is strange! If I tell you I see things, people, even the Lady—especially the Lady—I don't know what you will think. If I try to consider it with my rational mind, I don't know what I myself think.

The Lady's at the corner of my consciousness all the time, coming out of the billows of steam, slipping back into them. I felt dizzy this morning, when I first sat up, so I lay back down again, and I felt her put her hand on my brow—just like you used to do, whenever I had a fever, but your hand was always so cool, and hers was very hot.

"I'll work a miracle for you," she said. I heard the words in my mind. "It will be wonderful!" I felt her confidence—it became my confidence. Her joy was my joy.

So you see, you don't need to worry. I'm promised a miracle.

Love,

Your daughter Kayamanira

September 24 (Kaya's journal)

The Lady was here again just now. She came to me as I brooded on the news of new violence that mother sent.

"Poor Kaya, how can the words and actions of those little wisps of bone and flesh disturb you so?" she asked me.

"You're forgetting that I'm one of those wisps," I said. How she forgets! That her touch can burn, that her breath is noxious. And yet in her eyes, such love. "We wisps know best how to hurt one another."

"Shall I punish them for it? Spill heartfire blood down on them where they sleep?"

"No! You mustn't do that!" I said, but she pressed me:

"No? I have to shine forth somewhere, sometime. I must dance. Waiting makes the desire all the sharper. Almost irresistible."

"Well … someplace with no people, then," I said.

"That hill where I left my streamers drifting," she said, rising and lifting her left hand, like a dancer.

"The fissure to the north, in the foothills," I murmured. "There were people there, last time, hikers."

"Annnnnd … the cup of my treasures," she continued, swinging her right hand down, then up, and lowering her left to meet it, forming a cup. I knew she must mean Jarakasan Lake, where it's said she once shed ruby tears.

"That's near the field headquarters of Adze Forest Products." Adze Forest Products—the American company with a timber concession for half the eastern mountain district. "There are people there, lots of people!" I said.

She showed me her empty palms—*I'm sorry*—but with a smile on her lips. And spun round again and disappeared.

Is this real? Has she really told me where the next eruptions will come? Can I act on this knowledge?

September 25 (Kaya to her mother)

Dear Mother,

Please, find Grandmother Jemenli and ask her if there is anyone in the resistance who can make their way to the hillside in Taneh District where the new fissure opened up. If someone can get there today or tomorrow, they should raise a flag there, and take a photo and send it to the papers in Palem. They should do the same by Jarakasan Lake, but be careful, because the State Security Service will be thick there, protecting Adze Forest Products' field headquarters.

The Lady means to dance in these places, and soon. Our flags will tell the prime minister and parliament that the Lady's strength is our strength.

But warn people, too, especially by Jarakasan Lake. Not that anyone at Adze's field headquarters is likely to listen to the warning, but we have to try.

I imagine my words must be hard to believe. How can I know? You must think I've lost my mind. Sometimes I fear it myself. But what have we to lose? Even if the Lady doesn't bestir herself in these next few days, to raise our flag is an act of defiance. And eruptions and exhalations will *come, are coming, and we should claim them. Her power is our power.*

There was something more I wanted to write here, but my thoughts have dissolved in the steam, and I haven't got the cool head to precipitate them back out again, so I will just close, as always, with love, and send Sumi on her way.

Kaya

September 28 (Kaya's journal)

More sulfur dioxide from the Taneh fissure, Mother said, but the area has been off limits since the last release, so no casualties. Not so lucky with Jarakasan Lake. Someone did get a warning to Adze's field headquarters, but the bosses told everyone that if they failed to show up for work, they'd be out of a job. Seventeen were overcome when a huge bubble of carbon dioxide rose from the depths of the lake and settled in the gorge there, asphyxiating anything that breathes. Mother said the newspapers and radio stations are buzzing with the rumor that it was a massacre by our people, an attack with poisonous gas! Insane. And now fear of violence—or the government?—is keeping reporters away, so no one's learning the truth. The story of our warning has made the papers, though, along with a grainy photo of our flag by the lake, and these are being taken as proof of the vicious plot.

Where are the volcanologists? They must know the truth. Why aren't they speaking up?

The rest of Mother's note mentions more arrests, an exchange of fire at the Kemiyamin crossroads … I can't take it in now. Dry heaves this morning; all I want is to lie down with my cup within reach, so I can take some sips of water now and then. It's for the best that I can't eat much, as the helicopter won't be able to come until the wind changes again.

(From the September 28 transcript of the post-sentence interview with Prisoner 118, State Security Service files on the insurgency)

Lt. Sana: Not bitter? Nothing you want to say about Kayamanira, in light of the sentence? She roped you into this and didn't speak a word on your behalf.

118: [no response]

Lt. Sana: She practically ordered your execution.

118: [laughs]

Lt. Sana: It's amusing to you?

118: That you take orders from your own detainees?

Lt. Sana: She could have stopped it.

118: Nobody could have. I knew from the time I was four years old that this day would come.

Lt. Den: What about Kayamanira?

118: What about her?

Lt. Den: You're happy to have her follow in your footsteps?

118: [no response]

Lt. Den: This is your chance to save or sink her.

118: [no response]

Lt. Sana: You're a cold-hearted bastard, aren't you.

118: She belongs to the Lady. What I want or feel doesn't matter. But—

Lt. Sana: Same type of nonsense she was spouting. Two monkeys drunk on the same palm wine.

Lt. Den: But what?

118: Nothing. It doesn't matter.

Lt. Sana: Answer the question!

118: [inaudible]

Lt. Sana: Speak up!

118: I hope she lives. I hope she lives to dance on your graves.

(From the W— State Security Service's files on the insurgency: email records)

From: Tema Baii
Subject: Execution?!
Date: September 30
To: Hetan Baii

We just got a press release from the Ministry of Law and Justice saying that Ramiratam Kelkaniye was executed this morning. The sentence was only handed down Friday! It's got to be because of the Jarakasan Lake disaster. I swear the government's encouraging the story of a gas attack, even though it makes the State Security Service look incompetent. The rumor's definitely solidified public opinion against the separatists, and judging from the overseas press, it's put the Americans on the government's side, which I suppose is worth appearing like bumblers. I wonder if there's any truth to it. Maybe the separatists took advantage of a natural event to cause more trouble?

It's making me very worried about Kaya. The State Security Service can't have been happy with that speech of hers two weeks ago—not the unedited version, anyway—and everything that's happened since seems to justify their fears. I wish I could understand her better. She was always so sweet in school. But now? I'm not sure what to think. Still, whatever misguided ideas she has—even if she really does favor an autonomous mountain state—I don't want her to end up in front of a firing squad.

If I could cover the Jarakasan Lake story, I could help dispel the rumors and humanize the separatists a bit, but Kar said no way. He said he's not letting me anywhere near the mountains. So it looks like I'm stuck with the fishing negotiations, which are completely stalled—I'll be home late again tonight.

Tema Baii
Correspondent, Prosperity Television

October 1 (Kaya to Ramiratam, unsent)

Dear Rami,

I know from my mother's note that you are gone. I know it, but I can't accept it. They'll be lighting incense and sprinkling salt on the fires at home.

I can't do those things. I can't! I can't wish your spirit well, I want you *to be well, body and spirit both, I want you to be beside me—you, not some wish-fulfillment vision-dream—telling me you love me. I want to take you by the hand and tell you that I love you.*

Do you hear me? If I shout it from the edge of the platform? Do you hear me, wherever you are?

There were six blank pages at the back of Trees of Insular Southeast Asia. *I ripped them out and tore them into strips, and on each strip I wrote your name. I took them to the edge of the platform and let them loose, a flock of paper birds. I thought they'd wheel and sink, down to the Ruby Lake, and I even thought for a moment maybe I might join them, and maybe my spirit would catch up with yours, but no: the people in the mountains deserve better than a silly broken-heart immolation. I have promised to be fierce, and I will be.*

The bits of paper with your name on them—they didn't fall into the Ruby Lake. An updraft caught them and carried them up into the steam clouds. The wind's from the south now. I wonder how far it will take them.

Ramiratam, Ramiratam, Ramiratam. May your name be everywhere.

October 2 (Kaya's journal)

Along with her note about the hordes of State Security Service troops now inhabiting town, Mother has entrusted Sumi with two letters from Em. Here's an irony: in the first letter, Em says my words on behalf of her village have saved it. She calls it a miracle. Reading that, for a moment I feel happy. Not all my actions bring death and misery: here's some good I've done. But I can't stop the thought from coming: *Is this the miracle you promised, mother of all fire? What about the people who sing your songs and honor you, here? What help for them?*

And then the second letter. Em has heard about the violence, the deaths. She asks about Rami. I can hardly bear to read her questions, let alone think how to answer them, but I must try. I must find something to say that isn't too discouraging. Her home is safe, but her family is in pieces. I have to try to offer her hope, somehow.

October 2 (Kaya to Em)

My dear Em,

I was so happy to get your letter of September 24 and to read that Mermaid's Hands has been spared. That's the power of a multitude of eyes turning to look your way: everyone, from the smallest child to the largest government, behaves better when it knows it's being watched and judged.

I think I understand a little of how you must feel, wishing that your mother and Jiminy might be with you too. Joy isn't the same when you can't share it with the ones you love best—my bones ache day and night from the truth of that. You ask, why can't your father pull Jiminy home? Perhaps this will give you some consolation: your own actions may well be the line and hook that reel him in. Maybe by thinking of your loyalty, your father will find the heart to forgive your brother. And maybe by thinking of your loyalty, your brother will recall who it is who deserves his deep allegiance.

As for your mother, I cannot think of her without feeling pangs for my own mother, who I'm sure I've caused as much suffering as Jiminy has caused yours. Your mother's ways may not be Mermaid's Hands ways, but I can tell from your letters that she loves all of you very much—you children, of course, but your father too. I wish I could tell you that she will come home, but the future is like a rainbow we see on the far side of a deep gorge: the path to it twists and turns, and when we arrive on that far side, what we find is very different from the glimmering bow we first saw. Your mother's love, though, that's certain.

I also have before me your letter from September 26. I see you've heard news from my country, about the violence and my friend Rami. You are right to disbelieve what you read about Rami! His confession was not genuine. They forced it out of him—or forged it outright—and then on the strength of that false confession, they executed him. Earthquakes and poisonous gases are nothing to the evils people visit on one another.

As for those earthquakes and poisonous gases, don't worry about them for my sake. Was Mr. Ovey afraid of the sea? Are you? Maybe just a little, when the storm is all around you (maybe I am a little afraid, just a little, sometimes, too), but you know the Seafather's with you. And the Lady's with me. I didn't feel it before, but I do now.

I am afraid this will be my last letter for some time. The government will no longer let me receive or send mail—it's only thanks to Sumi's willingness to act as a messenger that I have your letters today—and I fear my mother's mail may be subject to tampering. In truth, I'm a little surprised the State Security Service let your letters through to her, but perhaps I've begun to overestimate their power, or maybe they saw no harm in her receiving them, believing she has no way to send them on.

They must continue to believe that. So, though it pains me to say it, I must ask that you don't respond to this. I am so sorry. One day, ~~if I ever leave here~~ when I leave here, when times are better in my country, I will write you again. I will invite you for a visit! Till then, please know how much your letters have meant to me. I wish you a bright future, filled with possibilities.

Always your friend, Kaya

October 2 (Kaya to her mother)

Dear Mother,

I'm enclosing a note for Em; you'll understand my thoughts when you read it. You mustn't try posting it; there has to be another way to get it out of the country.

~~*Maybe Piyu at the research station*~~ *No, don't try Piyu; he was friendly in peaceful times, but as a lowlander he's too much of a risk. But talk to Kalasia—do you remember her? Her father works for Nawalam's family. She's on the cleaning crew at the research station. She might be able to slip a letter in with the others destined for overseas.*

I wish now that I had thought to write my adviser at Cornell, or my colleagues there, back when we were first arrested. Maybe they could have raised a stink, put some pressure on the government. Too late for that now.

Has there been any more gunfire? Casualties?

I'm waiting until sundown to send Sumi. I worry about someone from the State Security Service noticing her comings and goings.

Stay safe.

Your loving daughter,

Kaya

(From the W— State Security Service's files on the insurgency: email records)

From: Lt. Den
Subject: Tasan Bay transcript
Date: October 3
To: Lt. Sana

Here's the transcript of Tema Baii's interview with Suta Sen, the fisherman who found those bits of paper with Prisoner 118's name on them. Prosperity Television agreed not to broadcast it. Did you say Capt. Aran's got the paper scraps?

> Baii: Some unusual and rather unsettling detritus has washed up in a small fishing village on the edge of Tasan Bay—slips of paper inscribed with a mountain name: Ramiratam. It happens to be the name of the separatist executed earlier this week for crimes against the state. Suta Sen is the fisherman who first noticed the slips of paper. Tell us how you found these papers, Mr. Sen.
>
> Sen: Tide was just about all the way in. The waves were at their highest, lapping right up to here, see? Right about here. And one big wave came in and left these white wrinkled strips way up on the sand, just above the high tide line.

Looked like white ribbons, maybe. I noticed there seemed to be marks on them, so I picked one up, and I saw it had a name on it—the name of that fella that got executed the other day. The mountain separatist. And the next one did, too, and the next. They all did.

Baii: What do you make of it?

Sen: Well, it has to be the Lady of Currents, don't it. Guess she wants us to think on him. Guess maybe probably she's not happy about the execution.

Baii: That's the Lady of Currents, an ocean deity still revered in some coastal villages. Mr. Sen, can you explain to younger viewers in Palem and the inland villages, who may not be familiar with the Lady of Currents, why she might champion a self-confessed criminal and threat to the nation's stability?

Sen: Ah. Well. Well now ... It's a hard question to answer as you've asked it. Of course the government's working for the best for all of us, but even the wisest folk can make a mistake sometimes. The Lady of Currents' only sister, who stokes the fires beneath the mountains, she's fond of them little dark mountain folk. If I remember rightly, this separatist and them others that were arrested, they claimed they done what they done for the Lady of the Ruby Lake. That puts them in her hands, y'see? They're hers. You don't want to kill folks like that—it's stealing. The Lady of the Ruby Lake's going to take offense, and the Lady of Currents'll take offense in sympathy. And where's that leave all of us? Right in the middle, between the angry sea and the angry mountains.

Baii: So you think the government should give in to the separatists' demands?

Sen: I don't know about that. I'm not a politician. We've gotta stay strong as a nation. And from what I understand, them folk up in the mountains are pretty backward; they need guidance. They'd likely run themselves to ruin on their own. But the government's gotta be careful, that's all. The waves brought

```
us a warning.
```

Sen was taken into custody and released after Lt. Vell gave him a good talking to. I think he understands the importance of not spreading the story around any further, and I'm sure he'll urge others to let it drop too. As for Baii, what with the suppression of the story and her awareness of being under observation, she's not likely to risk breaking it on her own.

(From the W— State Security Service's files on the insurgency: email records)

From: Lt. Sana
Subject: Re: Tasan Bay transcript
Date: October 3
To: Lt. Den

Yeah, Capt. Aran has the slips of paper. I saw them. They can't have been in the water long—the ink Prisoner 118's name was written in was hardly blurred. I'll tell you what it means: the insurgents have operatives or agents on the coast. We should bring in any migrant workers for questioning.

What a lot of garbage from that old fart Baii interviewed. You expect idiocy from the primitives in the mountains but I keep forgetting that some of our own people are just about as backward. You grow up, wanting to be proud of your country, wanting to help make it **be** something on the world stage, and meanwhile there are old granddads like that out there. And now this damn insurgency. I'm going to recommend that Capt. Aran press for relocating Prisoner 116 and moving along with the purge. Setting her up in that temple was a big mistake: you give those people the slightest encouragement and they walk all over you. We have to assert authority. Aran didn't want a police action, but frankly, I'd prefer that to all the pussyfooting that's gone on up to now.

Chapter 11. Open Hands

October 1 (Jiminy to Em)

Dear Em,

How are you? I hope your good. I heard from Ma that you and Tammy went home to help rebuild. Pretty nice save Mermaids Hands pulled off for itself. Maybe the Seafathers good for something besides storms, ha ha. Sorry just teasing. I do think its cool. Good for you helping out too though maybe its a sight better then being stuck with Aunt Brenda.

Ma made a stink about me being in danger and so I got transferred to a different unit here so I never see Ace. Thanks for telling her. Thanks for taking my phone calls at Aunt Brendas and thanks for trying to come see me. Your a great sister. It really makes a difference knowing that people are looking out for you.

I'm doing three classes now, GED Preparation, ~~Responsability~~ Responsibility and Good Choices, and Dynamics of Addiction. If I keep out of trouble and the teachers say I'm working hard, then I might get reccommended for a work release program.

I dont think I ever wrote so much at one time. If you write me, I'll try to write back soon. Say hi to Gran and Tammy and Dad ~~if hes done hating me~~.

Love from your brother,

Jiminy

October 3 (Em's diary)

Dad gave me the key to the mailbox. He said I could be in charge of checking it, and today there was a letter from Jiminy! He wrote a whole letter. He said I was great!

But that ain't true, not really. I didn't make it all the way to see him, and I've written more letters to Kaya than to him. But I'm going to make a promise here:

I PROMISE I WILL WRITE JIMINY AT LEAST ONCE A WEEK

A great sister would write every week. If I write every week, maybe I'll deserve to be called great.

Jiminy's letter made me wonder some things though.

1. He said maybe the Seafather was good for something besides storms, but then he said "just kidding." What does he mean? What is he just kidding about?

People say "just kidding" sometimes when really they're dead serious. I can't tell: does he believe in the Seafather, or not? Does he hate the Seafather? Is Dad right that Jiminy hates Mermaid's Hands?

I guess I can ask him in a letter.

Please let him not hate Mermaid's Hands.

2. "Dynamics of Addiction"? Why is he taking that class?

I guess I know why. I guess I just don't like the reason.

I guess I was stupid to think he just one day up and decided to steal stuff. I guess there had to be other things going on. I've been sticking up for the Jiminy I remember, but can I stick up for this Jiminy, too?

I have to, because how else can he ever want to come home? ~~But~~

~~if he's so different, do I want him to come home?~~ I do want him to come home. No matter what stuff he did while he was gone.

I do want him to come home.

I do want him to come home.

I do want him to come home.

There, magic. It's true now.

3. Dad. Should I show Dad the letter? I can't decide.

October 3 (Em's diary, second entry)

I showed the letter to Gran and she up and called out, "Trace, you come see this letter your son wrote!" Bunches of other people clustered round listening as Gran read it out—Mrs. Ovey and Uncle Near and Auntie Chicoree and Cody and Jenya and Clara—it seemed like everybody, and I could see Dad clench his jaw, and I felt a little jaw-clenchy myself, I have to admit, a bit of hot shame, especially when I saw Cody looking all serious and frowning. I just about wanted to strangle Gran at that moment.

But when Gran stopped, Mrs. Ovey said, "You'll bring him home yet Minnow Em," and Uncle Near patted Dad on the back and said, "That's a hopeful sign." And then Small Bill reminded me that it was time for him and me to take over from Lindie and Fairchance thatching the roof on the Oveys' house, and Mrs. Tiptoe called up from outside that supper would be ready by sunset in the Tiptoes' house.

Houses that are done now:

Winterhulls'

Tiptoes'

Oveys' (almost)

Fearings' (partway)

Ikahos' (partway)

Ours and Uncle Near and Aunt Chicoree's are up next.

October 4 (Em's diary)

Getting this down quick before we have to leave for school. This morning my eyes opened, and I was just staring at the roof of the Winterhulls' house without really noticing I was awake. On one side of me I could hear Tammy's slow breathing. On the other was a rumpled quilt, so that meant Gran was already up. Next to that was Auntie Chicoree. I couldn't really see her in the dim gray, but I could hear the little sighs and swallowing noises of baby Dawn-day nursing. The sea sounded way far away, so it was probably low tide. Uncle Near's voice came floating in from outside, not loud, but when it's quiet and you're awake, you can hear things.

"Setting that out for Jiminy? 'sgood. Everybody been wondering when you'd bend toward the poor boy."

I sat up. It had to be Dad Uncle Near was talking to, but I didn't catch Dad's reply. I wriggled out from under Tammy's left leg, which she'd flung across me in her sleep. She murmured, but didn't wake up. I tiptoed past Auntie Chicoree and Dawn-day. Wade was on Auntie Chicoree's other side, not asleep either, and when I went by he whispered, "We don't have to get up yet." My nod and my shrug meant *I know, but—*. I slipped into the kitchen. Gran and Silent Soriya and Pearlheart's granny, Granny Blessing, were flaking yesterday's redfish and beating eggs for breakfast, no one talking.

"I'm going out," I mouthed to Gran, and stepped out the front door and off the veranda onto the mud. Uncle Near and Dad and Mr. Winterhull were tying sacks of oysters to the side of the house. There's more places to dig for them at low tide, so you get up early if you have to.

"Did you see Brett, Jenya, and Cody had a good haul, too," Uncle Near was saying, and then he caught sight of me. "You're up early. Feel like staying home from school and helping shuck oysters?" he asked, but Dad said, "She's gotta go to school. Gotta have some kids showing their faces there every day to keep all the dry-landers happy."

"Sooner they all forget about us again, the better," Uncle Near said, making a face, adding something quickly about being grateful and all.

"Tomorrow's Saturday. I can help all day long, tomorrow," I offered, and Uncle Near smiled. Sizzling sounds and good smells were coming from the kitchen, and Anna Winterhull appeared in the kitchen door and said "Daddy!" real loud, and Mr. Winterhull hopped onto the veranda and lifted her up and set her on his shoulders. Uncle Near went in too, and that left me and Dad alone by the sacks of oysters.

I glanced at our grounded dinghy—which made it through the hurricane, even though our house didn't (Dad found it near the gas station in Sandy Neck and patched it up). There was a Mason jar there, full of water, just waiting for the sun to rise. I hugged Dad tight.

"Sun'll be up soon," I said.

Dad smiled a pained smile, opened his mouth to say something, then closed it, then opened it again—and closed it. Then we both giggled.

"Talking with the catch again?" I asked.

"Practicing for best fish-out-of-water impression," he said. Then, eyes to the horizon, he added, "It's starlight I was catching, actually.

All those stars, pouring straight down into the Gulf each night … I'll leave the jar out, though. I reckon this is strong water and can carry starlight and fresh risen sunlight together."

I never heard of anyone making a charm with starlight in water before. "What'll the starlight bring Jiminy?" I asked.

Dad hesitated. "Starlight's for your mother," he said, after a moment. "She's so set against the ordinary charms, I thought something different, something real fine, real rare, real … real beautiful might …"

So he didn't set the water out for Jiminy at all. Jiminy's an afterthought. It was for Ma. He wants her back so bad he's trying to invent new magic to do it with. Star water. Whoever heard of it? But maybe it'll work.

"Come on in and get breakfast, you two. Em, you got school to get ready for." It was Gran, standing in the doorway. Dad tapped the top of the Mason jar with his hand, and I knew his wish was going from his heart down his arm and out his fingertips. I touched the jar too. Be strong, water. Hold sunlight for Jiminy as well as starlight for Ma.

Water *is* strong. I know it is. It holds all the fish, and the whales and the dolphins, and the kelp forests. It can hold both sunlight and starlight.

October 4 (Em to Jiminy)

Dear Jiminy,

Thanks for your letter! I will write to you lots! I'm glad you're not in the same part of the prison as that other guy, Ace. I'd say I hope you flatten anyone else who tries to bother you, but I guess probably you're supposed to do stuff like walking away and counting to ten instead, huh?

If you can get into a work release program, does it have to be in Louisiana, or can you get one closer? I wish you could be some place that was easy to visit.

Dad ain't mad at you no more. He collected the first light of day for you, the other day, for luck. And I showed Gran your letter, and—please don't get steamed, you know how Gran is—she read it out, and everyone is pulling for you.

Dad said something, though, when he was bringing us back here. He said you were sour on Mermaid's Hands.

Are you?

I hope you're not.

There's so much to do here now. Mr. Tiptoe had the idea of adding windmills to our houses. Think about it! We'd never have to be stingy running the generators. We could have power whenever we want. Sounds only fair, right? Wind battered us down, so wind can serve us to make up for it. The parents and grandparents are arguing about whether we should take help from the Minorities Mobilize people when it comes to designing them or just do it ourselves. I told Dad we could probably find directions on the computer in the library, once it reopens. He looked pretty doubtful about the idea, but the library's where I learned more about Kaya's country, and Kaya's the one that got the Minorities Mobilize people to save Mermaid's Hands.

I should tell you about Kaya. She's in prison too, ~~only she didn't do anything wrong.~~ only it's because of religion and not having any rights. She's all alone in her prison, and it's over a volcano. Pretty bad, huh. You said it helps just knowing there are people looking out for you. I've written Kaya a lot of letters, so maybe that counts as looking out for her? She hasn't answered recently.

Tammy wants to add something here. Tomorrow I promised Uncle Near I'd help with oyster shucking, but I'll go into the post office early and mail this.

Hi Jiminy this is Tammy writing. I miss you. Thank you for writing a letter. You remember my bottle cap collection? Its all gone now but there's all kinds of stuff coming in with the tide these days. Wade found a mirror that's a regular mirror on one side and a magnafine mirror on the other side, and I found a lisince plate. I'll show you when you come home. Em says that may still take a while but dint you say in your letter about work release? Now Em is talking to me and trying to explain and I can't ~~consintra~~ ~~concintr~~ think about what I'm writing you. Love Tammy.

And love from me, too. Write again soon, please!

Em

October 5 (Em's diary)

Mailed the letter to Jiminy. I wonder if it counts as lying, what I said about Dad collecting the first light of day. I don't feel like it's lying, but it don't quite feel like the truth, either.

Last night all the grown-ups got together at the Tiptoes' for a talk-it-out about people coming and staying in Mermaid's Hands, I think because of the Minorities Mobilize woman who's been spending so much time with Tomtale Ikaho and staying at the Ikahos' house. Marcela, her name is. No kids are allowed at a talk-it-out, and not Marcela or even Cody, because he ain't yet been sung into a genealogy. A lot of the older kids hung around in the water listening, though, three and four of us to a dinghy. I wasn't going to go at first; I was going to stay with Tammy, who'd been having breathing problems all day and was resting, but after I made her some of Mrs. Ovey's tea, she shooed me off.

"I'm minding Dawn-day. She won't stay asleep without a body to snuggle up to, Auntie Chicoree said, and this way Auntie Chicoree can go to the talk-it-out."

She looked so proud. Ma always says no whenever Auntie Chicoree or Mrs. Tiptoe offer to watch over Tammy on her bad days because, Ma says, "They'll just put her to work chasing the littles, and the child needs rest." But lying down with Dawn-day is a job you can do resting.

"I'm helping out," Tammy said, letting Dawn-day suck on her pinky finger, and it was true. She was helping.

"You go on, too," she said.

So I went.

We could hear some of the grown-ups saying that we shouldn't be letting people like Marcela stay here for days and days, as if they lived here, unless they're thinking of staying for permanent, like Silent Soriya or Cody.

They didn't mention Ma.

Mr. Tiptoe said maybe we could take paying guests, like a dry-land boarding house or hotel, but a lot of other voices, including Mr. Tiptoe's own father, said no no, never nothing like that.

"This place ain't a resort," Mrs. Ovey said, and Snowy said, "Asking money just to breathe the air here, just to stand under these roofs we're fixing? No."

"Marcy would pay," said a youngish voice. That was Tomtale. "She said people would like to come here and learn things, like how to thatch, or how to make nets."

Then there was some teasing, the grown-ups piling on questions about whether Tomtale was sweet on Marcela and why didn't he ask her to get married and come live in Mermaid's Hands? Then she could learn those things for free. And then Dad came back to Mr. Tiptoe's suggestion. "It wouldn't hurt to have other ways to earn a little money," he said. "Now that the state's watching us like sharks, where we put down nets, where we dig…"

Which is funny, because that's what Ma's always saying, that stuff about earning money, and Dad always argues with her. I wonder whether it's the dry-landers watching like sharks that changed his mind, or whether it's missing Ma that changed it. Or maybe it was never as barnacle fixed as I thought?

There was some murmuring and mumbling, along the lines of well-maybe and gotta-think-on-that-some-more, and then they were back to pressing Tomtale to get Marcela to marry him and come live in Mermaid's Hands, with only Gran an odd voice out, saying, "You shouldn't ask a soul to stay here that don't want to," and oh how loud I heard Dad's silence ringing in my ears after that, though I don't think anyone else did. Meanwhile Tomtale was laughing in an embarrassed way and saying well Marcy's a grad student and you can't ask someone like that to tie herself down here. And people were agreeing in a sort of regretful way and saying you can't be a part-timer here, or have a divided heart.

It was real late when we went back to the Winterhulls'. Tammy was asleep, only wheezing just a little, and Dawn-day was asleep too, and Wade too, because he'd lost interest and come back early.

"Dad," I whispered, as he settled down across from me.

"Mmm?"

"When you were working at the cannery, when you met Ma—that didn't make you a part-timer here? Working all day on dry land?"

"Nah. I was one hundred percent gone from Mermaid's Hands while I was working there. But I always knew I'd come back. More like I was a part-timer on dry land."

"You didn't come home at night?"

"Uh-uh." He yawned. "There was an abandoned shrimp boat in that town. Slept there. G'night, Em."

Gran must've felt me still awake and thinking hard, because she scooted over next to me.

"I never knew there were rules about living here," I said.

"There ain't so many rules. Just, if you're gonna be here, you gotta really be here. Not like those towns on dry land, abandoned all day long and folks just slinking home to sleep."

I was thinking about Ma and Dad. I was thinking, you can be in a place with your body one hundred percent, but not with your heart. Like Dad on dry land. And like Ma, here. I guess I sighed, because next I felt Gran's hand on my head, fingers combing through my hair. It made my bones go loose and my eyes close.

"Don't fret—, Em. Mermaid's Hands are open hands. You sleep now."

October 8 (Jiminy to Em)

Dear Em,

Maybe you shouldnt of said that about flattening people in your letter because there are these ~~asswipes~~ guys, two of them, always giving me the eye and in my space and always laughing and yesterday I couldnt take it anymore and I didnt count to ten or even five and now there are "consequences" is what the unit director says, like not being eligible for the work release program for another six months. I say ~~fu~~ fricassee that. Actually no I shouldnt say that. I need to own my actions. I shouldnt even of wrote that about you saying to flatten people because its not your fault what I did. I know that. I am trying but it is so hard and you make a mistake like taking a swing at someone and then your back to square one. But still, you gotta take responsibility for what you do.

Like your friend Kaya. Thats great that your writing to her but I gotta tell you Em, people always say there innocent but most have dirty hands one way or another. People on the outside, too. Even Dad and Ma, probably even Gran. So maybe your friend has things to own up to. And not having any rights, well nobody does in prison! Thats why no one wants to be here! But letters help. I reckon yours help her alot.

You asked if I was sour on Mermaid's Hands. Its not that I'm sour! You know your always talking about Sabelle Morning? She traveled around, right? I just wanted to see the world a bit, you know, live a little, try some different stuff, see something new. Now its like I can feel everyone back home shaking there heads, like that was a mistake. I feel like, when I get out, I need to show Dad and everyone thats not true. And ~~I aint a fu~~ that I can make something of myself. I'm more than just a jailbird! When I come home, I want to be able to hold my head up high. I dont know if you can understand because you never disappointed no one.

Tell Tammy thats cool about the license plate and the mirror. What state was the license plate from? Thats cool about the windmills too. If one gets built draw me a picture of it.

Love from your brother,

Jiminy

October 9 (Em's diary)

I picked up a letter from Jiminy at the post office today after school, and I read it right there, with Tammy hanging on my arm, but nobody else around. Small Bill and Clara didn't want to come in to the post office, so they waited outside, and Wade and Skinnylegs went on ahead.

I must've made a face when I got to the part about Jiminy getting in a fight, because Tammy said, "What's wrong?" and "Let me read."

"It's nothing," I said. "Look." I pointed to the bottom of the letter. "He wants to know where the license plate came from. If you write him a letter of your own, maybe he'll write you a reply of your own. We can still share an envelope and a stamp—that way it'll cost less."

She nodded, but I could see her eyes scanning the top part of the letter. Then she looked up.

"They won't let him out early," she said.

"Not in the next six months, anyway," I said.

We were both quiet a spell.

"Let's not mention it to Dad," I said at last, and Tammy nodded.

I don't want to hear what Dad has to say about Jiminy losing his chance for the work release program.

That's not what's bugging me now, though. It's what he wrote at the end, about not wanting to come right home when he gets out. (Which I do too understand, Jiminy, so there! But just because I understand doesn't mean I have to like it!)

Will he ever come back? How long will it take him to prove

himself? What if instead he messes up again? Gran said Mermaid's Hands are open. Right now it feels like everything slips right through the fingers. Can't a person ever hold onto anything, or anyone?

October 9 (Em's diary, second entry)

So I was out on the Winterhulls' veranda, writing that stuff about Jiminy and gnawing on the end of my pencil, and Granddad Winterhull poked his head out the window and said,

"You still doing homework out there? Too dark for that, ain't it? Come get some rest." And I said okay, just one more minute, and next thing I knew Dad was squatting down beside me. I closed my diary, but Dad could see I wasn't working on homework anymore.

"Things on your mind, Minnow Em?"

"Maybe a little," I said.

"Is it your brother?"

"Did Tammy say something to you?"

Dad laughed.

"Could be that I heard her telling your Gran how she was going to write three letters, one to your ma, one to Mandy, and one to your brother. Or could be that I spied that envelope sticking out of your diary. That a new one from him?"

There was no point lying, and anyway, it ain't like I really want to hide stuff from Dad. I just don't want him to get stormy. I let him see the letter.

He didn't press his lips together to keep angry words in or push the letter away or get up and start pacing. He just sighed. I waited to see what he'd say, which was, "Guess maybe I should write him a letter too. What do you think?"

I hugged him real tight and said some stuff about open hands and not wanting people to slip away, which Dad must of understood, even with me speaking into his T-shirt more than the air, because he said me neither, and then he said, but it's better to keep hands open than gripped tight shut.

"Things that are set on leaving slip out anyway, like water, and fists never did welcome anything." He sounded sad. "New things flow in, though, if you keep your hands open."

I looked at him sidelong. Is that really supposed to make me feel better?

"You mean, like someone new to replace Ma?" I know they were sharp words. But you can't just replace people! If Jiminy goes away, you can't just replace him with Cody!

Dad looked toward the horizon. "No, I don't mean like that," he said, and the words were part of another sigh. I felt as rotten as three-day-old fish.

"Sorry."

Dad gave a smidge of a smile and shrugged.

"I meant more like that other prison pen pal of yours, that Jiminy mentioned."

That was another thing that bothered me about Jiminy's letter: he didn't understand about Kaya. But I can tell him more next time I write.

"She flowed into your life, didn't she."

"Actually, I fished for her, with a message in a bottle."

Dad's smile got bigger.

"Good catch, Em."

"I think the Seafather helped."

"He always does.

"And then she saved us," I said, warming up. It's more fun remembering good things than thinking on bad ones.

“How’s that now?”

“Didn’t I tell you? She’s the one, the lady overseas who gave the speech about us. She knew about us because of my letters.”

Dad couldn’t of been more stunned if an anchor fell on his head.

“Well I … You should … we should tell her thank you,” he said, his words staggering a bit, like they were dazed, too.

And maybe I swam right into that same anchor, because my head was ringing with what Dad said: we should tell her thank you. We should go on camera, like she did. Talk to the news people, like she did. And if everyone paid attention to us saying thank you, maybe her government would have to let her go, or at least take her out of the prison over the Ruby Lake.

“Do you think we really could? Go on the news and all?” I asked. “The people who followed y’all around when we were at Aunt Brenda’s, could we get them back again?”

“We can ask. Marcela will know. They were eager enough to come the first time round—couldn’t keep’m away with flyswatters.”

I jumped to my feet. “Then we can save her the way she saved us!” I didn’t add *maybe* or *I hope*. I wasn’t even thinking those things. I was feeling too sure. It was different from storm-sure, different from tidal-sure: it was surprise-sure, like Sabelle Morning being sure she’s going to board a merchant ship, and them not even knowing she’s coming. Wild, gleeful sure. *Dancing-sure,* came the thought in my mind, a visiting thought, a red-hot heartbeat thought, from someone with a red-hot heart.

Kaya’s Lady?

Chapter 12. Saying Thank You

October 10 (Em's diary)

Why is it already 4 PM? Why did I walk so slow to the post office? Why is the line so long at the checkout counter here at the gas station store? If this line doesn't get a move on, I'm going to pull Clara and Tammy out and they'll just have to skip getting Tootsie Pops. If we leave now and I run fast, I can still get back to school before Mr. Dubois leaves, I think.

When I stopped by the post office just now, there was a letter from Kaya, one she wrote on October 2, and now I'm afraid that my thank-you message idea may already be too late. That's why I need to get to Mr. Dubois's room. I need to look at a computer. I need to find out what's going on in W—.

That man I read about, the separatist that confessed: he *was* a friend of Kaya's. I knew he had to be. And the government killed him.

Kaya told me not to write her anymore. She was saying goodbye. It's like the Sabelle Morning story where Sabelle Morning gets captured and she sends a message to her first mate not to try a rescue, because it'll just put everyone in danger. Not that Benny Brave listened! But if I don't listen, it's not me that gets hurt, it's Kaya's mother and the other separatists, and Kaya too, it sounds like.

I need to find a computer.

Okay, Clara and Tammy have their Tootsie Pops. More later.

October 10 (Em's diary, second entry)

Oh please, Seafather, you know the movements of all deep-swimming things and the flavor of each wave. Please send me your strength and power. Mr. Ovey, granddad, everybody who lives beneath the waves, please: you too.

Clara and Tammy went on home, and I told Small Bill to go ahead too. Then I headed back to school.

I checked the parking lot first, to see if Mr. Dubois's car was still there. He runs the homework club, so a lot of times he stays late. And it was there! But when I went round to the front door, Mr. Barnes and Ms. Tennant were just coming out. Ms. Tennant was the last person I wanted to meet up with, so I doubled back the way I came and hurried around the rear of the building, looking in at each window until I found Mr. Dubois's room.

All the homework club kids had already left. He was alone in there, putting a stack of papers into his backpack. The window was cranked open, so I called in to him, but he didn't look up, and as he zipped the backpack closed, I noticed white wires coming down from his ears and vanishing into his shirt pocket. I rapped on the glass and waved, but still he didn't hear. He was swinging the backpack onto one shoulder and striding for the door. I took a deep breath, getting ready to really pound the window and yell, when a hand came down on my shoulder. I jumped, and something between a squeal and a scream came out of me.

"You know you're not supposed to loiter here after hours, don't you? No one should be on school property unless it's for school business. You have mischief on the mind?" It was Mr. Barnes, and hanging back a good ten feet was evil old Ms. Tennant, arms crossed and eyes all knives.

"I have to see Mr. Dubois," I blurted, forgetting all about "No sir." Mr. Barnes frowned.

"Then why didn't you come up to the front door? Why'd we see you dart away like some sort of delinquent?"

"And now we find you back here, getting ready to break windows." Of course Ms. Tennant had to stick her oar in. She turned to Mr. Barnes, and started in like I couldn't even hear, about how Mr. Dubois had supported and trusted me, and this is how I repay him.

"Whoa, what's happening out here? Who-all's repaying me for what now? Hello Em. Hello Charlie, Grace." All our commotion must of done what my calling and rapping couldn't, because Mr. Dubois was at the window now.

"Is that necessary?" he asked, nodding at Mr. Barnes's hand, which was still clamped like a vise on my shoulder. He let go. I leaned in on the window frame.

"Can I use your computer? I have to check about my friend Kaya and what's going on in her country! I'm afraid she's—"

"Em, you need to let Mr. Dubois go home now. Maybe he can help you tomorrow," Mr. Barnes said, while Ms. Tennant grumbled about attention-seeking behavior and teachers who enable it.

"Please?" I couldn't stop thinking of Kaya, trapped above the Ruby Lake, with no visitors and now no mail, either, writing "If I ever leave here."

"Sure, sure, come round to the front," he said, and then, over my head, "It's not a problem; don't worry," to Mr. Barnes and Ms.

Tennant. I snaked between them, leaving them to shake their heads and sigh together, and jogged back to the front. Mr. Dubois met me there.

"Now who's this Kaya? You said she's in another country? Is that why you were looking up … what was the name? It was one of those tiny places you barely even know is a country, I seem to recall."

"Yeah, W—. It's an island, here, see?"

I showed him the map that comes up over on the right if you search on W—, but then I put my new search in, adding "insurgents" and "Kayamanira" and "Ruby Lake" to W—. I could feel myself breaking out in a sweat, even though it's a pretty mild day and a breeze was coming in from the window we'd been talking through just minutes earlier.

"Huh, so that's where W— is. Tucked right in there with all those Indonesian islands. So you have a pen pal from W—, huh?

"She's more than a pen pal, she's a real friend. She's the person who saved Mermaid's Hands and she's a, a, an activist? A kind of protester? And she's in prison in her country and …" and then, maybe because of all the running, or maybe because of Mr. Barnes and Ms. Tennant, or maybe just because of worrying about Kaya, but I retched.

"Whoa, whoa, Em, you okay? Gently does it—here, sit tight a sec."

He hurried out of the room and came back with a paper cup of cold water from Mr. Barnes's office. He pulled his wheelie teacher-chair around next to me.

"I'm a little confused," he said, but his voice sounded more serious-worried than confused, and if I hadn't been so focused on finding out what's happening with Kaya, I might of heard my mind's warning bell, the one that goes off when grown-ups think you're doing something stupid or dangerous. "Wasn't it those people from Minorities Mobilize that changed the state's mind about Mermaid's Hands? And what's this about protestors and prison? I think you want to stay clear of ..." I followed his gaze to the article at the top of the screen. "Seventeen dead at US-owned logging camp," the headline said. By poison gas—an attack by the separatists.

I couldn't believe that, and I said so, quickly, but the serious-worry was settling heavy and thick on Mr. Dubois's face, and while I was insisting that Kaya's friends would never do a thing like that, Mr. Dubois was shaking his head and saying that violence and terrorism are never the answer. I backed up and told him about my message in a bottle, and about Kaya's prison above the Ruby Lake, and about how she got there. By the time I was done, he was biting his upper lip, and his eyebrows still hadn't lifted.

"I have a plan to help her," I said, "but see here?" I pointed to a story further down. "The Ruby Lake's going to erupt someday soon, and I can't even find out if Kaya's still in the Lotus or somewhere else. What if she's still there? The government needs to let her out of there."

I could feel my stomach churning again. I swallowed a couple of times and pressed my arms against my middle, trying to make my insides settle down.

"And how were you aiming to help her?" Mr. Dubois asked, after a moment.

I told him my idea, about getting the news to come out to

Mermaid's Hands again, so we could say a big public thank you. Then I showed him Kaya's letter, and where she said at the end about inviting me to come visit her.

"So maybe I'll also say how I want to meet her one day," I said. I reread the last line of the letter.

I wish you a bright future, filled with possibilities.

Last words. Last wishes. *No,* not *Kaya's last words.* Not *Kaya's last wishes. Just the end of this letter, that's all.* I had to scold myself something fierce to stop those bad thoughts. After a moment I noticed that Mr. Dubois hadn't said anything. I looked up.

"Maybe …"

I've never seen a teacher hesitate. They're always sure of everything. I waited. He took a deep breath and ran a hand over his shaved head.

"Here's the thing. It's awful to be in solitary confinement over a volcano. Almost too awful. Honestly, when you were talking, I thought maybe your Kaya was just a clever liar making up stories to get you to feel sorry for her. But then there's that," he said, tapping the computer screen. His finger was on the old story of Kaya's speech. He sighed.

"So, I guess the Lotus on the Ruby Lake is real, and that's bad. But it's hard to tell about all the rest of those stories. Hard to know what's true and what isn't.

"I know she feels like a friend to you," he continued. "But sometimes you can make mistakes about people, especially if you've never actually met them. Anyway, it's not just about her and you and your friendship. Stop and think about this a moment: Right now nobody connects Mermaid's Hands with Kaya or the separatists in

W—. But if you do a big public thank you, and if the government thinks of Kaya and the separatists as terrorists? Suddenly y'all are linked to terrorists. See how that could be bad?"

I did see. Things that make Mermaid's Hands look bad are dangerous—things like the Sandy Neck fishermen dumping their illegal catch in the back of Mr. Tiptoe's truck—because if Mermaid's Hands looks bad, the state might decide to tear it down after all. We've got a lot to lose.

But Kaya had a whole lot to lose, too, when she spoke up for us, and it didn't stop her. I want to be like Kaya.

"I have to try to help her," I said. "No matter what."

"I understand how you feel," said Mr. Dubois, "but you know, there are organizations that do this sort of thing all the time, organizations just for helping political prisoners. They can do research, send letters—they've got years of experience. And they're not putting their homes at risk. You could get in touch with one of them." He typed "Amnesty International" into the search bar, and the articles about W— and Kaya disappeared.

"But I know her. And I *am* her friend." I couldn't get my voice above a whisper. It sounded babyish in my ears. Mr. Dubois had a sad, kind of wistful expression on his face, as if he was thinking about something lost or broken.

"There's another thing," he said. "There's, well, there's what it would mean for you, personally, if you went in front of the cameras … because they, the news people … you know, they like to find out all about a person and their family … And, well, Jiminy …" Mr. Dubois's gaze went to classroom's ugly speckled floor. "His situation … That might have an effect, too, on how people look at

Mermaid's Hands. It's possible it could even have consequences for Kaya."

The words were a punch in the gut. I wanted to be out of that chair, out of that room, out of that school. I wanted to be running across the mudflats home. But instead I just sat there, staring at six different links for Amnesty International.

"I'm sorry," Mr. Dubois mumbled. "That came out all wrong. That last part probably isn't even true. Listen, it's just that you're a bright kid, a good kid, and I want you to have the best possible future. Like Kaya said."

I pushed out of the chair and gathered up my things. "Yeah. Yeah, I understand. Thanks. I'll … I'll … Well, I gotta go now, but …"

"Okay." He looked pained. Why? It ain't like anyone just said to him that his family shame could sink his home and hurt his friends. "I'll see if Amnesty International already has a campaign for Kaya," he continued. "If they don't, I'll find an address for you to write to, okay? By email. You can use my computer."

I was at the door by then, but I nodded.

I think he started to say one more thing—I think he called my name—but I was already running, as hard as I could, until my lungs and legs felt like they were on fire, and I still kept right on running. Too bad I didn't burn up: I would of been happy if I could of turned into a flame.

I was panting and sticky by the time I reached Mermaid's Hands. A knot of grown-ups were standing outside the Tiptoes' house, so I slowed down to catch my breath and cool off some before I reached them. Small Bill waved from on top of the pile of salvaged corrugated steel roofing panels for our kitchen roof, and a bunch of heads turned my way: first Mrs. Ovey and Dad, then Mr. Tiptoe, then Auntie Chicoree and Tomtale and Marcela. They didn't turn back to their conversation. They just stayed staring at me as I got closer. The hairs on my neck and arms stood to attention.

"What's going on?" I asked.

"Can I see your letters?" Clara asked. "From the lady who saved Mermaid's Hands?" She and Tammy were sitting on the Tiptoes' veranda.

"I was talking to Marcela here about saying thank you," Dad explained.

"I'm so sorry Minorities Mobilize didn't follow through on advocating for your friend," Marcela said, voice full of regret. "I was all caught up with work here in Mermaid's Hands; I didn't think to ask if a campaign for W—'s mountain people had gotten off the ground. I know everyone was really busy with the Rohingya campaign … I guess it pushed the W— situation off the radar."

"Can we do something now? Can we make a Mermaid's Hands thank you?" I asked, turning to Mrs. Ovey. She was smiling—like she used to before Mr. Ovey went under the waves.

"I think we should dye some shirts specially, each one with a letter on it, so you kids can spell out 'thank you,'" she said.

I felt warmth spread through me, so different from the fire that had been raging in me on the way home. This was a *good* feeling. But there, still, at the back of my mind, were Mr. Dubois's words and warnings. Would everybody still want to say thank you if they knew about the risks?

I thought about not telling them. I know Kaya's not a terrorist.

But what if everything happens the way Mr. Dubois says it might? What if suddenly the state changes its mind and says *take down those houses*?

"Mr. Dubois said that some people might think Kaya's connected to terrorists, and that if they think that, thanking her may turn them against us," I said.

Mr. Tiptoe nodded. "I know. He left a message on my phone."

"He did?" *He was that worried?*

"Yep." Mr. Tiptoe shrugged. "She can be a terrorist for all I care. Somebody helps us, we say thank you."

"That's right," murmured Tomtale, giving Marcela a squeeze.

"Mmm hmmm," agreed Mrs. Ovey, nodding, and everyone else joined in with an of-course or a no-question. Each one was like a sun ray, and I was the cup catching them all. I was shining inside.

"I'll tell her how we never forget our friends," I said. "I'll tell her how we'll sing her name to—"

"Whoa, whoa, hold on," said Mr. Tiptoe, casting a quick glance Dad's way. "I don't know that the news people are gonna want to film each and every seachild saying personal thanks, Minnow Em. What do you think, Marcy?"

"Well, I …" Her eyes flitted from Mr. Tiptoe to me to Tomtale to Dad.

Of course: Mr. Dubois must of mentioned about Jiminy, too, when he left his message on Mr. Tiptoe's phone. The punched-gut feeling was back again.

"I think Em has to say something, though, don't she? Seeing as she's the one that made friends with Kaya in the first place." Dad's tone was light, but I know Dad, and I could sense his temper rising.

He and Mr. Tiptoe locked eyes in an invisible tug of war, each trying to pull something from the other just with the strength of their gaze. Dad won. Mr. Tiptoe shrugged.

"Well sure, that only makes sense, I guess," he said, like it was no big deal. Marcela grinned, and Small Bill cheered.

"Those T-shirts, do you think we can make them right away?" I asked Mrs. Ovey. And then, to Marcela, "Can we get the news to come on Sunday?"

"That soon? Don't we want to plan it out a little?" Auntie Chicoree asked.

Thoughts of Kaya and the Ruby Lake were making my stomach twist and flip-flop like a fish on dry land.

"There ain't time. She's in danger," I said. Everyone was quiet. It hit me: to them it's just a thank-you, not a rescue mission.

"We can get those shirts dyed in no time," said Mrs. Ovey.

"I'll call my friends in Cambridge," Marcela said, "and see if they can get any national-level news guys to cover the story. I don't know if we can manage Sunday, but I'll tell them time's of the essence."

We all broke up for supper after that. I've been writing this in the dark—but in our own new house. It's practically finished. But I have to sleep now.

I hope this plan works. I wish I had arms as strong as Vaillant and could swim to W— … or wings, like a seagull—or a crow. Or even a red-winged blackbird.

October 13 (Em's diary)

Today was the day. We got the T-shirts finished yesterday, and Marcela contacted the news people. I thought there were going to be bunches of them, with lots of lights flashing as they took pictures and lots of cameras with news station names on them, like we saw on TV at Aunt Brenda's house when that football player who crashed into a school bus gave an interview, but there were just two people from a newspaper—a photographer and a reporter—and two from a news station, one with a TV camera perched like a roosting duck on her shoulder and the other dressed in a bright yellow jacket and high heels to match, to stand in front of the camera and talk.

The newspaper reporter had hair like crimped copper wire and lots of freckles up and down his arms. Small Bill said he'd come here before, when me and Tammy were at Aunt Brenda's and everybody in Mermaid's Hands was clinging to the Winterhulls' house, hoping to get permission to rebuild.

The woman with the yellow heels was sinking into the mud each step she took, leaving a trail of dots like clam breathing holes. She looked cross about it. Too bad, because she was pretty, even though her hair was relaxed, which Gran doesn't like. Gran says in the merlands, everyone's hair floats in a cloud around their face, and seachildren should remember that.

Both the TV woman and the newspaper reporter talked a while to Mr. Tiptoe, while the photographer snapped pictures. Then the TV woman stood in front of us kids and said some words to the TV camera, and the camerawoman turned slowly from left to right so that the camera could get a good look at all of us as we shouted out

"Thank you Kaya!" I wanted to say something more, but the camerawoman was already detaching things and putting them in a bag, and the woman in the yellow heels was busy tapping something out on her phone.

The newspaper reporter came over, though.

"Hi there," he said. "You're Emlee Baptiste, right? My name's Justin Landau. Can I ask you some questions?" The lines by his mouth and eyes as he smiled matched Dad's. I felt my courage come alight.

"Can I say some things of my own, too?" I asked.

"Sure you can. What do you have to tell me?"

I took a deep breath and started talking as fast as I could because I didn't know how much space was on his recorder or when he'd decide he'd heard enough. Finally I figured I'd covered just about everything and said I was ready for his questions. He laughed.

"Well, I reckon you've answered most of them. That's one amazing story, about how you happened to start corresponding. A message in a bottle. What are the chances it ends up in the hands of a prisoner—sitting in a volcano crater, no less." He shook his head.

But the chances are one hundred percent, because that's what happened.

"Political prisoner," I said. Adding the word "political" turns Kaya from a bad guy to a good guy.

"Political prisoner," he repeated. He was looking at me like he was trying to guess my height or weight, and then, out of the blue,

"So Em, I heard you have a family member in prison, yourself. Your brother, right? Do you think that made you extra interested in writing to Kaya?"

Just like Mr. Dubois warned. I swallowed.

"Maybe," I said. "Maybe a little." Mr. Landau nodded and waited expectantly. What did he want me to say?

"Maybe it worked a little the other way, though, too," I said, finally. "Maybe writing to Kaya made me want to try writing to Jiminy more." I struggled hard to keep my voice from sliding into a mumble there at the end. Then, remembering what else Mr. Dubois had said, I added,

"Just because my brother … just because he's in prison don't mean only criminals or families of criminals support Kaya."

Criminal. I hate that word. Jiminy is more than "criminal." Only for Kaya's sake—just for her—I made myself say those words: *Criminals* and *families of criminals.*

"Lots of people in W— support her," I said. "And I bet lots of people all over the world would support her, if they knew about her."

"No doubt, if she's like you described," Mr. Landau said, nodding.

Will he think she's like I've described when he reads all the stories about the troubles in W—? Maybe he's already read them. He did his homework on me, so maybe he learned all about Kaya, too.

"Will you put what I said about Kaya in your story? Make people care about what happens to her?"

"I'll see what I can do," he said with a grin, making the Dad-style smile lines appear on his face.

And don't mention about Jiminy, I wanted to say, but before I could work up the nerve, Mr. Landau was sticking out his hand and thanking me for my time.

After dinner, I went looking for Marcela. I found her playing catch with Tomtale and Windward Fearing, Tomtale's baby nephew, half on the Ikahos' veranda and half in the incoming tide, with Granny Ikaho watching. The sun was nearly gone, and everything was rosy-flame colored. Windward was waving his arms and squealing every time the ball splashed in the water, and that was making Tomtale and Marcela laugh. If you pretended Tomtale and Marcela were married, and that Windward was their kid instead of Tomtale's nephew, then it would be like Ma and Dad and Jiminy, before I was born.

I'm glad Dad wasn't with me. I bet it would of made him feel lonesome and regretful, seeing that scene. It kind of made me feel that way.

"Hey Em," said Tomtale, tossing the ball to Marcela and steadying Windward. "What's up?"

"First stars," I said, pointing to the sky.

"You gonna wish on one?" Marcela asked.

That's a dry-land charm, wishing on stars. I wonder if Dad knows that. Maybe that's why he thought to catch starlight for Ma. I told Marcela I had at least as many wishes as there were stars shining, and she told me that you're only allowed to wish on the first one you see.

"But I noticed that one and that one at the same time, and that one too," I protested.

She shrugged and grinned.

"I dunno, then." She set the ball down on the veranda. Granny Ikaho nudged it with her foot and sent it rolling toward Windward, who crouched and caught it with his whole body.

"I came by to say thank you. For calling the news people," I said.

"Oh, you're welcome," she said. "Justin told me he'd email me the photos Ed took. He said it's all right with the newspaper if we put them on the Minorities Mobilize website. We'll link to the story too, when it comes out. Hopefully people will notice!"

"Do you think they will?" My voice sounded thin in my ears. "Will people in other countries see it? Will it be in Google News?"

Her smile faded to something small and apologetic.

"I can't say for sure. I think it went to the right department at the AP wire service—I think. And we did send a note to a freelance reporter we know who tries to bring lesser-known human rights situations to light, but it all depends on what other news is going on and whether the editors want the story. But you know, our website gets thousands of views each day, and it's a good story, an important story, so ..."

Her hand brushed mine, a light touch.

"Ba! Ba!" Windward squealed, pointing. The ball bumped up against Marcela's ankles, and she pushed it back toward him.

I cast around for words.

"I guess I know what to use my wish on, then."

"Use all three," Marcela said. "It can't hurt to try."

October 14 (from the Mobile *Press-Register*)

Small community, big thank you

By Justin Landau

The residents of the tiny offshore community of Mermaid's Hands issued a public thank-you to an unusual benefactor yesterday. After Hurricane Helga wiped out the collection of 10 houses last month, state officials, spurred by complaints from coastal fishermen and conservationists, issued an injunction against rebuilding in their controversial location on the tidal mudflats off the coast of Sandy Neck and the Sunset Bay Conservation Area.

Then came intervention from the other side of the globe, in the form of a speech by Kayamanira (Kaya) Matarayi, a separatist leader from the Southeast Asian nation of W—. Kaya mentioned the plight of the people of Mermaid's Hands in connection with the situation of her own people, W—'s mountain minority.

Her remarks brought Mermaid's Hands to the attention of Minorities Mobilize, whose advocacy has been credited in the state's change of position on the village.

"We've already thanked our friends at

Minorities Mobilize," said Mr. Brett Tiptoe, the community's spokesperson. "Now we want to thank Kaya."

The children of Mermaid's Hands donned special T-shirts with letters on them to spell out a thank-you message. [photo]

But how did someone on the other side of the globe come to know about a community that almost none have ever heard of, even here on the Gulf Coast? Apparently through correspondence with one young resident of Mermaid's Hands, Emlee Baptiste (12), who has been writing to Kaya since July. While the US government has not taken an official position on the ethnic conflict in W—, Emlee is understandably supportive of her friend.

"I want to visit her one day," Emlee said. "I'd visit her tomorrow if I could. I hope she's okay."

There has been no news out of W— about Kaya for several weeks. It is not even clear whether she is still occupying the volcano temple where she was originally held or has been moved to a different location. The level of the lava lake in Abenanyi's crater has been rising steadily, and volcanologists say the volcano is likely to erupt within the next month.

Chapter 13. Without Friends or Family

October 5 (Kaya's journal)

A supply helicopter came today. It's been fifteen days. The clouds from the Ruby Lake are not much changed from yesterday and the day before, so I'm grateful to the powers that be that they decided today was a day they could risk a flight. My water ran out yesterday. Two from the State Security Service came as well, the Bully and a new one, not Friendlier. A shorter man with an angry pout and frightened eyes. They stood between me and the replacement water tank.

"Are you in contact with the insurgency?" the Bully asked abruptly.

I spread my arms. Nothing of the outside world was visible beyond the cloud towers rising from the Ruby Lake. No outside sounds reached our ears, only the Ruby Lake's own unquiet voice and the slowing blades of the helicopter.

"How?" I asked, glad that Sumi wasn't around to catch their eye and give them ideas. Though, what if she returned while they were here—worse, returned with a message? My pulse pounded in my ears.

"Three of the people we brought in for questioning after the Jarakasan Lake disaster said the directive to plant the rebel flag by the lake came from you."

"Did you know what was going to happen at the lake?" Pouty asked, his voice every bit as petulant and aggrieved as his lower lip suggested it would be.

"You wouldn't like my answer," I replied, but in the mountain tongue.

"Speak properly," snapped the Bully, and it was foolish of me to taunt him by saying "this *is* properly," still in the mountain tongue, because I was not fast enough to avoid his quick hand today. This time he grabbed my wrist and twisted my arm, making me stumble and, to my shame, cry out.

"Speak properly, or next time we'll bring one of the local brats along to translate for you, and you wouldn't want that."

"You know my circumstances. You put me here. You know every object that's in that house." The pounding of the blood in my ears, my eyes. I was seeing red, Ruby Lake red. "But if I *could* pass a message along, it would be to plant flags everywhere within the Lady's reach."

"Anything in there that could be used for signaling?" Pouty asked, addressing the Bully, not me. The Bully released my wrist and strode past me and into the house, leaving Pouty behind, hand resting on his pistol, as if he were afraid I might charge him.

"He thinks you know when and where eruptions are going to happen," Pouty said, pointing with his elbow at the pilot.

"I'm not a volcanologist," I said.

Pouty glanced past the platform railing at the Ruby Lake. "It's been letting off steam up to now, but the whole thing's going to blow one day soon," he said, grinning slightly.

"Even a botanist can predict that much," I replied. Pouty's grin widened.

"And yet here you sit. Getting pretty warm, eh?"

I looked away. The Bully was returning, carrying the metal cup, plate, and bowl I'd been provided with when I was brought here. He held up the plate, which winked in a stray beam of hazy sunlight.

"You can't be serious," I said. "A tiny pinprick of light like that can't pierce these clouds."

Could it? The plate was stainless steel; it had a high shine. Could I have been sending messages with flashes of light to watchers on the crater's edge, if I had thought to do so?

"Are you in contact with the insurgency?" the Bully asked again.

"I'm not sending messages with my dinner plate, no."

From overhead, the sound of wingbeats on the air. *Not now!* I prayed, but I couldn't stop myself from glancing skyward. It wasn't Sumi. It was two cuckooshrikes, already disappearing from view. My eyes returned to the Bully. He was smiling.

"That pet of yours. The crow. That's how you've been communicating," he said triumphantly.

"I think you have crows confused with homing pigeons," I said, but the Bully just shook his head and laughed as he headed for the helicopter, waving for Pouty to follow. He pulled a phone from his pocket, and although I couldn't make out what he said, I caught the word "crows" and the name of my town. He looked back over his shoulder.

"You're finished now," he said, voice positively mirthful. "I imagine we'll be back shortly to bring you in. Leave those by the water tank," he added as the pilot approached him, small sacks of cornmeal and rice under one arm and a net bag filled with vegetables dangling from the other.

"How about my cup and bowl, and my plate?" I called.

"Confiscated," he called back, climbing into the cabin.

"I'm sorry," the pilot whispered as he set down the food. "Please—" He looked in pain, his forehead was so creased, but it must just have been anxiety. He raised clasped hands, but was called back before he could make his request.

As if I could grant requests.

I must warn my mother, but the only way I have to warn her is through Sumi, and the State Security Service will be watching for Sumi now.

And even as I write, here Sumi is now, black bedragglement on the guard rail, and with a note tied to her leg.

October 5 (Kaya's mother to Kaya)

My dear girl,

I don't know how to tell you these things. There is no honey to be had if you bear with the sting of the news—it's wasps who rule the world right now.

Grandmother Jemenli has said I should leave town, Tatamaneh says so too. Captain Tata, we're calling him now—he's become the de facto leader on the ground here—but I remember when he was known as the Limping Boy, the last time round. They've told me they'll take me to a safe spot in the mountains. Rami's grandparents are already there, and Jeteman's mother and brothers.

I said I couldn't leave you with no link to the outside world, but they reminded me of the watchers who sit in their jeep, smoking, and keeping an eye on our house, and the ones whom I always see if I look over my shoulder in town, while I'm shopping, or the ones I catch lounging by Satmelelin's snack stand, when I take washing down to the river.

"They prefer meat, you know," one of the men called up to me last night, when I was scattering corn for the crows. "There's a dead rat here you can have. They'll love the taste." The other two laughed. I didn't answer, but it was unsettling.

I do that—feed all the crows—as cover for Sumi. I leave the door ajar, and while the other birds are pecking and fluttering, she bobs right into the house, unnoticed. Or did.

Captain Tata said you'd prefer to have me safely hidden away than arrested. He pointed out that by taking myself out of danger, I'd deprive the State Security Service of a tool to use to coerce you. Put that way, it seems like my duty to leave, much as I dislike hearing it.

The rest of what Captain Tata says, what he hears from the capital, I like even less. The word "purge" keeps on turning up, which seems to indicate the worst for all of you. But then he says there's talk of ringleaders taking advantage of naive youth—which sounded at first to my ears as if perhaps they were looking for a way to pull back from their harsh position, as if maybe Rami could be the sacrifice for all of you—except Captain Tata says that since the Lake Jarakasan disaster, Rami's name never gets mentioned without yours being mentioned too. They're making you out to be a wild-eyed religious fanatic who's trying to drag the mountains back to the Stone Age and who's likely to bring the nation down in the process.

For so long I've been petitioning for your transfer to somewhere safer, but now I'm frightened that a move would be prelude to a death sentence. And yet it's certain death if you stay where you are. What can I say. If you do get moved to the prison, keep your eyes open. Some of the young firebrands who've joined the resistance are talking about staging a breakout. They've never left the mountains and don't realize how dangerous it is to have a mountain face in the lowlands right now. And yet foolish daring may well be our best hope right now.

I wish Sumi could lend you her wings.

If you can send her back to me tonight, after reading this, do. Then I'll know you've had my message. I won't leave here until the dark hours of earliest morning.

Thinking of you always,
your mother

October 5 (Kaya's journal, second entry)

Where are you, Lady?

October 5 (Kaya's journal, third entry)

I don't think I called to her out loud. It was just within me, my cry, and I wrote it down, right there, underneath the pictures of the flowers and fruit of *Schima wallichii,* the needlewood tree.

What happened next … I closed my eyes to keep back tears, and suddenly there were the Lady's hot hands, pressed against them, as if we were playing guess-who, and her voice right in my ear, saying "Did you misplace me?" Then she let her hands drop to my arms, turned me round, and pulled me close, like a mother with a worried child.

I thought I was on fire. She let go and frowned, looking me up and down—I felt so insufficient!—but she said only, "I keep forgetting how fragile you are and how quickly fierceness wears you out." She sighed. "I do wish you could dance with me, little Kaya."

"I wish I could, too," I said.

Then her glum face brightened, and I realized I wasn't looking up at her anymore, but down on her. She was child-sized and shaped, with eyes full of mischief and the corners of her mouth lifting in the beginnings of a wicked grin. "I'm going to make more trouble for your enemies," she said. "Smoky farts from my butthole in Taneh! They won't like that!"

I couldn't help laughing.

"I guess they won't," I said.

She closed her eyes and let the grin spread across her face.

"They'll be busy putting out fires," she said. Then she opened her eyes wide, and we were face to face, and she was not a child or a bride or an old woman; she was ageless. And she said, "So they won't be ready, when I pour out my heart."

My own heart caught in my throat.

"If you pour out your heart, it will hurt my friends as much as my enemies."

"No, Kaya. No it won't, because you'll teach me the way to move. You'll trace me a path, and I'll follow. See? We *will* dance together."

It came to me then: I am going to die here. I don't mind. I think the heat from the Lady's gaze has burned all fear out of me. Death will be an embrace, her embrace. I see there are blisters on my arms where she held me just now, but strangely, they don't hurt.

October 5 (Kaya to her mother)

Dear Mother,

Captain Tata is absolutely right—I want you safely away from the State Security Service's clutches. As for me, I promise you: I will never sit in that lowland prison, and they will never execute me. Religious fanatic, am I? If so, they have only themselves to blame. Build a temple and you'll get a priestess. So they can say what they want. If blaming me makes them go easier on the others, all the better.

Here: let me prophesy a little. The vents in Taneh that have been releasing steam are going to release ash soon, and more land will burn. Tell them that. They may want to evacuate. Send that message to the media. Let everyone know that the State Security Service may have troops and weapons, but we have the Lady.

Your loving fanatic—

Kaya

(Report, Darwin Volcanic Ash Advisory Center)

On October 7, dark ash plumes erupted from the recently opened Taneh vents, 30 km north of the lava lake in the Mt. Abenanyi crater. The plumes were blown to the NW; ashfall in the foothill town of Rai is blamed for two wildfires and significant property damage.

Seismic activity is up markedly since July, and the level of the lava lake has risen precipitously.

(From the October 8 transcript of interviews with Prisoner 117, State Security Service files on the insurgency)

Lt. Vell: We want to talk to you about the situation in the mountain districts—

117: What about my wife? How is she doing? Is she okay? How's the baby? It's due any day now. You've got to release her, at least for the birth! A baby shouldn't be born in prison.

Lt. Sana: Oh no, I don't think a release is possible. Her charges are more serious than yours, what with her threats against the MP from the western mountain district.

117: What are you talking about? You've never said anything about threats before. All these months, coming in here, all the questions, all the accusations ... This is insane. Mirasan never threatened Mr. Gana; none of us did. Hell, I invited him to come to the festival.

Lt. Sana: The *demonstration*.

Lt. Vell: Kaya said that she proposed having the mob attack him.

117: That's the craziest lie I've ever heard

in my life. Mirasan can't even bear to swat flies or crush spiders. She'd never suggest such a thing, and Kaya would never say she did! You're just making things up!

Lt. Sana: She confessed.

117: What?

Lt. Sana: Your wife confessed.

117: She couldn't have. Why would she, when it's a lie? You must have ... What did you do to her? I swear I'll crush every bone in your body with my bare hands if I hear that you hurt her, you piece of sh—

Lt. Vell: Assistance in here please!

[Prisoner 117 subdued and restrained]

Lt. Vell: Well that wasn't a very promising display. But I understand; you're feeling emotional. Now listen. Maybe something can be arranged for your wife. Maybe we can have her transferred to a hospital for the birth, and possibly we can see about a reduced or commuted sentence, but that depends on you.

117: [no response]

Lt. Vell: Can we have some towels and water, please? Clean off his face. And bring in a cup of water as well. There. That's better. Go ahead; drink up.

Lt. Sana: It's bad in the mountains right now. The worst sort of unscrupulous, opportunistic troublemakers have surfaced, and they're preying on you people's ignorance and superstition, vandalizing property and inciting violence. It's a volatile situation, and it's getting worse.

Lt. Vell: You're interested in public service. You've had the benefit of a good education. You made the mistake of letting your childhood pals rope you into a foolish venture, but you're no separatist, are you. You know the mountain regions can only prosper as part of a prosperous W—. That's how *you* will prosper. If charges against you were dropped, you could go back and advocate restraint. Help steer things back in a rational direction.

117: I won't be your tool.

Lt. Vell: It's in your interests too, you

know. Your family owns a fair amount of property, doesn't it? If resentments are fanned high enough, the mobs may not limit their attacks to government offices and lowland-owned businesses. You don't want to collaborate, but your wealth and education mean you're already a collaborator. It's just a matter of time before the mobs realize that.

117: Then they're hardly going to listen to me, are they.

Lt. Vell: Right now they think of you as one of the heroes of their cause.

117: That won't last, not if I start singing your tune.

Lt. Sana: You're a clever man. You'll find a way. You have to; you have your wife and child to think about. You want to secure the best possible future for them—certainly you don't want any harm coming to them.

Lt. Vell: And don't think of it as our tune. Think of it as your tune. It's a better future for you, too. The man who brought peace? Nice ring to it. A better future for everybody.

117: [no response]

Lt. Sana: Well?

117: Mirasan will deliver in a proper hospital? With proper medical attention? And charges against her will be dropped?

Lt. Vell: Safe delivery of the baby, yes. No promises about the rest. It depends on your commitment and efforts.

117: [no response]

Lt. Sana: Don't keep us waiting.

117: All right. All right, I'll see what I can do.

October 9 (Palem *Courier*, online English-language edition)

New State Security Service contingents sent to Eastern, Western Mountain Districts

Mr. Bal (MP, Eastern Mountain District) and Mr. Gana (MP, Western Mountain District) welcomed the deployment of two more units of State Security Service troops to restore order in the increasingly anarchic mountain regions. Troops have also been assigned to protect the field headquarters of US-owned Adze Forest Products and the operations of China's Shanyan Logging, which obtained a concession in the western mountain district just last year. The Kaiten copper mine in the east and the major coffee and cardamom plantations in the west will also receive protection.

There are unconfirmed reports that reconnaissance helicopters fired on sites deep in the mountains that are believed to be bases for insurgent operations. Tempering military action with a conciliatory gesture, the government announced the release into house arrest of Nawalam Sashirayi, one of the instigators of this round of agitation. In a prepared statement, Mr. Sashirayi said he regretted the descent into violence that has followed the agitators' initial demonstration in January, and he explicitly repudiated recent separatist actions. A spokesman for the State Security Service wouldn't comment on the fate of Mr. Sashirayi's coconspirators except to say that those who undermine the well-being of the country deserve the harshest punishment.

(From the W— State Security Service's files on the insurgency: email records)

From: Lt. Sana
Subject: Re: Re: The situation with Prisoner 116
Date: October 11
To: Capt. Aran

Yes, I admit it was my responsibility to bring her in. It's a very temporary setback that will be corrected as soon as it's clear enough to take the helicopter over again.

With respect, no one could have predicted 116's behavior. That volcano's going to erupt in what, a week? two weeks? I'd bet a month's pay that it blows before the month is out. She should have been desperate to get the hell out of there. Instead, we order her into the helicopter, she says no. Vell and I go to grab her, she climbs up on the guard rail and starts spewing monkey talk at us, reverting to intelligible speech just to say that if we come one step nearer, she'll jump.

That would have suited me just fine, save us time and effort, but Vell pointed out that self-immolations are the sort of thing that set the human-rights crowd weeping and hand wringing. And I agree that we need to make it clear that no one dies unless we say so. We let 116 dive into the lava lake and this miserable lot are likely to whoop and cheer and count it a victory.

By the time it's safe to take the helicopter back there, her food and water will have run out, and I doubt she'll be in any state to make grand gestures. Just give me another week or 10 days.

(From the W— State Security Service's files on the insurgency: email records)

From: Lt. Den
Subject: useful re: Prisoner 116?
Date: October 15
To: Lt. Sana (attachment)

I know it's none of my business anymore, but this news brief might be useful to you. The girl mentioned in it is the one 116 was sending letters to, remember? See where she says she wants to come here? She'd come tomorrow, she says. I wonder if Aran could get her issued an invite. It would be a PR win for the government, and I bet it would make 116 putty in your hands.

Makes you almost think twice about having opposed the correspondence, huh!

Chapter 14. Casting a Strong Net

October 15 (Em's diary)

I saw Mr. Ovey last night. Maybe it was a dream, but it didn't feel like a dream … though I don't remember going out to sit on the veranda, which is where I was when I saw him. My feet were hanging over the edge, just above the water. I was watching a huge squashed-egg of a moon sinking in the west. Fish were jumping. I could hear the splash of them over the sound of the sea, and here and there I caught sight of their glint. And then there he was, breaking the surface just like a fish, right by the house. He put his elbows on the veranda and rested his chin on his hands and looked up at me. I was afraid he might choke or gasp, what with being up in the air and all, but he didn't seem to mind a bit.

"Hello, seaheart," he said. Not sweetheart. Seaheart.

I felt so many questions bubbling up in me, things I wanted to ask about the Seafather and the merfolk and life under the waves, and about hurricanes and families, and about your heart aching for people, and that last one made me realize that I might ought to go fetch Small Bill, because here was his father, but just then Mr. Ovey said,

"You cast a strong net for family, just the way a seachild should. Good girl. Sea families have all kinds of members, don't they. Seawater's blood, blood's seawater. You grip that net tight. You'll bring'm all into the boat safe." Then he slipped his arms back into the water, and he was going to go back under, and I don't know if I said it or thought it: "But Small Bill!"

I meant, *don't go yet!* I meant, *Small Bill and Mrs. Ovey and Lindie and Jenya'll want to see you too.*

Why'd you come to me when your own family's missing you so?

"Nice job he's done with the kitchen roofing for your place, and your uncle's," Mr. Ovey said. Called out, more like. He was already small, far away in the water, but I could hear pride in his voice. "Deena's gonna have a heart attack if she catches him jumping from up there, though, even if it is high tide. Tell'm that, and keep'm in your net!"

Then it was just waves and stars out there, and the fish weren't jumping anymore.

I don't remember how I got back to my bed, but that's where I woke up this morning. I know it sounds like it must of been a dream, but I don't think so. It was extra real. It felt more real than lots of regular days have felt.

On the way to school, I asked Small Bill if he'd seen his dad ever, since his dad was called under.

"Once, I think," he said, squinting into the sun. "He was way out … way out there. But he waved at me, and even though I couldn't see his face, I could tell he was smiling."

I nodded hard, remembering how it was last night, when Mr. Ovey was swimming away. "Yeah! like you could feel or hear it." Small Bill looked at me with raised eyebrows—double question marks. I told him about seeing his dad and gave him the message about not jumping off the kitchen roof.

"You saw me do that?" A smile flashed across his face, but what stuck there was a kind of glare, angry-embarrassed.

"I didn't see! Bet it was sweet, though." I wanted to get him to smile again. Plus, I bet his jump *was* sweet. I kind of want to try, myself.

Small Bill's smile didn't exactly reappear, but the glare faded into something near.

"It was … You didn't see it at all? So it really … really was my dad. My dad saw me."

Our eyes met. His were wide and brimming, but he didn't look away.

"He doesn't want you to give your ma a heart attack," I said, and that made him laugh—which made me feel like I'd scooped sunshine off the waves.

Small Bill's part of the family I've caught in my net. Don't you worry, Mr. Ovey. I ain't tossing him back.

October 17 (Em's diary)

I can hardly believe this. It's like I've wandered into a dream and forgotten to wake up—which is good. I need to stay in this dream a while longer!

It started in second period, when I got called to the principal's office. At that point it was setting up to be a bad dream: as I walked down the hall, I was going over everything I'd done all week long, trying to think what it was that I was in trouble for, but I couldn't come up with a single thing.

It didn't seem much better when I was face to face with Mr. Barnes. Both ends of his mouth were sloping down and it was choppy seas up there on his forehead. He had some papers in one hand and a stiff, shiny cardboard envelope in the other. The envelope had a red swooshing line across the front, with words that weren't English, and there was some kind of official-looking label on the front, and something stamped over the corner of that.

"It's from the government of W—," Mr. Barnes said. He held out one of the papers, and I could see the letterhead underneath a circular seal with an image of a bird whose tail swept over its head, its tips in flames. Government of W—, Ministry of Law and Justice it said, and then under that, another seal, a round shield with little flowers curling around it. State Security Service, it said. Panic juice spread out from my heart to the ends of my fingers and toes. I licked my lips.

"It's for you," Mr. Barnes said, pushing the letter closer. I took it. "They didn't know how to reach you, so they sent it care of the school."

I took my eyes off the words *State Security Service* and made them read the letter. *Touched by your concern … desire to foster warm relations … untangle domestic problems here … extend an invitation*

Extend an invitation?

In light of circumstances … expedited travel arrangements … and then a lot of details.

"They're inviting me to visit Kaya," I said, looking up at Mr. Barnes, who pursed his lips and said,

"I'm afraid I don't know anything to speak of about current events or political figures in W—, but yes, that seems to be the case."

"Because of our thank you," I said, even though I don't suppose Mr. Barnes paid much attention to Mermaid's Hands' thank you.

The sound of arguing floated in from the main office, where Mrs. Evans sits. She answers the phone, marks down kids who arrive late, and ushers us in to Mr. Barnes's lair when we get in trouble. This time, though, she seemed to be trying to keep someone—lots of someones—out, but it didn't work: the door behind me opened, and a bunch of people with cameras piled in, with Mrs. Evans following and scolding. There was all kind of flashing and popping, way more than for our Mermaid's Hands thank you, and questions coming at me and Mr. Barnes too quick for us to catch them all. I recognized the copper wire hair of Mr. Landau, the newspaper reporter I'd talked to back on Monday. He winked at me when our eyes met and called out,

"You like this turn of events, Em?"

"It's beyond my wildest dreams," I said, and then there were more camera flashes, so many that I was seeing black and red dots in front of my eyes.

I never thought I'd get a chance to say "beyond my wildest dreams" in real life, especially seeing as I have pretty wild dreams.

The questions were things like how long had I known Kaya and would my parents let me go, and would they travel with me, and mixed in with those, a few I didn't like the sound of—one asking did Kaya ever say anything in her letters to try to justify the loss of life and damage to property the insurgency had caused, and someone asking Mr. Barnes what he thought of his students being made into pawns in political games—but by this time Mr. Barnes's and Mrs. Evans's raised hands and raised voices were starting to have an effect, and everyone was quieting down. Mr. Barnes said he was sorry, but this was really too much of a disruption for a school that had already had plenty of disruption this year, and perhaps they could come back for twenty minutes or so when the school day was over. Then Mrs. Evans shooed them back out to the foyer and the front door. I could see the heads of teachers and kids peering out from nearby classrooms.

"… trouble with the law, like her brother," someone said, and "you see any police cars out front?" Hearing that kind of thing is like being force-fed rusty nails, but right then it couldn't hurt me. The letter in my hand, inviting me to W—, was like a double hull of stainless steel.

Mrs. Evans shut the door to the main office. She and Mr. Barnes exchanged a look.

"Well, that's not something that happens every day," Mrs. Evans said.

"I'd like more of the everyday days and fewer of the extraordinary ones," Mr. Barnes muttered. He handed me the rest of the letter from W—, along with the envelope, and just stared at me a moment or two, not saying anything.

"Come back after the buses have all left," he said. "You can talk to them then. Though maybe we better see about getting your father in. I know I wouldn't want a child of mine talking to reporters unsupervised."

"He won't be able to come in. Him and Mr. Tiptoe and my uncle are out at sea today." That wasn't exactly true. They were hugging the coast, going salvaging for windmill bits. But it was true that he wouldn't be able to make it in to dry land by the end of school.

"Brett Tiptoe is the one with the phone," Mrs. Evans reminded him, "so that means there's no way to reach any other adult out there." A disapproving sigh slipped out with the "out there." Mr. Barnes shrugged. "We'll just keep it short," he said. "You run along now," he added, and Mrs. Evans let me out.

Mr. Dubois was waiting for me in Mr. Barnes's office at the end of the day. "I don't want you answering these questions alone," he said, and I wasn't sure how I felt about that, but I guess I'm glad he came, because every time the reporter with the harsh questions about Kaya spoke up, Mr. Dubois said something smooth and bland about how my correspondence with Kaya was nonpolitical and how I was a true blue American through and through, laying it on so thick that if the window wasn't open we might of suffocated from all the patriotism building up in there. Eventually the reporter stopped asking those sorts of questions.

But Mr. Dubois also interrupted me if I tried to say anything about Kaya not getting to honor the Lady, or about her friend's execution, or even when I tried to talk about her saving Mermaid's Hands. He ran over my words with stuff about how great it was to have friends around the world and how wonderful it is to share traditions and how Kaya went to college in America and how he hoped I'd go to college, too, when I got old enough. I don't know how much the reporters wrote down, but I'd say half of what got said came from Mr. Dubois, not me.

About the time I was beginning to wonder how many more questions I could answer, Dad and Mr. Tiptoe showed up. I don't recall Dad ever coming to the school before. It was strange to see him and Mr. Tiptoe in Mr. Barnes's office. They seemed too big for that room, even though some of the reporters were taller and Mr. Barnes is fatter. Maybe it's that everything about them seemed realer to me: the salt stains on their arms and the warm, safe smell of sunshine, mud, and fish on their clothes.

"I'm taking my daughter home now," Dad said, eyes moving between Mr. Barnes and Mr. Dubois, like he wasn't sure who he should be talking to, which maybe he wasn't.

"Hey, Lightfoot, isn't it? Twinkletoes? Tiptoe! Still fishing in restricted areas?" one of the reporters called.

"That's pelicans you're thinking of, not us," Mr. Tiptoe shot back, flashing a barracuda smile. "Seen how many fish them and the herons been swiping from the restricted areas? You maybe better get the Fisheries Service on it."

Mr. Tiptoe drove me and Dad down to the shore, then went back inland to pick up some things at the hardware store that you can't come by in salvage. The tide was pretty far in, and our dinghy was bobbing and rocking where Dad had tied it.

"What is all this?" Dad asked, nodding at the letter as he pulled on the oars. "Saying thank you wasn't enough? Now you want to fly to the other side of the world for a visit?"

"It wasn't my idea! They invited me!" I protested, but my cheeks got hot as I was speaking, because it might not of been my idea, but it was definitely what I wanted.

"You'll have to tell them you're sorry, but no," Dad said. "We got a life to rebuild here, there's things that need doing. I can't go gallivanting across the Pacific, and I ain't sending you off halfway round the world on your own."

"But …" I never thought that Dad might say no. My dad, sitting across from me, muscles flexing as he rowed, was more powerful that W—'s Ministry of Law and Justice and its State Security Service. They could ask me to come and pull strings to make it possible, but Dad's *no* stopped everything.

"Maybe Ma'll come with me, then," I said. Dad didn't rise to the bait.

"I'm gonna ask Mr. Tiptoe if I can use his phone, and I'll call her. Call her new number," I said, my voice getting a little louder. Dad still didn't say a thing, just kept rowing.

When I reached Ma, when I finally got her to understand what I was saying, what I was asking, she laughed a little.

Why did she laugh? I don't like it when people laugh when there ain't nothing funny to provoke it.

Then she said, "I'm sorry, hon. I can't do that. I just started at a new job. I can't take time off now; I might as well quit if I did."

"But if I don't go, who'll save Kaya?" I asked, the words coming out all wobbly. I swallowed a couple times. Mr. Tiptoe was standing right there. I didn't want to cry.

"Not a sparrow falls to the ground without your father in heaven knowing about it," Ma said. "You leave saving Kaya to him."

I swallowed again. I didn't trust myself to speak.

"Don't you have a brother you're on fire to save?" Ma asked. Not accusingly. Kind of gently. "Last time I talked to him, he said he'd just gotten a letter from you. He sounded so pleased. Now that I have this new job, I can save up some money for a visit. How about that?"

I nodded—how dumb is that? You can't see nods over the phone. So then I croaked out, "Yeah, that sounds good," like the world's saddest frog.

"She has a point, though, about Jiminy," Small Bill said, a little later, when I told him. This was on the way to the Ikahos' to see if Marcela maybe might could come with me. I figured, she's part of Minorities Mobilize, and she said Minorities Mobilize wanted to help Kaya, so maybe? Small Bill was keeping me company, just the two of us in the dinghy.

"I mean," he went on, "about him being your own flesh and blood. Maybe Kaya's got ten brothers and sisters who're planning a rescue for her right now. They're nearer."

He can only talk that way about a rescue because he don't see the Ruby Lake in his mind's eye the way I do. He's never looked at pictures on the library computer. Me, I think about it, and I start to sweat, and I can practically taste the sulfur on my tongue.

"She never mentioned even one brother or sister," I said. "Or a father. I think it's just her and her mother."

We were right by the Ikahos', so I pulled in the oars.

"Look, Seafather's signal!" said Small Bill, pointing to the bright green flash where the sun had just sunk below the waves. We both waved back. Black specks, maybe gulls, were silhouetted against the flash, and suddenly Mr. Ovey was in my mind, maybe because of what Small Bill said that other day, about seeing him way out there, waving. Then it washed over me:

"Your dad said that sea families have all kinds of members. He told me I cast a strong net for families and that I can pull everyone into the boat. I fished for Kaya, and the Seafather helped me catch her. And your dad's telling me I can pull her into my family, like y'all pulled Cody into yours."

"Yeah but—" he paused to tie the dinghy to the mooring ring at the end of the Ikahos' veranda "—Jenya's *marrying* Cody."

"But I think you can pull someone in just as a brother or sister, too. Your dad told me to keep *you* in my net, but it ain't like you and me are getting married."

(Squirmy thought. I don't want to think about marrying nobody for a long time.)

"We can be like brother and sister, though," I added. "Or maybe crew. You can be my first mate."

"Huh. I ain't nobody's first mate. You be my first mate," he said, flicking water at me. I jumped onto the Ikahos' veranda, unbalancing the dinghy, and if it had been anyone other than Small Bill, they would've been in the water. As it was, he got good and wet.

"You bringing us the ocean one splash at a time?" It was Tomtale, come out onto the veranda with Windward on his shoulders. Windward's mom, Tomtale's sister Sweet-rain, leaned in the doorway.

When Jiminy was in high school, he liked Sweet-rain, but she liked Tidal Fearing better, and now those two are married and have Windward.

"We'll take it, if you are," said Granny Ikaho, peering out the kitchen window. "When's your granny coming over for a sleepover with me, Em?"

I grinned and peeked over Granny Ikaho's shoulder. "You sure she ain't already in there?" Those two were best friends when they were kids, like Tammy and Clara, or me and Small Bill. Marcela appeared behind Granny Ikaho.

"Hey Em, I hear it was a big day for you today," she said, grinning.

"It was but—Marcela, can you come with me? To W—? I can't go by myself. My dad won't let me. But he can't come with me, and my mother can't either."

My words were like a magic spell, freezing everybody. Marcela's mouth was frozen in an O.

"Ma ma ma ma …" Windward said, breaking the spell. He leaned his arms toward Sweet-rain, who took him from Tomtale.

"Em, I can't. I gotta go back up north. My adviser wants to go over the first two chapters of my dissertation with me, and I have to have the next two done before Thanksgiving."

"She's already got her ticket," Tomtale said.

"But she'll be back soon, won't you Marcy." That was Nimbus Ikaho, Mr. Ikaho to us kids, emerging from the house with some of Windward's diapers, which he pinned to the clothesline.

"She'll come when she's able, Dad," Tomtale said, with a bit of heat in his voice, and Mr. Ikaho disappeared back inside, saying he didn't see the point of catch-and-release fishing.

"What about someone else? Is there anyone else who could come with me? From Minorities Mobilize, I mean," I added, as Tomtale and Granny Ikaho and even Sweet-rain started shaking their heads and talking about getting food for the table and making sure the roofs were snug over our heads for the cool months.

"Because y'all at Minorities Mobilize want to help her, right?" I pressed, keeping my eyes on Marcela.

"Em, about going to W—. I wanted to talk to you."

An unexpected voice. I nearly jumped out of my skin, and not just me, Small Bill and Tomtale nearly did, too. We had our backs to the water and hadn't noticed Cody poling up in the Oveys' dinghy. Sitting in it, with his arms wrapped around his backpack, was Mr. Dubois.

What's he doing here? Why can't he just leave me alone? I thought.

Cody threw a rope to Small Bill, who tied it to the mooring ring. Mr. Dubois stumbled a little, stepping onto the Ikahos' veranda, and Sweet-rain caught him by the elbow and steadied him.

"Thank you," he said. "I'm sorry to intrude … Em, I know I upset you last week, with the things I said. I've been trying to find a time and a way to apologize."

I know I should of been a big-hearted person at that point and said I understand and no hard feelings, but it would of been a lie.

He passed his hand across his head. "The thing is," he said, "I've been doing a little research on W—, and on your friend Kaya, and I thought I could share it with you … You know, so you could familiarize yourself—"

I cut him off. "I ain't going," I said, feeling angry heat in my stomach.

He stared at me, hand still on his head.

"Not going?" he repeated.

"Nobody can go with me, and I can't go alone," I said. And then, maybe because of the heat in me, I added, "Bet you probably think that's the wisest thing, anyway, huh."

"Em," murmured Cody, frowning, and all that heat went right to my cheeks. I felt worse than if Ma had swatted me.

"No … no, that's not what I think at all," Mr. Dubois said. He looked out toward the Gulf. "I was wrong the other day … sometimes being too careful just makes things worse. I think you *should* go—with an adult, of course, but …" He turned back to me. "Em, do you think you could stand it if I went with you?"

Well shatter me and scatter me on the waves. It was almost harder to believe than the invitation from the government of W—.

"Must be the Seafather's work," muttered Granny Ikaho.

"But don't you gotta teach, Mr. Dubois?" asked Small Bill.

"Maybe I'll just have to take a page out of your book, Billy, and miss a few days. If Em'll have me." He was waiting for my answer. Everybody else was, too. I gulped for air.

"Yes, yes please—I mean, Yes, thank you! I-I mean—" I was getting tangled up. Mr. Dubois smiled.

"Shall we go see your dad, then?" he asked, and I nodded.

"I thought you thought it wasn't good for me to try to help Kaya myself. What made you change your mind?" I asked as I poled us homeward.

"Reading more about her, partly, and her country. And thinking about you … and Jiminy," he said.

Jiminy. My criminal brother. Anger came up behind me and caught me between its teeth, its hot breath all sour in my nose.

"You said Jiminy's troubles could rub off on her and hurt her," I said, anger's teeth making the words come out sharp.

He looked me straight in the eye. "I'm really sorry about what I said that day," he said. "I was- It was a mistake … Judging from you, I'd say a bit of trouble in a body's life makes 'em braver. People without your troubles should be as brave." The left side of his mouth crooked up, half a smile. "Maybe that's part of why I want to come with you. Get some of your braveness to rub off on me."

My braveness? Rubbing off … on Mr. Dubois?

I don't know what I think of that, but him saying it shocked the anger into letting go of me, at least. And then we were gliding up to the house, and Dad and Tammy and Gran were on the veranda, waiting for us. Dad still didn't jump with joy at the idea of me going to W—, but he shrugged his shoulders and said, "Won't do for me to hold you back. You'll just slip out like water—like your brother and your mother."

"It's not like I'm going for good!" I protested. He answered me with a smile that was as full of sadness as a bucket of tears.

I'll come back, though. He'll see.

So it's set. I'm going to go to W—, and very, very soon. I'll ask the Seafather to hold my right hand and, maybe, if she can hear me, I'll ask the Lady of the Ruby Lake to hold my left.

Chapter 15. In W—

(From the W— State Security Service's files on the insurgency: email records)

From: Lt. Sana

Subject: Re: flying conditions, how to proceed

Date: October 22

To: Lt. Den

I don't want to make do with a filmed plea—a tiny image on a damn phone screen? That's supposed to get 116 to give in? That's not what I greased palms to get the kid over here for. If it's safe enough for us to put our lives at risk, landing there, it's safe enough for that damn kid to ride along.

(From the W— State Security Service's files on the insurgency: email records)

From: Lt. Den
Subject: Re: Re: flying conditions, how to proceed
Date: October 22
To: Lt. Sana

Tell that to the minister of foreign affairs and the US ambassador. Anyway, what the hell extra leverage do you think having her there in person would give you? You're not orchestrating a family reunion; you're trying to pry 116 out of the damn temple. If she knows she can meet the girl if she cooperates, and the girl's begging to see her, it'll still work—assuming conditions ever do improve enough to fly. The way volcanologists are talking, 116 may get her fiery exit whether we like it or not.

October 22 (Em's diary)

They say the sky's an ocean over our heads. It's weird to be sailing through it now, seeing all those white-cap clouds from on top instead of underneath. A plane ain't really like a boat, though. You can't feel the wind. A plane is more like a submarine. A sky submarine. I wonder if me and Small Bill could make a submarine. Not a sky one, just a regular water one.

Mr. Dubois is letting me use his electronic book-reader. It's about the size of the bottom of a loaf tin, just a thin rectangle that's almost all screen. It has books stored in it. Mr. Dubois tapped his fingers on the screen and made a book appear. Then he slid his finger along the screen a couple times, and the page changed.

"It's a phrase book," he said. "I figured you might like to learn to say 'It's a pleasure to meet you.'"

The heading on the page was "Greetings."

I slid my finger the way Mr. Dubois had done, and a new page appeared with the heading "Asking Directions." I slid my finger back the other way, and then two more times, and got to a page that said "Introduction."

"It's for W—'s national language," I said, after reading a couple paragraphs of the introduction.

"That's right," said Mr. Dubois.

"But that ain't Kaya's language. People in the mountains have their own language."

"Uh huh, I know. I couldn't find a phrase book for Kaya's language. But it wouldn't hurt to know a few words in the language of the folks that'll be meeting us at the airport, right? The folks that arranged for you to come? Kaya's fight, her people's fight, with them isn't yours, except as she's your friend. But as her friend, if you show the officials in W— just how charming you can be, well, that might help her, right?"

"I guess …"

I looked at some more headings: At the Hotel. Food and Drink. At the Market: Bargaining.

"There's no section for human-rights phrases," Mr. Dubois said with a half-smile.

"Maybe I could use this," I said, pointing to a phrase in the bargaining section: *Is that the best you can offer?*

Mr. Dubois's lopsided smile widened. "Maybe so. Let's see if we can't put together a polite greeting first, though, what do you say?"

I said okay. Then he handed me an actual book, with paper pages. *Footloose Traveler,* it said up top, in small letters, and then W— in bigger letters in the center, over a photo of a boat with a prow shaped something like a dolphin, but snarling instead of smiling.

"It's a travel guide. You can read up on W— in there," Mr. Dubois said.

Inside was a description of W—'s geography and plants and animals, and then it told about the arrival of humans, thousands of years ago, first one wave and then a second, which pushed the first up into the mountains.

Then came history: lots of little kingdoms all along the coast that kept on getting swallowed up by this or that bigger empire, until finally the whole island of W— was part of a sultanate whose ruler lived on a faraway island. Then W— broke free and was its own kingdom for a little while, but not for long, because then the British came and gobbled it up. After the British came the Japanese, and then the British again until 1961, when W— became its own country again.

The last few paragraphs, about the development of modern W— (industrialization, politics, international relations), were complicated and hard to follow. There was nothing in the history chapter about Kaya's people. The only mention the mountains got was for natural resources (timber and copper) and cash crops (coffee and cardamom).

I looked up "mountain region" and "mountains" in the index and found "Mountains, the Prince in," but that turned out to be just a picture in the folktales part of the culture section, a photograph of people in glittering costumes and elaborate masks on a stage, with a caption that said, "The banished prince enlists the aid of the pythons, the eagles, and the dark men of the mountains to guide him safely through the spirit-haunted forests to his allies on the far side of W–."

When I meet Kaya, I'm going to ask her to tell me proper mountain stories and history.

I tried one more lead from the index, "Mountains, trekking in the." "The mountain regions are not as developed as the rest of W—, but they are a rewarding destination for hikers and nature lovers, offering breathtaking views and abundant wildlife," the book said. The caption beneath a photo of the Ruby Lake bragged, "The 'Ruby Lake' in the crater of Abenanyi is one of the world's few persistent lava lakes and an awe-inspiring sight for the intrepid hiker." Like every other picture I've ever seen of the Ruby Lake, it was from before Kaya's lotus was built.

Another photo in that section showed a woman pouring something into tiny red clay bowls. "You can buy delicious roasted peanuts or piping hot honey coffee at market stands in the larger towns," the caption said, but what drew my eye was the woman's face and hair.

"The mountain people are black," I exclaimed, showing the picture to Mr. Dubois. *As black as Vaillant*, I was thinking.

Maybe I could sing Kaya into Vaillant's lineage. She could be my big sister—and Tammy's and Jiminy's, too.

"You didn't know that? You've never seen a picture of Kaya?"

I shook my head. Mr. Dubois pulled out his phone and made a photo appear on the screen, a smiling blond-haired woman with sunglasses on, her hands resting on the shoulders of a girl wearing a baseball cap and a striped shirt.

"Whoops, that's my wife and daughter." Mr. Dubois lingered on the photo a moment, then flashed through a bunch more before stopping at a black-and-white picture of five people on a stage. Underneath the picture it said, "Undergraduates in Cornell's Department of Crop and Soil Sciences present at the Conference on Soil Depletion."

"See that one? That's Kaya." The woman Mr. Dubois was pointing to barely came up to the shoulders of the others. She seemed like a kid beside them. At first I thought she must have her hair cut real short, but then I saw it was just pulled back tight: a puff of it showed like a halo behind her head. And she was as dark as I am. Darker, even.

I wanted to see her face better, wanted to look right into her eyes, but the picture was too small.

"Do you have any others?"

"Well, there's this, but it's blurry."

It was soldiers in green-and-black speckled fatigues, guns in their hands, one pointing and some others corralling a bunch of people who had crowns of flowers on their heads and long, bright-patterned cloths tied round their waists, the men and women both. In the background, more soldiers, a wall of them. Here and there between their shoulders, you could just make out the faces of onlookers.

"It's from the English-language version of the main newspaper over there," Mr. Dubois said. "It's from when they first arrested Kaya and her friends. I think that one's her."

Her face was half blocked by the arm of the pointing soldier, but I could see her eyes all right, wide and frightened. The force of that fear stole my breath from me.

"You okay?" Mr. Dubois asked.

"Yeah. Yeah, I'm okay."

I've gotta be okay. I'm gonna make myself be okay. I wasn't able to get to Clear Springs for Jiminy, but I'm going to W—. I'm doing it. And I didn't have to stow away in a truck or hitchhike. They invited me. So hang in there, big sister. I'm coming. I've got the Seafather's blessing and everything. I'll work a miracle for you, like you did for me.

October 23 (Em's diary)

It turned into tomorrow when we crossed the International Date Line. I practiced some of the phrases from the phrase book for a while, then slept for a bit, and the next thing I knew, the pilot was saying we were coming in for a landing at Palem International Airport in W—.

There were a handful of reporters waiting when we got off the plane, snapping pictures and shouting things, and just when I realized that one thing they were repeating was the word "statement," ("Statement! Statement!"), a stream of soldiers in pale green uniforms poured in and swept them all away. Three men in dark suits rode in on another wave of soldiers, and making his way through that crowd came a tall man in a paler suit, an American, maybe—he looked like an actor playing a millionaire in a movie.

"Fredrick Henry, staff aide to the ambassador, US embassy in W—" the movie actor guy said, sticking his hand out at Mr. Dubois at exactly the same moment one of the dark-suit men was saying, "Mr. Dubois, Miss Baptiste, welcome to W—," and introducing *him*self, an undersecretary of something or other. He and Mr. Henry both laughed awkwardly. I decided it was time to use the phrase I'd been practicing in the plane.

"*It's a pleasure to meet you*," I said, carefully as I could, in the national language of W—.

The undersecretary looked startled, then bowed his head a slightly. He said something I didn't understand, then said in English, "The pleasure is mine." Then he exchanged a few words with Mr. Henry, and the two of them worked out that somebody would take our bags to the hotel for us, so me and Mr. Dubois could visit the embassy first and then the Ministry of Law and Justice, right away. I'm keeping my diary with me, though, so I can write down everything I see and think.

At the embassy, Mr. Henry said he had to talk to Mr. Dubois alone. They left me in a courtyard with a big fountain that a crowd of sparrows was using as a swimming pool. I tried to sketch them playing there, to show Tammy, but before I got very far, Mr. Dubois and Mr. Henry were coming back out again, both of them with overcast faces. Mr. Henry put on a smile when his eyes met mine. He glanced at Mr. Dubois, then said,

"We're all set now, Emlee. Just had to talk over keeping you safe. I'll let Mr. Dubois fill you in on the details—" Flick-flick, his eyes from Mr. Dubois to me and back to Mr. Dubois. "—as appropriate," he finished. His smile wasn't looking very comfortable on his face. It constricted into pinched lips and disappeared altogether with a "well then. Here's to a safe and successful visit!" Then he escorted us to a spot outside where a bunch of cars with dark windows were parked. Idling near them was our taxi. Me and Mr. Dubois got in. One set of gates and then another opened for us, and then we were back on the busy streets of Palem.

"What did Mr. Henry mean, back there? What details was he talking about?" I asked, as the driver wove in and out between the scooters, bicycles, and tiny trucks that crowded the road.

"Everything's just a little more unstable here than our good government likes, right now. Volcano's unstable, situation in the mountains is unstable, and seems like Kaya's maybe not the most stable element in the mix, either. Mr. Henry doesn't want the government of W— putting you at risk in their efforts to get Kaya to be reasonable."

"Get *Kaya* to be reasonable? They're the ones keeping her over a volcano. How about *they* be reasonable."

"Well Mr. Henry says that W—'s State Security Service claims that they tried to take her to safety, but she refused to leave, threatened to jump when they came near her."

I couldn't believe my ears. *When I get out of here*, she said in her letter. She can't want to stay there. How could she?

"They say she's staying to encourage the insurgents, and that the insurgents are getting in the way of evacuating people in the mountains from the eruption danger zone."

"She would never ever put people in danger! The government must just be saying that as an excuse—because they want to leave her there!" I didn't mean to shout, but it was making me real mad, hearing the things Mr. Henry had said.

Mr. Dubois shrugged apologetically. "Apparently many people in the mountains think that Kaya speaks for the Lady of the Ruby Lake, that she can control the volcano. Even some lowlanders think that. Maybe Kaya's let herself believe it too."

"No way! She once told me she wasn't even sure she believed in the Lady! The government's just a bunch of liars!"

I would of been happier if Mr. Dubois got angry right back at me, but he just sighed. "People can change," he said. "Especially if they suffer a lot." His mouth crooked up a little, not really a smile. "It doesn't mean the government's not a bunch of liars. But it's also possible that Kaya hasn't told you one hundred percent—"

"Don't!" I said, covering my ears.

"Hey," Mr. Dubois said, putting a hand on one of my arms and gently pulling it down. "I'm not saying she set out to mislead you. But think about it: anything she wrote to you, she had to hand over to the State Security Service before it could get mailed, right?"

The taxi slowed to a stop in front of more gates, which opened to let it drive right up to the front of a grand brick building painted butter yellow, with white columns and arches: the Ministry of Law and Justice.

More men in green uniforms appeared, opening the doors of the taxi for us, speaking to the taxi driver and leading us inside. I was feeling too stormy to pay much attention to what my eyes were showing me. There was too much stuff going on between my ears—mainly replays of the things Mr. Dubois had said about Kaya.

Maybe she *didn't* tell me everything. Maybe she left stuff out. If I knew that someone like Ms. Tennant was going to read everything I wrote to Kaya, I wouldn't of written my letters the way I did. The stuff I wrote about Jiminy, or about Mr. Ovey dying—I wouldn't want Ms. Tennant's eyes on that.

Okay. So she didn't tell me everything. But the part about getting in the way of evacuation plans—that couldn't be true. What Kaya cared about most of all was people not getting hurt. There's no way she'd do things that would *make* people get hurt.

What if people are going to get hurt anyway? If people are already being hurt?

Where'd that thought come from, burning its way into my mind like a piece of hot ash?

"Em?" said Mr. Dubois.

We had arrived at a room that was almost entirely filled up by a long, polished table. Another Em and another Mr. Dubois looked up at us from within it as we came near. Their faces were solemn and nervous-seeming. Two men in uniform and the dark-suited undersecretary from the airport were already at the table. The undersecretary rose and motioned for us to sit, then introduced us to the officers: Lt. Sana (chest like the hull of a boat, hard face) and Lt. Den (a lot thinner, salt-and-pepper hair). Someone brought in coffee for the grown-ups and a cold, fizzy drink for me that had a flavor like coconut mixed with something sour-sweet.

The undersecretary cleared his throat and said what a remarkable young woman I was, and how my parents must be proud, and that he and the government of W— extended their heartfelt thanks to me for agreeing to offer my assistance and how, nevertheless, he wanted to reassure Mr. Dubois and, by extension, my parents and the whole US government that I'd be kept safe and sound. Then he looked to his left. "Lt. Sana, why don't you review the situation," he said.

Lt. Sana opened a folder and spread photos on the table: bodies sprawled on the ground, a burnt-out building, smashed cars. He didn't look at me or Mr. Dubois, just kept his eyes on the photos, and spoke in a monotone—well, mainly a monotone. Sometimes something treacherous-sharp would show up in his voice, like the edge of a broken bottle revealed when the waves pull sand and pebbles out, and sometimes his lips twitched a little as he described "separatist violence" goaded on by "insurgency ringleaders."

The room was air conditioned, but sweat was beginning to prickle under my arms and on my forehead. I felt like he was accusing *me* of the things he was describing. Maybe he was.

I caught Lt. Den looking at me with friendly eyes. "Don't be distressed," he said. "You could not have known about all this, when you were writing to Miss Matarayi—Kaya, as you call her. She wouldn't have admitted to it." He sighed. "She took advantage of your friendship."

She didn't, I wanted to say, but a tiny worm of doubt wriggled up through my mind. *Did she?*

Lt. Sana was speaking again. "Since the Jarakasan Lake massacre, it's become impossible—"

"Whoa, hold on a moment," Mr. Dubois interrupted. "I thought I read that the deaths at the lake turned out to be from a natural disaster, not separatist action."

It was one of Lt. Sana's glass-shard moments. "Yes. The initial deaths were from a bubble of carbon dioxide that escaped the lake," he said. "But then, *then* the insurgents exploited the situation." He jabbed one of the photos with his finger. "These people died from bullet wounds, not asphyxiation."

"Ah, I see," said Mr. Dubois, nodding, his eyes on the photo. Then his brow wrinkled. "I apologize for my ignorance, but aren't some of the people in this photo mountain folk? Why would the separatists kill their own people?"

"Punishing government collaborators, I suppose," Lt. Sana replied, a sneer in his voice.

"There may have been an exchange of fire; that's still under investigation," Lt. Den admitted.

"But that's a gunfight, not a massacre."

"A gunfight that wouldn't have happened if the insurgents hadn't taken advantage of a natural disaster to attack a US company," Lt. Den said, and now there were barbs in *his* voice, too.

"Terrible," Mr. Dubois said, shaking his head. I couldn't tell if he meant it or not, and I guess Lt. Sana couldn't either, because he was glaring at Mr. Dubois. Lt. Den carried on with the talking, explaining that one of the insurgents, a "confederate of Ms. Matarayi," was now helping the State Security Service work out a peaceful solution.

"It's hard, though, with Ms. Matarayi continuing to stand in opposition. And now, with Abenanyi on the verge of erupting, and the possibility of loss of life, it's more important than ever that we remove her. From the Lotus on the Ruby Lake."

Remove her. The way he said it made me shiver.

"This is where you can help," said the undersecretary, smiling at me like Granny Ikaho trying to coax her cat back into the house. "Our State Security Service would like you to make a … little film?" he looked questioningly at the men to his left. Lt. Den nodded.

"We'll do it with a cell phone. Very short. We want you to ask her to come away from the Ruby Lake, to come to safety," he said.

"Can't I … Can't you just take me there? Can't I ask her in person?"

"It's too dangerous for you to go to the Ruby Lake," Mr. Dubois said swiftly, before anyone else could answer. "That's one of the other things Mr. Henry said, when we talked. I meant to tell you in the taxi. I'm sorry." He sounded like he meant it, too.

I'm this close, but still as far away from Kaya as everyone else in W—. A Ruby Lake away.

"I do want her to come away from the Ruby Lake. I do want her to be safe," I said.

I want it with all my heart. So why is there a *but* bubbling up in me?

"Excellent! Then I'll leave you with Lt. Sana and Lt. Den," said the undersecretary. "Mr. Dubois, Miss Baptiste." He bowed slightly, said something quick to the lieutenants, and left the room.

"Just sixty seconds should be enough," said Lt. Den. "You're waiting in the capital, you want to see her, you want everyone to be safe: say those things."

They're always using people to get other people to do what they want, I realized. Before, they wanted Kaya to read their statement so the people in the mountains would do what they wanted, and now they want me to say things to get Kaya to do what they want. It's okay, though, because what they want and what I want are the same—Kaya away from the Ruby Lake, and people safe.

Right?

The *but* in my mind was growing bigger. *Is that really what they want? Kaya's made all this trouble for them—and they still care about what happens to her? The people in the mountains are fighting them, but they want them to evacuate to safety? Either they're lying, or … Or they're not as bad as Kaya said?*

I realized the room was completely silent. Everyone was looking at me expectantly.

"Okay," I said at last, and then, for reassurance, "And I'll really get to see Kaya? She'll come here?"

"Yes," Lt. Den said.

"And she'll be all right?"

Lt. Sana's jaw tightened, and he muttered something I couldn't catch. Lt. Den laced his fingers on the tabletop.

"Kaya has committed—is accused of committing—several

crimes, some serious. But W— operates under the rule of law, just like your country. I can't promise a particular outcome for her, but I can promise justice. And leaving the Ruby Lake voluntarily will work in her favor. It will be a sign of cooperation."

Not much comfort there! But what could I say or do? It was all they were willing to offer.

"Okay, then," I said. "I'm ready.

Chapter 16. The Ruby Lake

October 23 (Em's diary, second entry)

We repeated the filming over and over again before the officers were satisfied. The words I was saying stopped seeming real—it was like I was an actress playing myself, and even the myself I was playing wasn't real. It was just a me-shaped piece of bait, and the officers were perfecting their casting technique. I wonder if they've ever gone fishing for real.

"We'll send for you when we have her here," Lt. Den reassured me, when they were finally satisfied and me and Mr. Dubois were getting into our taxi. The sky had gone all shades of crape myrtle, turning Mr. Dubois's white shirt pink and the ministry building orange. The air smelled a little like oranges, too, or anyway, like something you could peel and eat, and my stomach growled.

"We can get a meal back at the hotel," Mr. Dubois said, once the doors were shut and we were on the road again. They'd brought in food while we were filming, but I'd been too wound up to touch it. Now I just leaned back in the taxi and pulled my knees up against my stomach.

"Do you think it's true, that stuff about people getting shot by the lake?" I asked, thinking about Mr. Dubois's argument with the officers. Something Jiminy had said once popped into my head: *Maybe your friend has things to own up to.*

Mr. Dubois tapped knuckles against his lips. "Hard to say. Those photos were definitely of people with bullet wounds, but we don't know how they got them, or even if they really died there by the lake or were brought there afterward. On the other hand, the separatists did put a flag there, like they were claiming it after a battle. So I don't know."

That didn't help my stomach much.

"Least nobody can say that Kaya was shooting people," I muttered.

"But Em, you know she doesn't have to shoot anyone to still be involved."

Mr. Dubois! I know that's true, but why'd you have to go and say it?

I kept that thought in my head. Instead I said, "I know. Like with Jiminy and his friends. In the end it didn't matter who had the gun. They were all in trouble." By then, I wasn't even feeling hungry anymore. I just wanted to close my eyes and not see anything or think about anything for a while.

"Well now, about Jiminy. I've been doing a little poking around, and I found some information about an interesting program that he'd be just right for."

My eyes flew open. I looked over at Mr. Dubois.

"You were poking around for Jiminy?"

That lopsided grin of his washed up on his face, then ebbed away. "I remember when he was your age. He didn't have the head for schoolwork that you do, but he'd come out with the most interesting ideas sometimes. And he's what? No more than eighteen, right? And never been incarcerated before—he deserves a chance at rehabilitation. There's this work release program—"

The hope Mr. Dubois's words had lit inside me flickered out.

"He already tried for a work release program. He lost his chance because of getting into fights," I said.

"This is a different program, something he has a special skill for, growing up in Mermaid's Hands. It's volunteer work restoring coastal salt marshes. Wouldn't he be good at that? Finding and protecting sea turtle eggs and pelicans' nests?"

I giggled a little. "He might take a couple eggs to eat, if he got hungry." Then, quickly, "not really. Never sea turtle eggs; they're our cousins. Gulls' eggs, though. We used to collect a basketful, get Gran to make omelets. Sometimes Ma would make pancakes." I was back to hungry again, but a happier hungry. I leaned toward Mr. Dubois and gave him a quick hug. He grinned again, a longer-lasting grin.

"What's that for? Don't you manhandle me, Em; you know delicate dry-landers like me aren't used to your rough ways."

At the hotel, he ordered us some food that got brought right to the room, spicy and delicious, but no sooner was the edge off my hunger than I found myself swamped by sleepiness, head bobbing like a buoy in the bay.

"We can save the rest of this," Mr. Dubois said. "Why don't you change into PJs and get to bed. I'll see you in the morning, bright and early." He headed for the door.

"Where are you going? You're not staying with me?"

"No, I have my own room, 412, right across the hall. I'm going to send some emails home, and then I'll go to bed too. Don't look so worried! You'll be fine. You're a young lady now; you need your privacy."

He coudn't know that I never slept alone before in my life, that there's always been the sound of someone breathing nearby, to lull and settle me. But there's gotta be a first time for everything. I nodded and let him turn on the TV to keep me company. It looks like it's doing American Idol, W— version. I need to brush my teeth but I'm so sleepy. More later.

October 23 (Em's diary, third entry)

Trying to get this all down. So scared, but it'll be all right. It'll be all right. I got the Seafather behind me and the Lady ahead of me, and Mr. Dubois next to me. It'll be all right.

So here's what's happened. I fell asleep without getting changed or nothing, and woke up sometime later because of a drumming sound—I thought maybe from the TV, but it wasn't the TV. It was someone out in the hall, knocking.

I opened the door: hard-faced Lt. Sana, with his tight uniform stretched over his big chest. *He's come to arrest me,* I thought, *to arrest me for being an accomplice, an accessory.* My brain said *run!* but my body wouldn't move. I just stared up at him.

"I need you to come with me," he said, same flat voice as back at the ministry. I shook my head fiercely and took a step back into my room. *This is a bad dream,* I thought, and I struggled to wake up, but nothing changed. On the TV, an old black-and-white movie was playing. An actress with swooping dark eyebrows was singing, but her high tones were half lost in hissing and crackling.

"Please."

Not a word I think Lt. Sana has much practice saying. "The little film we made—it will never work. It was a waste of time; 116—Kaya—won't let any of us get close enough to hand it to her." His lip curled. "Too skittish. And even if she does look at it, she'll think it's a fabrication. That's why I—we—need you. Otherwise, she goes for a swim in Abenanyi. None of us want that."

"No," I whispered.

"Then come. If she sees you, she'll listen."

I glanced back into my room and out the window at the far end, at the dazzle of nighttime lights—a city of fireflies.

"Now? In the middle of the night?"

"The wind has turned. The helicopter can make an approach. There's no telling how much time we have. This is the first time in days that flying has been possible."

I licked my lips and swallowed. "Okay. I'll come." My whole body chose that moment to start shaking. I wrapped my arms around my middle, trying to hold myself together.

The door across the hall opened sharply: Mr. Dubois.

"Lt. Sana. What are you doing here, at this hour? Em, go back in your room and shut the door. I'll talk to the lieutenant." Mr. Dubois's voice was cold.

"No, *you* g-go back in *your* room. I'm g-going with Lt. Sana to bring K-Kaya back," I said. I just couldn't stop shaking.

"You're absolutely not. I told you. It's not safe."

"I have to! There ain't m-much time. She'll die if I don't. She'll never even look at that little movie I made."

"Is that what the lieutenant said?"

"It's true," said Lt. Sana.

"If she won't listen and won't come, then that's her poor decision and a shame, but that's the way it goes, I guess," said Mr. Dubois, as hard and harsh as Lt. Sana, who he was glaring at. "But there's nothing gained by your risking your life, just a lot of potential grief and sadness for a lot more people. Do your superiors know you're here, Lieutenant?"

"I'm taking … how do you say it? Personal initiative," said Lt. Sana, not so much grinning as baring his teeth.

"Uh huh. I thought so. Well initiative yourself on out of here or I'm going to start raising a very loud stink."

"No!" I said. "Please don't do that! Just let me go." I could feel myself filling up with tears. "I'm always getting in trouble for things like this, running away, not stopping to think. You know I am! Let's just pretend you were sleeping the whole time and I ran off with Lt. Sana, and you never knew. No one could blame you. My fault. Please? If it saves Kaya's life, ain't it worth it?"

Lt. Sana pulled a buzzing phone from his pocket and flipped it open. He looked up. "Now. We have to go now," he said.

Mr. Dubois closed his eyes a moment, took a breath, and said, "I'm coming too."

"As you wish," said Lt. Sana. "Hurry."

We had to race to keep up with him, down to the ground floor by the stairs, not the elevator, then out to a car, which Lt. Sana drove fast and hard to a base, where a helicopter was already running.

"Get in," he ordered, opening the cabin door. "Here, take these. You may need them." He tossed us both gauze masks with loops for our ears.

"To keep out ash and particles in the air," Mr. Dubois explained. Lt. Sana climbed in, said some words to the pilot, and the helicopter lifted into the air.

And here we are, in the air.

*   *   *

I think we're getting close. It's been pitch black for a while, no lights from towns, but there's a glow up ahead.

*   *   *

It's all clouds and smoke. Lt. Sana said the wind had changed, but has it? Or maybe it's already changed back. There's nothing solid, just columns and towers of cloud wherever the pilot directs the searchlight. You can't even see the Ruby Lake, just a cherry red glow deep in the clouds. I definitely don't see no platform or nothing like that. How can the pilot land?

* * *

I saw it! I saw the Ruby Lake through the clouds, and a black silhouette right in the middle of it that must be Kaya's Lotus. The pilot's taking the helicopter down.

* * *

He's tried twice but had to pull away both times. Clouds keep drifting by. We're really pitching and rolling. How long before we get too low on fuel and have to give up?

* * *

These masks don't do no good. I can't stop coughing, and Mr. Dubois is wheezing when he breathes, like Tammy on a bad day.

* * *

I think we raked the lip of the crater on this pass. I saw Mr. Dubois looking at the picture of his wife and little girl a minute ago, but now his head's dropped, and he's just concentrating on his breathing.

Maybe we really are going to die. I don't feel like writing no more right now.

October 24 (Michael Dubois to Kelsey Dubois)

From: Michael Dubois

Subject: what really happened

Date: October 24

To: Kelsey Dubois

A follow-up to my call, just to reassure you again that I'm alive and well (should be a doctor along soon to say I'm free to go) and to try to get down everything that happened while it's still fresh in my mind, so that you know the real story and don't have a heart attack when you hear whatever it is that they end up saying on the news.

While the pilot was trying to land the helicopter, I was trying to quell my panic at the air being practically unbreathable—should have expected as much, it being a volcano on the brink of erupting and all, but I confess, I wasn't thinking very clearly that night. Call it poor response to pressure. Anyway, I was running through my breathing exercises, and next thing I knew, we'd touched down and Lt. Sana was opening the cabin door.

At first I couldn't make a move. It was like being asked to step into a furnace. The air was shimmering; each breath seared. But I took the plunge, and Em followed, face all squinched up against the heat.

The Lotus on the Ruby Lake was nothing more than a long wooden platform, maybe 50 yards long. Around it on every side, too bright to look at for long, the crusting, weeping sore of the lake. Every now and then a fountain of lava would spurt up somewhere on the lake's surface, which had risen perilously close to the platform.

At the far end of the platform was a tiny structure not much bigger than our tool shed. It had roof finials like you see on coastal shrines here in W—, but as near as I could make out, they were in the shape of flames instead of fish. Gotta give the government credit for attention to detail there.

Once Em was safely out of the helicopter, Sana shouted something up to the pilot, then drew a gun.

"Is that necessary?" I asked. Even those three words took it out of me.

"She's dangerous," Sana said grimly. He started down the platform. "Matarayi! Kayamanira Matarayi! Someone's here to see you!" he shouted. Something cool and damp touched my arm—Em's hand.

"I changed my mind," she said, anguished. "I don't want to be bait for Kaya. She put her hands over her face. "I'm as bad as Jiminy, getting my friend in trouble."

"She's already in plenty of trouble. Nothing they can do ..." (had to pause for breath there) "is any worse than what's going to happen right here ..." (pause) "any minute now. You're not betraying Kaya. You're saving her. Remember? Let's go."

Sana opened the door to the little shrine-thing without so much as a knock, but before we could look in, he'd pulled it shut again.

"Empty. She'll be on the rail," he said, which I didn't understand until we walked round to the back of the shrine. There, sitting on the guard rail that ran the perimeter of the platform, was Kaya. She had a white cloth covering her head and wrapped tightly around her upper body. She held it over her mouth and nose with her right hand and steadied herself on the rail with her left.

It hurt to look at her: impossibly thin wrists, sharp cheekbones showing even through the white wrap, eyes sunken—but bright. Fierce, even. She said something quick and sharp to Sana, who stopped in his tracks. I was relieved to see that he'd lowered the damn gun.

"Look who I've brought to see you. Your pen pal from America," he said. He added something in his own language, then pushed Em forward.

"Go on, talk to her," he said.

Em took off her gauze mask. "Kaya, it's me, Em. Your friend," she said. I can't explain how it felt to hear her. It was a voice that belongs splashing through incoming tide, or joking with friends, or shouting angrily at me about injustices. It didn't belong in that inferno. All the same, Em spoke up clearly.

Kaya let the white cloth drop away from her face.

"I recognize you," she said, tilting her head slightly. "You're exactly as I dreamed you." She smiled, and I could see the ghost of the woman she must have been ten months ago, when she was just a botanical researcher, excited about her plans for a festival. But her eyes moved to Lt. Sana, and the smile didn't linger. "How is it that you're here? *Why* are you here?"

Em's eyes fell and she hunched her shoulders. "He brought me," she mumbled, with a small jerk of the head toward Sana. But then she straightened up and said, "It's because I want to rescue you. Please? Will you come with me?" She took a step forward, the sole of her sneaker peeling stickily up from the platform. The wood was that hot; I could feel it through the soles of my shoes, too. Kaya slipped down from the guard rail, then gasped as Em pulled her into a hug. I winced, thinking like as not Em would crack her ribs, but apparently Kaya's less fragile that she looks. I suppose she'd have to be. She rested a hand on Em's cheek—such a tender gesture.

"I can't," she said. "There are things I have to do here."

My heart sank. How can you argue with a ridiculous assertion? How long would we be there pleading before Lt. Sana lost patience—or one of those lava fountains ignited the platform?

Em took Kaya's caressing hand in both of her own and held it clutched to her chest.

"There ain't nothing to do here. You'll die if you stay here."

"Stay or go, that will happen, I'm afraid. Isn't that so." The last remark was directed with jutting chin and narrowed eyes at Sana. Em twisted round and looked up at the lieutenant. He rocked back on his heels.

"That's for a tribunal to decide," he replied with a shrug and the faintest trace of a smile.

Kaya shot him a defiant look and turned to Em.

"If I go with you, and I'm executed, then he and his friends get to tell the story of who I am and what I've done. A horrible story, a shameful story—and everyone I know, everyone I've grown up with, will be punished for it. But if I stay here, stay with the Lady, give her my thoughts, my memories, my everything, then what I gain for them is such power. No troops, no armored vehicles, no helicopters can withstand it. Do you understand?"

Em looked frightened. Poor kid. I wonder if she grew up with warnings about the dangers the drowning pose to the living. Maybe not, because she said,

"I- I think I understand. But—" She took a gulp of the molten air. "I remember when I found out we couldn't rebuild Mermaid's Hands, I remember thinking, wishing we could just go down under the waves and live with the seafolk. We're seachildren!" She ran her tongue over her lips. "If we did that, though, we could never come back up again. Maybe I'd've tried anyway, if I'd been with everyone at the Winterhulls' house instead of at Aunt Brenda's. But I'll never know, because instead you saved Mermaid's Hands, and now we're rebuilding, and there's gonna be windmills! And I want to build a submarine with Small Bill, and I want to show Tammy the picture I drew at the embassy, and I wouldn't get to do none of that if I went under the waves. So won't you let me save you, like you saved me and mine? Because I just bet your ma and your friends would rather bear some of the troubles and hardship they have if it means they can also keep you, the way you are now, in this world right here."

Kaya gazed into Em's beseeching face, brow furrowed. Her eyes went distant, and she murmured something none of us could quite hear. Then she shook her head slightly. "A miracle," she said, still barely audible. "The Lady promised me a miracle. I thought it was to be the other thing ... but maybe *you* are the miracle."

Em nodded vigorously. "Yes! Me for you, like you were, for me."

Kaya pulled her white wrap tight around her with her free hand. "All right," she said. "For the miracle that appears, rather than the one I imagined." Her voice shook slightly. Lt. Sana stirred. There was a clink and click as he opened handcuffs.

"For crying out loud, handcuffs, too? Not safe enough with the gun?" But the force of my sarcasm was lost in a fit of coughing that left me woozy.

"Just protocol for transporting a prisoner, Mr. Dubois," Sana said, his satisfaction evident. "I believe it's standard practice in your country too. Come then, Miss Matarayi," he said, lingering on each syllable of her surname, "Mr. Dubois thinks you're a reasonable creature; let's see who's right." Kaya didn't move.

"Well? Coming?"

Kaya's eyes met Sana's for a moment. His smile—predatory, triumphant—deepened. Kaya looked away. Em still held Kaya's hand clasped in hers; now Kaya closed her fingers tightly around Em's. Sana advanced a step. Kaya retreated, and Em with her.

"Now, now," said Sana, a note of warning in his voice. He raised the gun a fraction. I forced myself to exhale slowly, slowly, then drew in a superheated, sulfurous breath.

"Kaya," I said, "It's going to be all right. You may be in his custody, but we're here too; we're witnesses. We're not going to let anything bad happen. We're going to make sure your side of the story gets told. When I get back stateside, I can get in touch with your professors at Cornell to vouch for you; I can see if human-rights organizations want to get involved. We won't let them—"

Lt. Sana was staring at me with a look of such hot fury that the rest of my words shriveled in my mouth.

"Her side of the story! Human-rights organizations? You want to keep her from justice? She ordered vandalism, sabotage, murder. Destabilized the country, made W— appear weak and chaotic in the eyes of the world. And you think you can shield her from the consequences? Because she wrote letters full of lies to a little girl? You're a fool; you know nothing." Then, to Kaya, "Get over here right now or—" Face flushed with emotion, Sana abandoned English for his last few words. Kaya gasped and then—well, it was very confusing, everything happening at once.

"She's going to jump! She's going to take the girl with her!" Sana shouted, raising his gun in earnest and taking aim, while simultaneously Kaya screamed, "He means to shoot Em! Em, drop!"—but that last part was lost in the crack of gunfire.

"Are you out of your mind?" I choked out. Both girls were down, but I couldn't see if either had been hit. I threw myself at Sana, missed, and went sprawling, knocking whatever wind my sad lungs contained clean out. My vision cleared enough to see Em roll free of the melee and get to her feet—unharmed, thank God—and I saw Kaya stagger to a stand as well, right hand clutching her breast just below her left shoulder, red blossoming between her fingers on the white wrap.

"Em, run for the helicopter!" I heard her say. And then—I swear I didn't imagine this—Sana took aim again, but not at Kaya. At Em.

I couldn't yell a warning, couldn't even offer a distraction, having barely managed to lever myself onto my elbows at that point and still struggling to draw breath. There was a gunshot and a blur of motion that must have been Em, diving for the protection of the little shrine.

"Your death's upon you, lieutenant!" Kaya called, and eerily, a white web descended, shroudlike, over his head. Kaya's wrap—she'd unfurled it over him.

He flailed wildly, trying to tear it off, and when finally he was free of it, there was Kaya, so close to him that her upturned face practically brushed his chin. Her lips moved, a message for his ears only. Whatever she said provoked him; he lunged. She stepped to one side and he skidded on something slick and wet—her blood. His hands flew open as he tried to catch his balance, and the gun slid across the platform. Seconds later his desperate dance ended, as with top-heavy force he fell against, and then went over, the guard rail. The Ruby Lake swallowed him before he had a chance to scream.

Em had reemerged from the shrine and stood trembling, eyes fixed on the place where Sana had vanished. I managed to pick myself up and take a shallow breath of the poisonous air.

"The Lady is coming. We have to leave," Kaya said. As she stepped over her crumpled wrap, I became aware of the trail of blood down her left side.

"You need medical attention," I said.

"In a hospital in Palem? No." She bent to retrieve the gun. "Quickly!" We hurried to the helicopter; Kaya disappearing for a moment into the shrine and returning with a heavy volume—*Trees of Insular Southeast Asia.* At the helicopter, she trained the gun on the pilot.

"Do you have to do that?" Em asked, voice quavering.

"Yes," Kaya said softly. "It's better for the pilot this way—he can say he was coerced, and it will be true." She gave orders, and as the helicopter lifted off, the far end of the platform burst into flames.

Behind us, the mountain rumbled and shook; we felt the

vibrations in our bones. Then came an explosion, and for a moment the pilot lost control of the helicopter. Huge clouds of ash filled the air. "The Lady's changed the shape of Abenanyi," Kaya said. "She's dancing, now." Kaya stood beside the pilot and pointed out over the mountains, speaking rapidly. He followed her directions, and sometime later set the helicopter down in a fallow field beside a narrow dirt track across from the corpse of a hut—three walls and a collapsed roof, broken ribs still showing but thatching long gone. In the dawn light—or maybe it was still the eruption that was lighting the eastern sky—we seemed to be deep in the middle of absolute nowhere. Kaya opened the helicopter cabin door. Even after the distance we'd traveled, the air was still ashy; I still couldn't take a deep breath.

"I have to leave you here," she said. Her eyes were on Em and her voice was full of regret. Em nodded, long-faced.

"Don't you want to get a little closer to your destination?" I asked. "You're not in any shape to be hiking." Kaya glanced at the helicopter, with its State Security Service medallion, and shook her head. "No, no nearer."

I heard the beat of wings and saw a shadow resolve itself into a glossy black bird. Kaya held up her right arm, and it landed just above her elbow, then hopped up to her shoulder.

"It's your crow!" said Em, brightening a little.

"Yes, it's Sumi. I'm glad you're safe, friend," she said, kissing the crow's head. It made a series of low clacks, more conversation than bird call, then flew off over the broken hut and into the trees.

Kaya turned to Em. "You really are a miracle," she said, "everything about you, from the start. I wish … I'm so sorry …"

"I wish I'd've learned some words of your language," Em mumbled, dropping her head. She plowed a narrow ditch in the soft earth with the half-melted heel of her sneaker. "Then I could say goodbye properly."

"I'll teach you. Listen."

It was several syllables.

"It means, literally, 'When the sun next comes.' Like 'See you tomorrow,' in English, but with tomorrow standing for some day, one day ..."

Em tried out the unfamiliar sounds. Kaya said them a second time, and Em repeated them again.

"Good," said Kaya, with a trace of a smile. She released another stream of syllables.

"That's, 'I'm so happy to see you,'" she said. "A greeting for when we meet next."

"Can you say it again?"

Kaya did, and Em repeated the phrase back. Kaya's smile deepened. Then she turned to me.

"The book I brought with me. There's a record in it. I don't know if you can find anyone who can read my language ... It will probably be hard. But if you can, it has the truth of what I've done, this past month and a half. You said you'd see that my side of the story got told. Even if no one will listen, if you can share it with Em, at least ..." Kaya trailed off. She seemed to be shivering. Shock?

"I wonder if there's a blanket or something in here," I muttered, looking back into the cabin.

"I don't want anything from the helicopter," Kaya said, somewhat sharply.

"All right, but take my jacket, at least." Kaya let me drape it over her shoulders. With its sleeves dangling halfway down her thighs, she looked more like a refugee, like some child abandoned by the roadside, than a separatist leader.

"Now you should go," she said. "Here." She handed me the gun. Em went to give Kaya another rib-crushing hug, but stopped short.

Kaya's face was tight with pain.

"You aren't going to die, are you?" Em asked.

"After you've gone to all this trouble to keep me alive? How could I?" But Kaya's smile this time was wan, and Em looked unconvinced. Still, she let me guide her back into the helicopter and tapped on the window and waved furiously as the helicopter ascended. Kaya, however, had sunk to a squat on the ground, head down, and didn't wave back.

"What if she does die?" Em asked, a sob in her voice, as we leveled off and headed northwest, toward Palem.

"She not die, this time," the pilot volunteered, startling both of us. "Her people maybe probably nearby, hidden, waiting we go."

We'd already flown too far to tell if he was right, but it's worth hoping for.

Must close now. I see Mr. Henry and some other suits in the hallway talking to the nurse on duty. They don't look happy. Time to face the music, I suppose. I'll write or call soon.

Love you,

Justin

"Dramatic escape amid Abenanyi eruption"

October 24 (Reuters) — A young American girl and her chaperone narrowly avoided death in a volcanic eruption in the tiny Southeast Asian nation of W— early this morning, W— government sources say.

The two were visiting separatist leader Kayamanira Matarayi, under house arrest at a temple at the volcano since January, in hopes of persuading her to comply with a transfer to a safer location, but the visit reportedly degenerated into a standoff that ended with one State Security Service officer dead and Matarayi's escape in a State Security Service helicopter. The helicopter pilot was able to bring the Americans safely back to the capital city of Palem, where they received treatment for minor injuries and smoke inhalation.

A staffer at the US embassy in W— would not confirm the W— government's story and said only that the United States condemns the endangerment of its citizens and the increasingly violent actions of the separatists and urges both sides to work toward a peaceful resolution of differences. Prime Minister Ija Vin has vowed that separatist actions will not be allowed to destabilize the nation.

Chapter 17. The Sea Heart

October 28 (Em's diary)

I'm glad to be back home. I was afraid they wouldn't let us leave W— at first. The State Security Service kept wanting to talk to me and kept asking the same questions over and over again and picking at what I told them. *What makes you think Lt. Sana was shooting at you? Didn't you say you went into the temple? If you went into the temple, how could you know what was happening?* They got me doubting myself and my memory. Mr. Dubois said it was the same for him: *Wasn't it Kaya he was shooting at?* they asked. *Didn't you say she was the one who was wounded?* Like that. When Mr. Dubois wouldn't change his story, they started asking if we were planning a rescue attempt all along. *Either you were aiding and abetting an enemy of W—, or you were hostages. Which is it?* For a while I thought they might arrest Mr. Dubois, and I didn't know what was going to happen to me. Mr. Henry and the people at the embassy sorted stuff out for us, but they were real angry, too, because we did the one thing they'd said not to do: go to the Ruby Lake. They said we'd caused "diplomatic difficulties," and they told us not to talk to any media people.

So that leaves two wrong stories about what happened at the Ruby Lake out there in the world. One: Kaya tricked me into thinking she was my friend and used me to escape from the Ruby Lake so she could keep on making trouble for the government of W—. Two: Me and Mr. Dubois tricked the State Security Service into taking us to the Ruby Lake so we could help Kaya escape and keep on making trouble for the government of W—.

Even people who want to understand and believe our story get snagged on the details—like what Lt. Sana was up to. Small Bill asked about that after school (which I didn't have to go to today, Dad said, on account of it only being my first full day back).

"He really tried to shoot you? I don't get it, though. Why?"

"I don't know. Mr. Dubois thinks the only reason he wanted me to go to the Ruby Lake was to keep Kaya from dying there and becoming a martyr. But it ain't like he wanted to save her life or anything. He just wanted her dead his own way. So then when Mr. Dubois started promising that her side of the story would get heard and talking about human-rights groups and things, Lt. Sana just … Well, Mr. Dubois thinks he went kind of crazy-mad and was hoping to make it seem as if Kaya had committed an unforgivable crime, like, like jumping into the Ruby Lake and pulling me with her. Something that would make everyone hate her and her cause.

"But then again, maybe the heat from the Ruby Lake just boiled away Lt. Sana's brain juices, and he just wasn't thinking straight. Maybe he really did think Kaya was going to jump and was trying to save me. That sure ain't how it seemed to me, but maybe I was influenced by Kaya shouting out that he was going to shoot me. That's what the State Security Service thinks."

"And now Kaya's free. Even if you didn't set out to rescue her, that's what you ended up doing, huh. It's like a Sabelle Morning story."

Which is why half the news stories say that's what we did. And maybe that is what I really wanted, if I think about it honestly—but I didn't plan none of it, and it definitely ain't what Mr. Dubois planned. I wonder if any of the real life behind Sabelle Morning's stories is this complicated.

"You reckon her friends found her and patched her up?"

"Yeah. Yeah, I'm pretty sure they did."

I'm going to just keep saying that and thinking that because I can't bear thinking about the other possibility: that we flew away and she died there on the mountainside, by herself, away from everyone, even the Lady of the Ruby Lake.

There's a commotion coming from the kitchen. I can hear Dad and Tammy and Gran all talking at once—I think Ma just arrived, and it sounds like Uncle Near and Wade, too. I'll write more later.

October 28 (Em's diary, second entry)

Ma said I never cease to amaze her. She was smiling when she said it. She smiled her whole visit, leaning back against Dad's chest, and Dad smiled pretty much the whole time, too, his hands on her shoulders, then sliding down her arms, then holding her hands in his. There was some kind of secret conversation in those touches, just between the two of them, even as they were talking with all the rest of us about Kaya and the Ruby Lake, and about what's been happening here at home, and about Mr. Dubois's idea for Jiminy, and finally about Ma's job and the money she was earning.

Ma said she was aiming to save enough to get tickets for all of us to go to visit Jiminy during the Christmas school break.

"That includes you, Trace, if you want," she said. At that point I thought they might start sparring like old times, because Dad didn't say yes or no about going to see Jiminy. Instead he said it was all well and good, in a dry-land sort of way, to be making money and such, but when did Ma think she'd come home? The kitchen got very quiet then, everybody waiting on Ma's answer. The palms of my hands started hurting, and I realized it was from my fingernails—I had my hands clenched that tight. Not open hands, not Mermaid's Hands. Nervous Hands. Em's Hands.

What Ma said surprised all of us: "Ain't red-winged blackbird the genealogy I got sung into? It's a dry-land bird, even if it loves wet places. Like me. I got dry-land stuff to do. I want to go to college. I want—well lots of things. But you can't keep a red-winged blackbird away from water, and nothing'll keep me from flying out to visit you, if you'll have me. I'll fly right in at your window."

It's the most Mermaid's Hands-like thing she's ever said. Now that she's living away from home, she sounds more like she belongs here than she ever did before—what does *that* mean?

And how did Dad answer? He said, "Well as you might recall, it gets a little chilly on the water in winter. Sometimes we gotta close the window. But if you fly in and find it closed, you just tap, and I'll open it."

Nothing else! And then Ma left! Hugged and kissed us all, gave Dad an extra squeeze, then opened the kitchen door, stepped down onto the mudflats, and started walking back toward dry land.

November 25 (Jiminy to Em)

Dear Em,

Its my first day at the Coastal Reef Restoration Project. They mainly just showed us around and explained what they want us to do. Lots of heavy lifting because they're sinking these sections of concrete pipe into the sand underwater and then piling big net bags of oyster shells in there for other oysters to grow on. We'll be doing a lot of that but also we'll inventory which is when we go out and count all of each kind of bird or fish or other whatever we see, even types of grass and seaweed, anything. They asked me to show everybody how to look for nests and eggs and how you can tell one-year-old gulls from two-year-old ones, things like that.

Its so good to be by the water. I didnt know how much I missed it. I been telling myself it didnt matter so much to me, the sea and all that, but now I'm here and it just feels right. And this work we'll be doing is work a person can feel good about, too. It has a meaning, you know? For the sea and for people who make there lives with the sea, like us at Mermaids Hands. I'm going to send a letter to Mr. Dubois and say thank you for fixing me up with this, but can you tell him, too, when you see him? Tell him thank you from me.

I know I'm in the right place because I already found something special. I gave it to my supervisor to send to you and Tammy. Its a giant bean seed, bigger than a babys fist, in the shape of a heart. A sea heart its called. Finding it was like getting a present from a secret admirer. You think someone under the waves has a thing for me?

My supervisor said a jungle vine makes these seeds. He said it floated all the way from Costa Rica to here. Its hollow inside. You could put a message in it if you once opened it. Then you could close it back up with wax and set it afloat in the water again, like your message in a bottle. Sounds like you got your hands full with just the one pen pal you fished for though, huh. Anyway you and Tammy can keep it or pass it on to someone else who needs some sea love.

Love,

Jiminy

November 29 (Em's diary)

Jiminy sent a letter and a package! The package had what I thought was a shiny, smooth, heart-shaped wooden box in it, but there was no way to open it. Then I read Jiminy's letter. It's a sea heart—a love token from the ocean. Seaheart. That's what Mr. Ovey called me, before I went to W—. Jiminy said we could keep it or pass it on. At first Tammy had an idea to make a jewelry box out of it, but then all of a sudden she changed her mind and asked if I wanted maybe to send it to Kaya.

I guess she knows Kaya hasn't been out of my mind since I got home. I still don't even know if Kaya's alive or dead. Each day I can, I go to the library and use the computer to search on "Kayamanira" plus "W—", but there hasn't been anything new about her or the mountain people since the eruption at the Ruby Lake. Dad and Mr. Dubois say no news is good news, but what's good about this empty blankness? I wish, I wish so hard, that I could just know how she is.

December 2 (Ibrahim Bakar to Em)

Dear Emlee Baptiste,

My name is Ibrahim Bakar. I'm a student in the Arts and Sciences College at the University of Southern Mindanao in the Philippines. I have been traveling in W— this past month for a documentary I want to make on the separatist movement there. I got to meet some of the leaders of the movement, including Kayamanira Matarayi, and she asked me if I would send this note to you when I returned home. I promised her I would. You will find it enclosed.

Yours respectfully,
Ibrahim

November 20 (Kaya to Em)

My dear Em,

I have been longing for a way of letting you know that I am alive and well and for a chance to thank you, with all my heart, for saving my life. Your courage and friendship make me most humble. These past weeks, your face has been always in my mind: whatever I do, whatever course of action I contemplate, I think of you, and I think, how would this seem to Em? How would I explain it to Em? You have become my conscience—half the world away.

It's strange now. Very busy, very confusing, very noisy. *Very different from all those months alone, with only my own thoughts, and then the Lady, behind me and around me and in me. I don't feel her presence now. Sometimes this makes me lonely, but there is too much to think about, too much to argue about, too much to fight for, to feel lonely for long. Right now I'm trying to persuade my new colleagues that we should not remain in hiding here in the mountains, that we should move back to our towns and villages. They say it's too dangerous, for us and for "civilians," but I don't want there to be such a division. We are not, should not be, separate from the people on whose behalf we seek to act.*

One of my school friends from childhood, who helped plan the festival that began all this, has gone over to the government's side. This pains and angers me for more reasons than I can share in this letter, but I am hoping to make some good come of it. I want to try to meet with him. Whatever has motivated his collaboration with the government, there must still be, at his core, something of the boy I grew up with. If I can persuade my colleagues to trust him, and if he truly can act as a good-faith representative of the government, then maybe together we can find a road away from civil war and still secure rights for the mountain people. That would be an outcome I'd be proud to show you, an outcome worthy of your bravery. Do you still remember how to say "I'm so happy to see you"? I am determined to gain a chance to say those words to you, and to hear them from you, here in the mountains.

Sending you all my love,
Kaya

28867385R00212

Made in the USA
Charleston, SC
24 April 2014